Guil

Dr. K]

Book I

Diana Scott
Published by Diana Scott

"You came into my life without waiting for you. I received your comfort with suspicion, and your smiles were stronger than all my promises. Your chocolate eyes reached me where no one could, and today, as a slave to your perfume, I wonder when you will return..."
Akim Dudaev

Don't do what I do
Day after day
You and I
Dreams
I will catch up with you
Wake up
Theft?
I can't
Don't miss Book II Dr. Klein Series

Foreword

The whole week turned out to be much harder than usual. Brenda was exhausted. The weekend didn't turn out to be much better than the rest of the days. Her body was crying out for a well-deserved rest. The fluffy mattress enveloped her in its sweet warmth as she organized next week's tasks on her Iphone. Work and patients followed her wherever she went, like crazy ants looking for shelter. Some days could be long, but others were simply exhausting.

A psychologist by profession, and a caring person at heart, her successful therapies were sought after by London's socialites. Brenda loved to feel recognized and was proud to be so. Many people may have thought they knew her, but very few knew even the surface of her secrets.

Brenda Klein was much more than an educated, high-class doctor. She found great comfort in working with the Association for Victims of Abuse. There she felt truly alive. Dr. Klein offered her services completely unselfishly and, although Max often tried to persuade her to become less involved, she did not let herself be persuaded. In the company of these women she felt useful and free. Brenda may have helped them with her professionalism and self-improvement therapies, but they offered her restless spirit a sense of fulfillment she rarely felt anymore.

The coolness of the night came through the slits in the half-open blinds of her tidy room, and the woman closed her eyes sighing with a busy Monday coming soon. Bombon, her caramel brown kitten, licked her hand before purring and lying down beside her enjoying the softness of the fluffy quilt.

For the past two hours she had made great efforts to stay awake, but her delicate, drowsy eyelids were closing exhausted in an increasingly dark night. She wanted to stay awake, but it was getting harder and harder. Just today, despite it being Sunday, she received a call from an authoritative voice on the other end of the phone that turned out to be none other than that of the prime minister. At first he thought it was a practical joke from Connor, although the conversation and the problematic nature of the matter was too convoluted even for a Scottish madman like his friend, so he had no choice but to surrender to the evidence. On the other end of the line was the prime minister himself.

With a request that was more like a demand, the man "requested" an appointment for a very close person. Very close? she thought curiously. A strictly private consultation, the man said, causing even more intrigue in the doctor. At first she could not deny that, although she resented the impositions, the case interested her greatly, and then she simply could not resist. Curiosity got the better of him to such an extent that he readily agreed to make room in his crowded schedule.

First thing in the morning I would attend to such an important patient. Whoever he was.

Brenda Klein was a professional with capital letters, but curiosity was one of her flaws to overcome, and that Sunday was not the right day to overcome it, she thought amused. Who could catch the prime minister's attention enough to make him reach for his phone and call her on a Sunday afternoon? And why such urgency?

Brenda, with ample experience in listening to inappropriate embarrassments, at first intuited that it would be a consultation for the prime minister himself, but the latter dismissed the idea. First thing in the morning, someone would arrive for her consultation on her behalf, but who, and why all the secrecy?

The prime minister cut the call short with a terse thank you, while the woman assimilated the information. A little over a year ago, her life had taken a turn towards a fame that did not dissipate with the passing of time. Since her participation in the rescue team of that bus full of children kidnapped by a father bomb, the fame of her practice had skyrocketed to such an extent that today her phone number was in the address book of the Prime Minister of the United Kingdom. Wow, and a thousand times wow, she thought, looking at the clock on her computer and realizing how late she was running late. At first, she thought about waiting for Max to wake up, but her good intentions turned out to be history when she closed the laptop.

She was sleeping soundly when a warm, hard body and settled next to her, though she did not wake up.

Max slipped under the soft cotton sheets, happy to be home. Brenda was everything to him. His future and his beginning, his friend and his home, his whole orange. He smiled as he imagined what she would think if she knew how poetic he became when he didn't have her by his side. Of course he would never tell her, they were so much more than those platitudes of cloying poems and flowers wrapped in cheap cellophane. They were an established couple who didn't need empty frivolities to show each other what they meant to each other.

Gently he approached her to admire her, in the freedom offered by finding her in the arms of Morpheus, and to his regret, he had to admit that he was terribly aroused. It had been days since he had had her by his side and he felt intoxicated. It was enough to see her long cinnamon-colored hair scattered on the pillow, or the smoothness of her full lips, to show him that the years did not pass for women like her. If at twenty he already considered her beautiful, what could he say now? The years had given her the intelligence of experience and the curves of adulthood, what more could she ask for? She was a complete woman, special and irresistible. "At least for me," he thought libidinously.

Sleepily, she tried to open her eyes and tell him how glad she was to have him home, but her tired little eyes didn't respond. Her hair covered her own face, and Max couldn't remember ever seeing her look more lovely than she did at that moment.

Wishing not to wake up, she mumbled a barely audible 'sorry' between her teeth, and the man smiled instantly thinking how the demanding doctor of the day, could become the delicate nymph of his nights. Unable to contain himself a second longer, he coyly extended his long fingers clearing her face. She shifted, settling better into her fluffy pillow, but he did not cease his attempts. With delicate and provocative caresses he enveloped her in his warmth. He kissed her tenderly on the forehead while with the softness of his fingertips he ran his fingers from her shoulder to her small ear, to which he dedicated special interest. His hands recognized her wherever they went, she was Brenda, his wife. He caressed her again and again, accompanying them with small kisses scattered here and there. She sighed and squirmed in her sleep and Max carefully slid the sheets down causing a soft shiver in the tender body that bristled instantly.

Brenda looked beautiful in that delicate champagne silk nightgown with thin straps that he had chosen himself. At first she had shown interest in a light blue satin one, but this was certainly the more suitable choice, he thought as he stroked it with two fingers slowly so as not to wake her up. And starting to slide it down.

The freshness of a spring night just beginning peeked through the night and Brenda let herself be caressed, enjoying a passion that seemed to begin to awaken.

Hands caressed tender pink breasts, seductive and the perfect size as the juiciest of apples. And Max loved apples.....

His fingers, which with a life of their own moved enthusiastically over the smoothness of her skin, caressed her with desperation, but with the prudence of a man who did not want to wake her up. He wanted to take her like this, dozing and babbling her name in her sleep. They had been together for years, but he adored the way she said his name in those moments when she lost control. The intonation she put on when she said the M or the way she elongated the letter A. Yes, that was her. Brenda Klein, the perfect woman for him.

She stretched her neck back wishing that dream would not end. She needed it. She had been asleep for a long time and it had nothing to do with work fatigue. Months passed and her body didn't wake up. At least not as it should.

In the darkness she searched for that mouth that would devour her and those hands that would return her to the place from where she had escaped. She had lost her way and was looking for the hand that would guide her back. Her body burning with desire lifted her hips and rubbed longingly in search of what she could no longer find. She squirmed as her hips rose hoping to satiate a permanent hunger. With her eyes still closed and enveloped in the haze of sleep she weakly raised her arms and clung to the hard back that began to cover her completely. The heat was enveloping her and her nails began to dig into the tanned skin as she silently begged to find what she was looking for. Her delicate body became more and more agitated wanting to express with movements what her words dared not say.

Max reacted promptly to her requests and, thirsty for her warmth, threw himself on the wetness of a body that claimed him like a bee to honey. Brenda received him with a little moan and hoping to find that something that would make her wake up. Her eyes closed, now tightly, she struggled to find the necessary concentration.

I've got to get it, I've got to get it, she told herself impatiently. Max murmured two affectionate phrases and she squeezed him tightly. He was Max, her mate, her friend, her everything. He would rescue her. Sinking again and again into the burning heat of her sinful body, he would receive all that only she was capable of offering him, and she let herself.

Brenda moved between nervous and excited. She was looking for him, wanting him, wanting him, needing him.... Not yet... not yet... she murmured desperately, but he wasn't listening.

Max moved ardently again and again offering his best, but Brenda was lost again. Desperately she tried to move, maybe if she matched his rhythm, maybe like this... she thought enthusiastically. She wanted to follow him, she really wanted to, but how? The wetness of her body told her that his intentions were real, so why couldn't he get her back? Passion wandered lost in a limbo she could not reach.

She needed Max's hand to rescue her, but she said nothing. How do you explain to another what even you are not able to understand?

The man moved in and out, in and out, again and again, ecstatic in a wave of splendorous sensations, expressing with his body his absolute need for her, but the woman was no longer there. Her body may have enjoyed a pleasurable moment, if little else.

His teeth bit his lips to keep from speaking while his mind, now awake, wandered in who knows what directions. Again and again he tried to concentrate, but all efforts fell on deaf ears. It wasn't worth the struggle. Not now. Thoughts like whirlwinds of uncontrolled storm tried to offer her solace, solution or simple despair, whatever it was, she was no longer making love to her partner.

Max grunted as a resounding yes! escaped his lips. Gently he fell onto her body and she covered him in a sweet embrace with a lot of tenderness, but none of passion.

The days

Max, in a state of complete drowsiness, embraced her and pulled her to his chest trying to lengthen those moments, but she gently pulled away, and so, separated, they ended up falling asleep.

It was early morning and a new Monday was beginning to dawn. Being very careful not to wake him, she pushed the sheets aside and set off. Max would be exhausted and there was no need to wake him so early. She tiptoed and, with the utmost stealth, made her way to the bathroom.

Stretching her still numb muscles and adjusting the water to just the right temperature, she stepped into the magnificent stone and glass shower Max had designed especially for the two of them. The warm drops ran down her body from beginning to end, traveling unperturbed from her delicate neck to reach the tiniest of her fingers. With the sensation of coolness on her skin, she lifted her face to the sky and her thick hair slid over her delicate shoulders seeking the comfort of the morning water.

The squirts slid down her face and she breathed deeply, trying not to think. The feeling of guilt overpowered her completely. Her hands heavy with self-doubt leaned against the wall waiting for the tiny drops to wash away stupid sensations. Guilt, uneasiness and fear gripped her brain, driving thoughts too confused to be clarified even more maddening.

She bitterly remembered the failed love encounter with her husband and tried to find some logical reason for his apparent indifference, but she couldn't find it. If there was one person she loved with all her being, it was Max, so what was happening to him? Hormones, age, boredom, monotony? What was the right answer, she wondered, overwhelmed, and mainly, who had her passion and how could she get it back?

Many times in her practice she had dedicated entire sessions to patients with serious relationship problems, but now a very complex dilemma confronted her with her own reality. She had to apply her own advice and decipher the enigma on her own. When dealing with her patients, she was a cold spectator offering her knowledge, this time Brenda was the protagonist of her own movie. She had in her hands a script of which she did not know the ending and of which she did not know if she would be able to rewrite with good handwriting.

It wasn't so bad, she thought trying to console herself, I had an orgasm, a small one, but an orgasm nonetheless. That must have meant something.

"If I were indifferent to the act I wouldn't have felt it. Besides, I feel like it and a lot, the problem is..." she paused, scolding herself for her own foolishness.

She was alone, in the shower, and arguing with her own thoughts, but that didn't mean she was crazy or anything. She loved Max and that wouldn't change.

"Everything has a solution," she thought optimistically, the only problem was finding it. "Maybe if you talk to him?" her little inner voice tried to scold him, but she dismissed it instantly. Max adored her and she knew it, there was no reason to worry him. No, this was her problem and she would solve it herself. She was Brenda Klein for a reason, one of the best psychologists in the country. Her desires and passions evaporated one morning and it was her duty to get them back. And she would.

She closed her eyes tightly and moved her hands with excessive energy over her frothy mane wishing the jets of water would wash down the shower drains, her concern.

A few liters later and large amounts of soap, achieved the miracle of returning it to its natural state. That of optimism. The one that told her that she was a prestigious professional, lived a serene and organized life, balanced and totally in love.

Much more cheerful, she quickly dried her body, wrapped herself in a soft, fluffy bathrobe, and headed down the long hallway in search of her much-needed caffeine fix. The solid wood door creaked a little before closing and leaving her in the solitude of the kitchen. With her usual speed, she turned on the coffee pot, prepared the toast in the toaster, heated the milk in the microwave, and got some jam and butter from the fridge. She spread the delicate pale pink placemat on the table, and waited while she watched the horizon through the huge window. The day was beginning to wake up and it was a beautiful spring morning. Joy was evident in the flight of birds, the elegant greenish hue of the lawn, and the life blooming in the colorful flower boxes. Bonbon scratched at the door, and she, smiling, opened it for him while he treated her to the cup of milk she loved so much.

The intense aroma of the excellent South African coffee covered the kitchen and memories of a childhood she did not wish to recall appeared unbidden. The image of her, tiny and sitting undisturbed, admiring the hard profile of her father drinking strong coffee from his porcelain cup while reading the newspaper uninterrupted, assaulted her. He always read while drinking that coffee, and although she tried very hard not to imitate him, little details made her think that a part of him, even if she didn't want it, would always be part of her own essence.

The renowned lawyer Oliver Klein had been living in South Africa for more than fifty years now, specifically in Cape Town, the legislative capital of the country and the center of major political decisions. As an undisputed prosecutor and a famed despot and even more profound egoist, he never had time for his annoying little daughter, who drove him crazy more than he would have liked to admit.

From the moment they arrived in South Africa, his father felt at home. It was in countries where inequality was palpable and differences were perfectly defined by the tinge of well-defined social classes that Oliver Klein felt the most powerful being of all. It would be for that, and a few other reasons, that he never tried to return to London and Brenda never asked him to. They hadn't heard from each other for months. Exactly two, the time in which with a cold five-minute phone call he would have learned that his mother had died of terminal cancer.

She could have traveled, she could have said goodbye, but he didn't see fit. "You couldn't do anything," he said. And maybe he was right, but why not let her say goodbye to those eyes that always looked at her with sadness and resignation?

Brenda took a sip of her coffee and tried to remember only the good things, but the truth was that those moments were few and far between. Maybe the few happy times were at the girls' boarding school, maybe they were when Rachel, that little dusty girl with huge red hair braids, would sneak around the nuns' room looking for romance novels hidden under the mattress, or maybe they were when the screams of a shy Johana, with curls the size of huge conches, would meet those undesirable, merciless and murderous beings called spiders. Brenda smiled as she remembered those two, her best friends, who to this day were her inseparable. They had returned to London and were now a motley trio. Max couldn't stand Rachel and swallowed Johana without chewing, but they all behaved socially polite and responsible when they had to share the same room, and for Brenda that was more than enough.

The toaster threw a crispy slice of rye bread into the air, sending Brenda back to the planet of current realities. She glanced at the time on the wall clock and cursed under her breath. She sucked down her coffee and hastily bit into the delicious toast slathered with red berry jam, eager to start the day and stop the nonsense that was getting her nowhere. The past was in the past and her current idleness would be solved as soon as she applied one of her famous therapies to herself. Excited, she checked her cell phone and organized her week.

If you knew

Akim dried his freshly shaved face. Today he was starting on a new crew and he really needed the change. It was urgent for him to disappear from the previous job. For a moment he stared at the reflection of a hard, half-dressed body and felt sorry for himself.

"No wonder you intimidate." He thought as he looked at the tattoos on his shoulders and the scars he kept on his arms, or hands, the fruits of years of hard work.

Some women considered his broad shoulders, his square jaw, or his black eyelashes, as a special and masculine attraction but surely not her. She would never notice a body as coarse as his. She was finesse, delicacy, poise, politeness, while he...

The bathroom was illuminated with only a small light bulb because of an account almost always in the red, but, even so, and despite its scarcity, he was able to see exactly every detail that separated him from her. Muscled arms achieved by the effort of carrying indecent amounts of debris, hands cracked by the corrosion of materials, a chest too broad to follow the current canons of masculinity, and waves that were neither curly nor anything else, simply unruly. He snorted as he tried to fix with his fingers that wavy and unruly hair of an intense black, but he gave up the attempt. Her hair, like its owner, woke up insurgent and hopeless.

He stroked the softness of her chin wondering if she would like him better with a beard or without, he immediately dismissed it from his heated mind. She wasn't his, he wasn't to imagine her, he wasn't to keep thinking about her or he would go completely insane. He was twenty-six years old and he couldn't keep making mistakes and suffering their consequences. He had to get on with his life and leave her forgotten in the past. It seemed possible, after all nothing at all ever happened between them. Absolutely nothing, he thought dissatisfied.

He shook his damp head trying to remove the last drops from the shower while with a quick movement of his arms, he put on his T-shirt, tucked it over his worn jeans and cursed as he felt the new wound on his wrist, and unwillingly remembered it again. That wound that was beginning to heal was a true reflection of his distraction every time he saw her.

He shook his head twice with a loud shake as he begged his mind to please help him forget her. She was too much, something unattainable that would only make him suffer.

"I shouldn't complain, but fuck...". He thought knowing that, although in his world he was lucky, he couldn't help but feel sorry for himself.

He rested his hands on the sink and for the first time since he had left Chechnya, he felt limp. For the past five years he had led a life quite different from that of a normal young man, but he was not a normal young man.

When others were beginning to enjoy themselves, he was fleeing a country at war with a baby in his arms, and an aging and sad father. He looked at himself again in the faded mirror and cursed aloud, angry with life, destiny and with her. She, who provoked him even though she did not recognize it. Before her he would never have bothered to spend even five minutes of his time on a past he couldn't erase or a damned present he couldn't rewrite, nor would he have asked for a transfer even though he knew his heart was tearing at the thought of never seeing her again, but there he was, suffering for love for the first time in his hard life, and he hoped it would be the last time.

Those little chocolate eyes had him bewitched, and although he wanted to erase her from his memories, he could not. Just last night, Lola, in her eagerness to conquer him, gave him the most prodigious attention, but what's the use of a couple of well earned powders if when you put on your helmet and get on your bike her smile comes back even sharper than before?

Ever since that damned day when she walked through the doorway, and got lost behind the architect's office wearing an impeccable black dress, and those heart-stopping heels that would drive any mortal crazy, her image had not left his thoughts.

The young man put his hands under the faucet and washed his face with freezing water, again. He tried to forget what seemed to be an impossibility. What was it about her that, despite being everything he shouldn't, was the only thing he wanted? For days, like a crazed stalker, he waited to see her, walked up and down hallways, climbed stairs, threw debris, even offered to paint one of the new offices. Everything to see her again. Nervously he moved material from one floor to another looking for an opportunity to bump into her and talk to her, but she did not appear. Like a young man in love he prayed to heaven to hear his cries, but as was usual for men with his background, it never happened. God did not listen to men like him. Bitter and disappointed after two weeks of fooling around the building, and believing himself capable of forgetting her, he saw her and his hopes were reborn in front of him.

She was there. In the same office and under the same roof. His throat went dry, his heart shot out of control, and his hands petrified at the sides of his frozen body. He didn't move, he didn't speak, he simply looked into her eyes with a stupid smile that even he didn't know he had. Since when did he know how to smile so enthusiastically? Even he himself was surprised at such an unrecognizable attitude.

Trying not to look like a championship jerk, he looked down to see himself and tried to spruce himself up with a few hard shakes on the dust-covered coveralls.

His image wasn't one of the best, but maybe with any luck she wouldn't mind. He quickly tossed the paint brush into the bucket trying to look less workmanlike, while opening his mouth he prayed the words would come out and he wouldn't look even more stupid than he already felt.

She had been imagining that first meeting for days and was about to make it a reality when the architect, whom she had forgotten she had at her side, stepped forward and with the movement of only three steps, stood in front of her, and kissed her. In front of her incredulous eyes, he kissed her.

-Dad, will you take me to school? Dad!

A little boy, barely six years old and with the same sky-colored eyes, made a place for himself in the bathroom.

-We agreed that it was not polite to enter the restroom without knocking.

-But we are boys. There are no girls at home. He replied as if that justified everything.

Lucien's mother abandoned him at birth and Akim, at the age of twenty, became a single parent and together with his father the child's sole educator, which is why the little boy often came to such crazy conclusions.

-Just because no woman lives at home doesn't mean we don't have rules.

The little boy shook his head as he answered confidently.

-Paul says that when their mother isn't home, their father gives them candy, they drink Coke, play Play Play, and have burping contests. His dad can do it for a minute straight," he said in amazement. One day when he was at home, Paul and I measured him with a stopwatch. His dad made us promise not to count it.

Akim looked at him curiously while trying to hold back a smile.

-If his wife found out she said she would cut off his manhood, although I don't know what that means. Lucien lifted his shoulders and his father could not contain himself and burst into a loud laugh.

-Knowing Paul's mother, I can imagine his father's fears. Now go with Grandpa. You will go to school with him. She replied, lifting the little boy into her strong arms and giving him a smiling kiss on his rosy cheeks.

-Are you going to another building today?

-Yes.

-Did you finish the other one?

-Let's say I needed a change.

-Ah," he said as if he understood something, "Will you build it?

He was no famous architect but his son refused to see him as a simple bricklayer.

-I'll help a little.

-Tell me again, come on, Dad," he said, pointing to the tattoo peeking out of his lower neck.

-Go drink your milk or you'll be late," he said seriously, changing the subject.

The boy pouted at not being able to hear the story again and left as happily as he had arrived.

Akim adjusted his jeans, grateful that he no longer cared whether or not they were too worn, or if his shirt was more than two springs old, after all he would never see it again and other opinions mattered little to him. He walked towards the door, picked up his helmet and the keys to his bike when his father intercepted him with a cup of coffee in his hand to offer it to him.

-I can't, I have to cross the whole city and I'm late.

-New crew?

-It seems so. He replied, putting on his helmet.

-Will Nikola work with you?

-As if I could lose it," he said amused, and his father laughed as he held out a twenty-pound bill.

-What is this?

-A few odd jobs I did," he said, lifting his shoulders. You still need it.

-It's not necessary. Save it to buy something you need," he said before walking out the door.

"Something you need," he thought as he started his bike. He knew perfectly well that for his father any purchase needed would be for little Lucien. His temper soured even more than it already used to. Thinking about his father and the sacrifices he was making to help him raise his son made him feel even more of an idiot and terribly guilty. He accelerated hard and left the portal with the roar of the motorcycle that, while deafening, didn't account for half of the fury and frustration in his raging heart.

Surprise

Without looking back, she hurriedly picked up her purse and started her convertible and headed for work. He had a busy day ahead of him, and he didn't have time to continue to waste on unwarranted rambling about a marriage that had no problems at all.

She recalled with enthusiasm that, ever since her negotiation with that father bomb on the school bus, she had been continually approached by big names for therapy. The last year had been a fast-paced one, but she was thrilled. She felt that all her efforts were valuable to a society that needed her and she gladly attended. Her father had always told her that her sensitivity to the weak would bring her no good, but he was wrong, her work was useful. She remembered her successes with satisfaction. "It's on you, Dad," she thought wryly.

Enjoying the start of a new week, which came loaded with new stories to hear, he parked in front of his office and could not resist the temptation. The Starbucks in front of her office and the latte-macchiatto with caramel and a delicate hint of vanilla were a pleasure she could not refuse, especially on a Monday morning.

He got out of the car and his legs did not have to consult the destination. Latte-macchiatto you are mine, he said to himself with a smile on his face.

-The usual? -A young girl with a broad smile that looked like something out of a Japanese comic book asked enthusiastically.

-Please, Laura.

-And to go... -It was not a question. I knew her very well.

-Yes, thank you," he replied as he watched the employee capture a recycled cardboard cup with a lid and write 'Dr. Klein' without asking.

Brenda paid for her order and moved to the side so as not to get in the way of the line as she anxiously awaited her second caffeine fix of the day. Her cell phone rang at the exact moment the smiling employee handed her her hot beverage. With a perfect tightrope walk she managed to bite the handles of her purse while holding her coffee in one hand and picking up her cell phone with the other.

-Tell me," she replied as she held the phone with her shoulder and slipped the handles of her purse over her wrist to free her hand.

-Honey, you'd better come and soon. This is a mess." Someone was heard shouting on the other side.

-Try not to kill anyone until I get there," she replied amused as she thought it couldn't be that bad. A facelift, Max had assured her. Surely Connor was exaggerating as usual.

-Oh honey, I swear you have no idea what I'm looking at. I don't think I'm going to leave anyone with a head." He was heard to exclaim angrily.

-Connor!

Brenda raised her tone trying to get through the phone, but her friend had already hung up. With cell phone in hand, purse half-hung, and coffee mug in the other, she tried to open the exit door, only to realize its narrowness when it was too late. His recycled, eco-friendly cardboard mug collided head-on with a four-by-four wide body. The young man, who by now was dripping coffee on his hitherto immaculate T-shirt, stared at her in disorientation.

-I'm sorry, I'm sorry, I'm so sorry. I'm such a klutz.

Brenda brought the paper napkin she was carrying close to the cup and tried to dry it, but the young man's tension was increasing. She looked him in the face again, trying to apologize, but this time it was not anger or rage that she noticed on his face, but something like fear?

No, it was not possible. That young man had neither the size nor the appearance of a skittish bunny, but rather the opposite. His face was hard, he possessed a stature that forced her to look up at him despite his exaggerated heels, and the width of his well-fed arms did not show him to be the type of man who would be frightened of a petite woman like her.

"Brenda, you're losing your faculties. He's just mad as hell." She thought regretfully.

-A thousand apologies please, what can I do?

-I'm fine.

-I'm really sorry," he commented as he looked at the stain that was beginning to darken part of the fabric.

He barely looked her in the face and she could have sworn he hated her with all his might. She tried to move to the side as she commented regretfully.

-He opened his eyes wide again and Brenda wondered what other mistake he had made. Better to let it go and get out of the way. It was clear he had no desire to excuse her.

-Well, I'll let you in.

He turned in his tracks to make room for him when the man shook his head.

-No.

"No? No, I won't come in? No, I don't want coffee? No, you won't pay for the dye? No, I don't even want to see you? Which one?

She watched him in surprise as he, for the first time in their disastrous encounter, stared into her eyes. Blessed God, they were as clear as the most delicate of sapphires. Precious stones almost transparent, delicate and shining like sweet nature, yet sturdy and hard as rock itself.

He was watching her in concentration as if he wanted to tell her something else, as if they already knew each other, although that was highly unlikely. If she had ever seen those eyes before, she was sure she would remember them.

"Brenda please! That you're a lady." She thought in disgust.

-The prices. He said flatly and waking her up from her thoughts.

"Prices? coffee? t-shirt? dye?".

Akim did not clarify, he simply pointed to the blackboard hanging on the wall.

-I understand," she replied quietly. But I guess after the mess I've made for you, it's on me," she commented, understanding the situation as she slung her purse over her shoulder and prepared to go back inside. My coffee is all in your shirt and it's only fair that I at least pay you for one that you can drink," she said with a small pout. She said with a little pout.

"My goodness, it's a bit infuriating. It's nice that he looks like one of those punch and kick movie actors, but he's not to kill me with his eyes either." She said to herself.

-Shall we go? -A young man who appeared at his side asked in a foreign accent as strong and thick as his own.

-Yes.

The young man pointed to the board with the prices and his friend nodded without asking. They both turned to leave when she would have sworn that the one with her coffee on him for a few seconds hesitated as he left, so she dared to ask a second time.

-Please stay. I invite you. It's the least I can do for you.

The young man turned away without answering her. He looked at her as if she were a ghost, and in the most unforeseen and somewhat schizophrenic way, he smiled at her without a hint of desire.

-This can't be happening.... -He shook his head.

-I beg your pardon?

The man looked at the stain on his best shirt and replied ruefully.

-My souvenir. Thank you.

The men left and Brenda stood for a moment as she watched him go. What would happen to him?

"Do I remember, would I be right in the head?". She shook her head and tried to forget about it. She entered the premises again and approached the bar where her cordial, smiling waitress was waiting for her. She needed another latte-macchiato and this time with double the caffeine.

The chaos

To call the image before Brenda a catastrophe would be an understatement. Bags of who knows what were scattered around the reception area. Sand and other assorted materials were scattered at the entrances to the offices. Huge tangles of blue and black wires were draped under the frames like uncontrolled octopuses running the length of the hallway reluctantly up the main staircase. Paint pots and cement-filled buckets scattered between the entrance to his office and Connor's studio. The beautiful hardwood floors could barely be seen under a pile of dust worthy of central Sahara. Great slender iron giants, whose use would be impossible to decipher, were deposited in front of the door of what until then had been a beautiful late nineteenth-century elevator.

-God bless... -he muttered, holding his delicious late-macchiato in his right hand and trying to avoid the debris on the floor so as not to stain his delicate shoes.

-I told you. You shouldn't have married him. He's crazy.

"And here we go again," she thought bored. Connor never felt any special sympathy for Max, and truth be told, neither did Max for him. According to his friend, Max restricted her freedom and locked her into a world of well-adjusted social norms. Connor couldn't have been more wrong. She and Max represented the perfect marriage, the problem was not her husband, but that she was no longer the idealistic young woman Connor had met on the college campus. She had matured, he had not. That was exactly what their differences were based on. Max was poised while Connor was very.... Connor. Free as the wind, a Scottish artist without mincing words. One was the oil that was always ready to jump while the other represented the calm of a channeled river. Max, a perfect English gentleman if ever there was one, never left anything to chance, on the other hand Connor...

-I don't like you talking about him like that, and you know it.

Connor rolled his eyes and tried to bite his tongue to keep from talking back to his dearest friend, but his efforts fell on deaf ears. As usual.

-What was wrong with the building the way it was? And why the hell is he tearing it down!

The truth is that, although Brenda tried to answer with some reason to justify such a disaster, she could not. Max insisted that the offices were outdated and even though she didn't see it that way, the building belonged to her husband's company and she was entitled to the changes. "Just a little facelift," Max had said, but this was a full-body facelift, she thought angrily.

"The consultation should be commensurate with your newfound notoriety," her husband said, and she agreed. She trusted her husband's judgment completely, although at times like this, she wished she hadn't.

Connor snorted as he paced back and forth kicking every bucket he could find. Brenda understood his anger because, if she could have, she would have been kicking a bucket or two herself, but it was her husband who had gotten them into such a mess and she didn't think it was the right time to add fuel to the fire, even if she felt like burning Max at the very stake of Joan of Arc.

-When we talked about a small reform, I never imagined anything like that..." she commented in disgust.

Connor instantly regretted his bad temper. She wasn't to blame for having a selfish, self-centered, self-absorbed jerk like Max Brown by her side. She wasn't capable of seeing him for who he really was, he was. Brenda was not only his best friend since time immemorial but she was able to understand him beyond social conventions. When everyone turned their backs on him, she was always there. When she cried for that selfish jerk Jason, she was the one who dried her tears, when her parents turned their backs on her sexual condition, she was the one who opened her arms. It was up to her to support her and put up with her husband's imbecilities, even though she loathed him with a vengeance.

-Cari, don't worry. We'll manage," she said without conviction.

-You think so? -Where are we supposed to be working? -I have an appointment in an hour and this place is... it's... it's... -Her gaze shifted to the catastrophe in front of her and she shouted angrily, "Fucking bullshit!

Connor opened his eyes like two chestnuts and smiled softly. That was Brenda, the original Brenda, the one he knew and Max was in charge of formatting, and that very rarely, came to light.

-Dr. Klein?

They both turned in unison to face a little man just over six feet tall, with very tanned skin and blue work overalls, stained entirely by too many materials to be enumerated. He was wearing an orange construction helmet and dust seemed to be blowing out from between his boots with every step he took as he approached.

-It's me, and you are? -he commented in a soft voice and Connor smiled as he saw how the bricklayer took off his leather glove to offer him a most effusive handshake.

-I am in charge of the work. I belong to your husband's crew and it is an honor for me to be part of this renovation.

"Honor?" Brenda tried slyly, so as not to offend him, to wipe her hand that the attendant had squeezed and smeared with something yellow, paint?

-Sir... -she said trying to be polite.

-Samir, my name is Samir, ma'am.

-Samir," he repeated with a fake smile, "You say you're in charge?

-Yes, ma'am. Your husband has given the instructions to the quantity surveyor and he has left all the decisions in my hands. You see, I am the master builder," he said, proud of his position. I control all types of renovations, from masonry, painting, electrical and general plumbing. Some would say I'm the Rama of the works.

-The Branch of...?

-He's an Indian god of..." Connor replied, increasingly amused by the situation, but he couldn't finish because Brenda glared at him.

-I know who he is." She tried to take three breaths before answering, after all the poor man was trying to prove his worth and she valued his effort very much.

-Samir, and since my husband has left you in charge, you will know that we need the building to be completed as soon as possible.

-Of course, ma'am. He answered seriously.

"Good, good, we're doing well." She thought somewhat calmer.

-And how long do you say we have to stay in this... this...? -He looked for the best sounding word to describe that cataclysm, but he couldn't find it?

-Disaster, chaos, hecatomb? -Connor bluntly clarified and the little man narrowed his eyes in offense.

-In two weeks, sir," he said in a serious tone.

"Nothing else?" Brenda missed the deadline, but Connor started to shout before letting the man continue with his explanations.

-Two weeks. -Two weeks! But how the hell are we supposed to work in this nest of...

The little man stretched his shoulders, trying to keep up with Connor's six-foot-five-inch frame. His friend's green eyes flashed like a demon reincarnated from hell itself, but the little man was undaunted.

-Let me tell you again," he said annoyed, "that my crew and I are a team of professionals and we know perfectly well what we are doing. He replied offended, and Brenda admired him for his courage.

Anyone at the screams of a fearsome, flame-haired Scotsman like Connor would have run for miles without looking back. The

architect made provisions for Mrs. Klein - he emphasized every letter
of her last name - to have a temporary consultation.

-And for me? The "architect" didn't make any forecasts? -he
asked obfuscated and with smoke coming out of his nose.

-No one mentioned any secretary," he commented, making it
clear that he did not know who he was nor did he care.

-Secre... secre What!

Now it was Brenda who was smiling. Max, with this oversight,
was taking a lot of Connor's comments towards him in spades.

-Samir, let me explain that Connor is an internationally
renowned sculptor who works in one of the studios they are
renovating," his friend nodded in agreement with Brenda's
description.

-Ah, one of those artists.... -he said, making it clear how much he
disliked him.

Connor nearly lifted him off the ground by the scruff of his neck
if Brenda hadn't intervened with her own body.

-You see, Samir, we both need a place to work and if possible it
should be free of.... - "Dust, dirt, cement, paint, wires, sand..." - "so
much hustle and bustle," he said dryly. so much hustle and bustle,"
he said, wiping his forehead. Looking for less offensive words was
proving to be a real challenge.

-Dr. Klein, your husband didn't say anything about - she glared
at Connor - him.

-Of course he didn't do it. The artist bit his tongue so as not to
insult to the four winds.

-I'm sure my husband forgot to mention it..." Brenda looked
at Connor in disgust as he continued to curse. -Brenda looked at
Connor in disgust as he continued to curse, "but I'm sure we can
work something out. Samir have any ideas? -she asked almost
desperately, squeezing her forehead.

-Dr. Klein, what you are asking is not easy," the little man took off his helmet and wiped the sweat from his forehead with a gray rag hanging from the pocket of his overalls, "but I think we can work something out.

Brenda breathed a sigh of relief.

-Thank you very much Samir. You don't know how much you are helping us. So there are two free offices? -she asked hopefully.

-No, just one, but we can put up a screen to divide it.

-A screen, a screen? A screen!

Connor raised his voice to such an extent that even the walls shook from his screams as the doctor squeezed her forehead even tighter.

The worker smiled with satisfaction at the giant's fury as he walked along humming to the bollywood beat, and waiting for them to follow him. Totally confirmed. The artist had not gone down well at all.

A screen in your life

-I plan to leave you a widow.

-Max did not want to...

Connor arched an eyebrow and the friend preferred to keep quiet. Her husband had wanted to and that was undeniable.

-I have a consultation... -she expressed in alarm as she looked around the small room that Samir proudly showed her. The beautiful passion red couch, which Max had given her for her last birthday, presided over the modest but delicate office. On one side the files were guarded by a delicate modern piece of furniture made of wood and painted in a delicate off-white that matched perfectly with the small but exquisite desk. Everything was perfect for her, but only her.

Brenda was rearranging her files when Connor appeared through the door after a little over an hour. It was clear from the ferocity of his insults that he had not yet calmed down. His friend didn't need to ask what state his study was in, he knew full well how dire the situation was. Yes, Max had intentionally forgotten Connor.

-In about fifteen minutes a model will come for his first session. He said desperately.

-Model? -He asked, pausing to look at his friend curiously. You don't usually do portraits.

-A nude to be more precise. He commented bitterly.

Brenda opened her mouth, then closed it and opened it again.

-Connor smiled mischievously and Brenda grumbled in annoyance as she set her laptop on the desk.

-So this whole mess is because you didn't have your riding arena ready? Connor! I'm going to have to agree with Max in the end. He said pounding on the keyboard as his friend became disgusted at the mere mention of the stuffy architect.

The artist studied every nook and cranny of the office and Brenda looked at him curiously over the reading glasses. What was he up to? Connor patted the couch, watched the morning light stream in through the window and nodded reassuringly.

-It will do.

-What the hell are you talking about? -The doctor found out when she saw the mischief in his smile. No way. I have an office and mine is a bit more serious than yours.

-Cari, please, please! -she begged with clenched hands. I've been cajoling that fireman for a little over a month.

-I don't care if the entire fire department shows up.

Connor gave one of those little pouts that left a little dimple in his face and brought out the emerald green of his eyes, but Brenda resisted. The consultation with the prime minister's friend was rather more important than any hot fireman. Brenda shook her head emphatically as she typed on the computer an email to her secretary Clotilde to take the day off. Better the month, she thought as she looked at the chaos from behind the door.

Connor cursed loudly before replying angrily.

-I'm not going to cancel!

-Please be reasonable. Mine is a serious case.

-And mine is a case of extreme necessity! I plan to throw myself at the fireman with or without your help.

They both looked at each other with blood injected in their veins.

-Let's be reasonable," she said, getting up from her chair and rounding the desk to lean back exhausted and trying to calm herself. Why don't you take him to your apartment and enjoy a memorable morning? -she commented, trying to cajole him.

-Impossible." He shook his head emphatically, "I don't bring strange men home.

-What are you talking about! -Brenda lost what little patience she had left. I've seen more naked men in your house than at a stripper show.

-That was before.

-Three weeks! -Only three weeks ago!

Connor raised his lip in amusement as he remembered Brenda's face when she saw that handsome waiter open the door to her apartment covered in a simple kitchen apron.

-I am a more mature man.

-Since when?

-Today.

-And that's why you want to hook up with a firefighter in my office. Because you're more mature?

-Cari, mature, not an idiot. That boy wants to meet the great artist and I'm going to show him," she said with amusement in her voice.

Brenda tried to grumble, but Connor's nonsense unhinged her as intensely as it amused her.

-Change the schedule," she said defeated, "let me have my session and then....

-Permission. The door opened wide as strong arms and a black T-shirt appeared, carrying a huge piece of wood that covered the man's entire face.

-What is that? -. He said pointing to the hideous piece of old wood.

-I guess the screen," Connor mumbled through his teeth.

Brenda closed her eyes, trying to calm the pounding headache that was beginning to set in the center of her brain.

The muscular arms left the furniture on the floor and the man was starting to leave when Brenda's scream echoed through the room, startling the artist.

-Think about leaving it here!

The man turned around with complete parsimony.

-Samir's orders," he said in a thick voice with a strong foreign accent. Before turning around and staring into her eyes.

-You.

-You?

They both answered at the same time and were perplexed to discover how short life's twists and turns turned out to be.

-He looked at his chest and checked the traces of his clumsiness -the one with the coffee... the one he couldn't buy...". -Brenda shut her mouth instantly and Akim glared at her, surely offended by her second clumsiness.

That man managed to get her to make one mistake after another. For his part, Akim felt very hurt by the reminder of his lack of purchasing power. On his lips the truths were even more painful.

-We're not all so... superficial. She mumbled through her teeth as she scanned up and down her top of the line dress and her perfect elitist shoes.

The experienced psychologist, accustomed to mastering attacks with total professionalism, answered emphatically.

-Fuck you.

Connor opened his eyes in disbelief and she closed her mouth the instant his words had left her lips.

"Goodness gracious, did I say that? Must be the stress." She thought unable to accept her most natural and unpredictable reaction. She was not like that, she was an educated and controlled woman. She never gave free rein to her base impulses. She began to rearrange her hair behind her ear, trying to calm herself when the young man counterattacked.

-He shows me the way doc-to-ra.

Her good intentions as a controlled, respectful and diligent psychologist went down the drain. He was provoking her in every way.

-Put that wood somewhere else. She ordered authoritatively, and Connor leaned against the wall with his legs crossed, watching in amusement.

The worker not only did not move, but crossed his arms in defiance.

-And where do you want me to stick it, doc-to-ra? -He replied wryly, and Connor guffawed shamelessly.

Brenda glared at her friend. She felt insulted. He might throw his coffee at her, compare him to a beggar and treat him in an overbearing manner, but that didn't mean he should treat her so rudely.

-Back it up against that wall. I don't need a little boy like you for much more. I'm on my own... for everything." She replied proudly with her answer.

Akim smiled sideways accepting the challenge.

-This little boy has lived a lot, when you want I'll show you.

The young man approached with his eyes fixed on her and Connor felt compelled to interfere with the situation. Although this young man seemed to be playing games, his double wide back and those overly muscular arms, put on alert a friend prepared to defend the doctor above all else.

-You can leave and try not to stain the doorknob with those hands full of paint.

Brenda said this, pointing to her dust-covered overalls as she turned her back to him and raised her hand in the air, closing the discussion. The young man who had a lot of pride and little calm, shook his head as he walked away slamming the door loudly.

Connor approached from behind to ask cautiously.

-Are you all right?

-Perfectly, I don't know why you ask," he said as in a fit of rage he ran to the door and opened it to shout at the top of his voice.

-When will they give birth to us?

Akim stopped in the middle of the hallway in disbelief. She was calling him a brat again, damn it! How wrong he had been about her. That woman was uptight just like all of her kind. He turned around and with a look that would have set hell itself on fire and answered her in a gravelly voice.

-I don't know, and I don't care.

-Then go and ask. I need it." He ordered defiantly.

The man looked at his watch and as he looked up from his wrist he replied viciously.

-Time for my lunch.

That young man provoked her to an extreme degree. He brought out the worst in her.

-I don't give a damn! This is my work and I'm the boss. If I ask you to give me a light, you give it to me, and you can shove that damn lunch up your ass!

Connor's eyes widened in shock.

"Where do you fit? Did Brenda say that? Her Brenda? The sweet, polite, overly supportive Brenda?

-First I will eat," he replied seriously, retracing his steps and approaching threateningly. And then, if I want to, if I really feel like it, I might meet the demands of my "uptight boss".

-Stretched me? Did you call me stretched? He called me stretched! -Brenda looked aghast at Connor for logistical support, but he was too amused to come to her aid.

It was the first and only time in twenty years that he had seen his friend lose her temper and he was delighted. Brenda shook her head and snorted at the lock of her hair that stood between her eyes, determined to stand up for herself.

-Look at your pretty face. I'm no stiff and just so you know, I do charity work.

Connor covered his face with both hands and Akim turned to leave in utter disappointment. He had no desire to talk to her anymore. Brenda Klein turned out to be a huge disappointment.

He walked down the long corridor without looking back, wondering how he could be so unlucky. He had asked for a change of gang trying to forget her and all he had achieved was to get even closer. Could one have worse luck than his own?

-Don't worry doctor, I will look for the electrician myself.

A bricklayer of equal size and stature, but with light brown hair, spoke behind her.

-And who are you? -He answered with his blood boiling as he watched Akim leave without speaking to him.

-My name is Nikola and I'm part of Samir's crew," he replied with a huge and most pleasant smile. If you'll excuse us, we only have half an hour and we've been working all morning without a single cup of coffee, but I promise that as soon as we finish we'll fix your little problem with the electricity.

The worker smiled politely at her and she wanted to die right then and there. But what had just happened? Why had he attacked this young man? At the very least, he was more than a decade younger than her. How could he have been so cruel to talk to her like that?

Brenda ducked her head and her shoulders slumped in regret. She spilled coffee on him at the Starbucks and they hadn't gone in because they couldn't afford the expense however seeing him had reacted as if his presence threatened her. "I have no apologies."

Without being able to look up, he thanked Nikola quietly and went back into the office, closing the door with guilty parsimony.

-Someday you could stop meddling where you're not wanted. Akim spoke in annoyance.

-And let them fire you? You need the job as much as I do.

-I'd rather lose him than put up with women like that.

-Maybe, but Lucien and your father need the salary, now stop this nonsense and let's eat. He said lifting the two sandwiches wrapped in silver paper.

Brenda behind the door heard it all and felt terrible. She had behaved like an idiot.

-I'm not like that... I'm not like that," she stammered, leaning back against the frame and squeezing her forehead with two fingers, totally regretful for her behavior.

-And are you going to explain why?

-Because what?

-You know perfectly well. You're not like that and we both know it. You don't lose your temper with anyone. Damn, Brenda, you've managed to reinsert a bomber into society. You have nerves of steel, but with that man you lost them all.

-He is a child.

-How?

-An impulsive kid and he got on my nerves, that's all. He answered unwillingly.

-I have seen a man and not a child, but what has that got to do with the subject that concerns us?

"What's that got to do with it? How should I know? I don't even know why I said it."

-Let's forget absurd discussions and tell me exactly how we do it. This is my practice and you're not going to seduce any heart attack firemen here.

Connor reacted as Brenda had predicted and quickly forgot about his bricklayer to focus on the really important problems. Dr. Klein smiled at her ability to manipulate - after all, so many years of college studying minds was worth something.

-I have an idea," she said hopefully.

-Do you want a threesome? -He replied with one of the many jokes that Max couldn't stand, "Honey, you know I'm not into women, but I'd make an exception for you.

-Don't be silly, besides, I'm a married woman," she said with amusement in her voice.

-Yes, the stupidity of being faithful to the glanders.

-Don't call him that. Brenda tried not to smile, although she couldn't.

Many times Connor's descriptions of her husband were reckless, but very accurate. Max was a good man, although I know no one would call him the king of the party.

-Bring your agenda and cut the bullshit. We have a lot of work ahead of us and your firefighter will be on his way out.

Connor nodded as she sat down in the only chair there and his friend leaned back on the couch and opened the calendar on his Iphone.

The weather

After taking off her heels and arranging all her files for a little over an hour, Brenda rested. The doctor had not finished relaxing when, magically, the lamp on the table turned on by her own choice.

"Perfect timing." He thought as he looked at his wristwatch, another wonderful birthday present, from Max.

-Everything all right, doctor? -said a voice from the door.

The woman jumped in place as she was interrupted just as she was putting on her shoes to answer hurriedly.

-Eh, yes, yes, everything is perfect.

-Great, her husband is my boss and I don't want to look bad. The Nikola winked at her with such confidence that the woman was somewhat taken aback by his total lack of self-confidence.

-The light is on. The deep, deep voice of her companion made her look him in the eyes to check the presence of that worker so... so and so....

-Thank you very much. She said softly as a sign of peace, but the man left without even looking at her. The doctor took a deep breath, knowing that his disdain was totally justified. Samir appeared behind them down the hallway, carrying a huge bucket of paint.

-Well ma'am, I'm leaving

-He's leaving? Leaving us? Like this?

Dr. Klein surveyed the complete mess in the hallway and looked at him so perplexed that the man smiled in amusement.

-My crew will stay and work. Don't worry, when we're done with this place the Pope's church will look like a shack.

-The Pope's Church?

-Yes, the one in France, I think? -. He scratched his chin.

Brenda closed her eyes without answering.

-And when do you say the great completion of the Basilica will be?

The man looked at her as if she had suddenly sprouted two heads and four horns. It was clear that he had not understood a single word of her irony.

-I say, when will the work be finished? -. He asked, pointing to the third world war.

-Oh, that. The woman rolled her eyes as the worker replied in all seriousness. In two weeks.

Brenda opened her eyes in surprise but very very happy with the answer.

The walls were bare brick, the cables were in the air and the floor was half raised, but if the site manager said two weeks, why not believe him?

-Only two?

-Yes. He answered, and she almost kissed him.

-Now if you'll excuse me, I'm leaving. Your husband is waiting for me at another construction site.

-Yes, yes of course," he answered happily. Two weeks... two weeks...

Connor would have his precious art studio and she would have a practice worthy of her level.

-Two weeks and like the Pope's.

The master builder commented as he left and this time Brenda was not offended by his ignorance. She was happy. She had never imagined that such a mess could be undone in just two weeks. When she told Connor he would be as happy as she was.

"Connor...," she thought somewhat disgusted. "Poor guy had to cancel the session with the hose god." She thought amused.

Brenda bent down to plug in the cord to the second desk lamp, when a most masculine voice interrupted her. The woman, on all fours under the desk and reaching for the wall socket, lifted her head over her shoulder and tried to look back, but was puzzled.

-I'm looking for Connor McNeal. You wouldn't happen to know where I could find him?

The doctor was only able to shake her head. That man was not a God, he was "The God". For heaven's sake, such a man could not be of this world.

-They told me you were waiting for me in your studio," he commented, looking at the cement bags, "but clearly I've got the wrong address.

-No, no... it's here... me, him... -Please, I'm not a little girl to get stuck". We're in the works. She answered as best she could while looking at her long legs wrapped in jeans that fit her like a dream.

The wonderful male specimen raised an eyebrow uncomprehendingly and she bit her tongue for becoming perfectly brainless.

The woman got up as best she could from the floor and tried to regain her composure while shaking off her wrinkled clothes.

-Connor is my friend and he has his office here. I mean next to me, I mean next door. And you must be?

-My name is Angel. We're meeting for a modeling.

"What a well placed name," she thought, choking on her thoughts and never ceasing to admire those little honey-colored eyes.

-You see, Connor is not here, I understand he left a message for you at home. We've had a problem with dispatch and unfortunately he had to cancel the appointment.

-I came straight from work and haven't listened to my messages. Anyway, I will call you back. Thanks for the information.

-I, uh... you're welcome.... - She replied sighing as she watched him leave and found that he was as perfect when he came as he was when he left.

"Will all gays be like this one? Because I think I might make an exception and..."

-When you stop drooling I need your opinion.

Akim didn't mean to sound so angry, but seeing her look at that guy made him burn even hotter with rage. She was not only an unscrupulous stiff but she was also into the typical brainless handsome guys. Please! How wrong he'd been with her daydreaming about a woman who wasn't worth the trouble.

-No, I wasn't, I wasn't.... -Yes, yes, I was, and why does that damned bricklayer show up when you least expect him?"

-Whatever you say. Which of the two? -He commented angrily, holding up two pieces of stone?

-What am I supposed to answer? -He said, looking at the material the man was holding in his hands.

-Polished white or off-white," he replied hastily. Having her around upset him.

She was a stiff, cold and ruthless woman, but those little chocolate eyes captivated him like a trained puppy.

-Are there any differences? -The doctor narrowed her eyes, trying to clear them, but nothing.

Akim did not answer, he just watched her waiting for an answer. He wanted to leave the place as soon as possible. At such a short distance he was able to perceive a delicate vanilla scent that began to intoxicate him and he was not sure he could contain himself.

-The target... Broken? -He said, looking at one of the pieces and hoping that it was the right one.

The worker was about to leave when Brenda asked him curiously.

-What are they supposed to be? The truth is I don't know much about materials," she commented amused, trying to gain the man's trust and start from scratch. She was not as he imagined her to be and for reasons out of this world his opinion mattered to her.

-Decoration of the bathrooms. He answered sharply.

Of course, I'm absent-minded, but it's hard to understand, you see, once I...

-Doctor, I have work to do.

-Of course, and I don't want to interrupt you. After all, finishing this mess in just two weeks won't be an easy task.

The bricklayer watched her with a small gesture on his lips that seemed to be a hidden smile, amusement? Brenda couldn't decipher it.

-Two weeks? -he asked amused.

-Yes, that's what Samir said. Isn't it incredible?

Akim left without answering and deepening the gesture to something more akin to a soundless laugh.

Dr. Klein looked at him confused and uncomprehending. She and the young man had gotten off on the wrong foot and it would not be easy to straighten him out, but she would do her best. The poor man had not been to blame for his outbursts. It was clear that the nerves of the calamitous play had gotten her out of control, but she was not like that. She was sweet, kind and understanding, she repeated herself once again.

-Brenda, Brenda Klein? -A perfectly coiffed man in an impeccable suit approached her, dodging long wooden slats as he asked somewhat fearfully.

-Yes. She said perplexed when she recognized the character.

He had in front of him the president of the Liberal Democratic Front, the country's current majority party.

-I'm Michael, Michael Murray.

-I know.

The man passed into the consultation room without looking back at the complete chaos. Brenda pointed to the couch as she closed the door.

-We are in the middle of a small renovation.

-You'd think so... -he said as he brushed a sand stain off his spotless jacket.

-We will be comfortable here.

-If you say so...

The man kept looking at everything with his eyes wide open like saucers.

-Please, Mr. Murray, if you would do me the favor of sitting on the couch.

The man tried to sit down when at that very moment blows from beyond the grave resounded throughout the office, shaking the foundations of the building.

Politically incorrect

The man didn't look a day over fifty, and in spite of being so well preserved, he still had that constipated look on his face from the moment he walked through the consultation room, looking like a constipated man on the verge of wanting to and not being able to.

-What was that?

Brenda tried to calm down and explain to him that her unconscious husband had started a pharaonic work without consulting her, but he preferred to skip the explanations and beg her to take a seat while she headed for the door.

-I wonder what the fuss is all about!

The woman screamed at the top of her lungs, but no one heard her. The crew pounded and hammered incessantly while the hateful bricklayer in front of the column, with his back to her, turned on and off the damned tool from hell. He didn't know what the damn thing was called and didn't care, he just wanted it to stop the infernal sound it made as it cut through the steel. He walked with his arms up in the air and his eyes injected with hatred when the crew, noticing his anger, began to make way like the Red Sea before Moses, and stopped making noise. Everyone stopped except him, who, with his back to the spectacle, continued working with the utmost concentration.

"I don't give a damn if I'm not like that, I swear I'll kill him." He thought as he stopped behind Akim's back who excited to see the steel split in two continued at full speed sending sparks flying through the air.

Brenda, with two strong taps of her index finger on his back, got his attention. He took off his goggles placing them on his forehead and turned around smiling. He thought it was Nikola and he was ready to tease him by demonstrating how he had finally managed to bend the blissful spine, but the smile was instantly wiped off as he noticed how the doctor, with both arms up in a crouch, was looking at him on the verge of murder. He turned off his noisy radial saw and deposited it on the floor. That woman was looking for war and there was no question of leaving a weapon near her, he thought amused as he watched the colors of fury tinge her delicate face, further highlighting those melted chocolate eyes. Please! Could he ever see her for the uptight, hateful woman she was?

-You tell, doc-to-ra.

"Now you're talking to me as you and with a twist, well, so be it".

-You see, o-bre-ro -suck it -I'm in a consultation and I need a little quiet.

Akim narrowed one eye as a sign of war. She would throw down the gauntlet, well, he would pick it up.

-You don't know how sorry I am, doc-to-ra, but we have orders to finish as soon as possible. As I understand it, these are your own directives, or am I wrong? -he commented with a rogue smile.

Brenda no longer had patience, she had lost it first thing in the morning and she didn't give a damn about education and good manners, she wanted to kill someone and that bricklayer fit her like a glove.

-And now I want you to stop. He said biting his tongue to keep from swearing.

Akim was most amused. Apparently the uptight woman had blood in her veins. Too bad she was such a shallow woman.

-He said with apparent seriousness as he picked up his tool from the floor.

Brenda, thinking seriously about the legal consequences of committing murder, decided to take three deep breaths and let her angry feelings escape to a farther place. Her yoga teacher said that was the best strategy for subduing the grudges of the flesh, and she tried it.

"One, two, three, let him escape...". She thought trying to regain her calm and speak logically to the man. If she explained serenely, he would surely understand her.

Akim, who kept watching her with increasing amusement, knew he had to collaborate, after all she was the boss, but how nice it was to have her in front of him, even if it was only to discuss. He had been dreaming about her for so many months that resistance to those little chocolate eyes was impossible.

-Well, doc-to-ra? -Are you speechless?

Brenda thought that, if he spelled out the word 'doctor' one more time, she would kick him so hard in the very balls of his ass that it would knock the wind out of him.

-Look... -. She looked at him doubtfully. Did he know her name?

-Akim, my name is Akim. He said with his thick accent that Brenda had not yet managed to locate.

-Akim, that patient is a very important personality and he needs me," the man focused his gaze on her and the woman breathed a sigh of relief. He was getting her attention. And to tell the truth, so was he. Those eyes were heavenly crystal clear. Like heaven...

-I beg your pardon?

-Nothing, it's just me. I mean, if you could please interrupt that infernal sound for at least my hour of consultation I would appreciate it very much.

Akim scratched his chin as if thinking about the answer and the doctor would have liked to pierce him with the screwdriver hanging from the pocket of his overalls, but he breathed, one, two, three... and let the anger escape... If only Master Yogi could see her.

-Do we have a truce?

Brenda gave him the most buying smile she was capable of and Akim had to lean against the pillar to keep from falling right there or doing much worse. He calmed his heart that wanted to jump out of his chest and answered with his characteristic coldness.

-I don't think so.

The doctor, who at this point was tapping her shoe on the floor, cursed so loudly that the workers, who were following the discussion with great interest, exclaimed in horror.

"No, no. I'm not like that!".

-Tell me who's in charge or you'll find out! I want some silence and I'll have it. I want you to tell me who's boss and I don't give a damn what happened to you in childhood or your damn badass traumas, I don't have to put up with you.

-What a psychologist, and so is humanity. Akim laughed cheekily.

-I swear I'll kill you. -Who!

She looked at the five around her as one fearfully pointed a finger at Akim himself. Brenda growled angrily as the worker was having the time of his life. Having her angry was better than not having her at all, ten thousand times better. The woman was about to start the third world war, when Nikola, standing behind her, made a gesture to her friend of the most significant kind. The man accepted the threat and decided to end the discussion.

-All right, doc-to-ra. We'll work for a couple of hours without making too much noise.

He removed his protective glove and extended his calloused hand toward her in sign of signing the truce. Brenda watched him suspicious of his sudden outburst of understanding, but accepted the hand in the spirit of peace in the working world.

Her delicate fingers barely brushed him, but he felt an unnatural tingle run through him. She was going to release him quickly and he wouldn't let her. His calloused hand enclosed her tightly trying to hold her back and stop time in that instant. She had never felt anything like it. Never. Her hard body reacted to the mere touch of his skin, was that even possible? They both looked at each other and Brenda smiled at him in a sign of truce and Akim felt the ground open up under his feet. Either that or his knees were shaking just looking at her. He hoped it was the former because otherwise he was disastrously lost.

-You three will work at the entrance portal! Nikola, Alexander and I will remain on this floor, quietly.

The crew nodded to Akim's orders as they each headed off to resume their tasks.

-What happened here? -Nikola asked with an arched eyebrow when she checked that the doctor was far enough away.

-Mind your own business.

Akim went for a wheelbarrow and Nikola thought no good would come of it.

Somewhat calmer and with a rather illogical smile, she entered the consultation room. She was confused, her manners and control were lost when she was in front of that man. She shook her head and closed the door, trying to forget what had happened. It would be the best thing to do.

-Well, we can begin. She said a little calmer.

The man, who thank heaven had not escaped, nodded resignedly. Dr. Klein gave him room to adjust while she started the recorder. He picked up his reading glasses and took a seat next to the patient's couch. Her first consultation of the day was beginning and what she sensed was an exciting story awaited her.

Session 1

-Mr. Murray, before we begin therapy I would like to offer you some guidelines for what will be our sessions from now on. I want you to know that what we talk to each other is subject to strict professional secrecy, so you should not hesitate to express anything you need or consider appropriate.

The man nodded, trying to lean back on the couch between nervous and cautious. His haughtiness and arrogance prevented him from fully trusting a stranger, and Brenda understood this perfectly. He continued with his lengthy presentation, because in spite of the many minutes he spent on it, it was usually the most effective way to get the patient to be sufficiently at ease to begin to explain his problem.

He talked for more than ten relaxing minutes and went on to explain the emotion chart they would be working on together.

-As you can see," he said, pointing to the sheet of paper he handed her, "it has a list of emotions ranging from number one to number fifteen.

The patient accepted the sheet and looked at it reluctantly, although he refrained from making any value judgment.

-The chart ranges from states of complete well-being such as joy, freedom, or love, to emotions such as frustration, irritation, or revenge," he paused a moment to continue. You don't need to read them right now, but I do need you to get used to the terms. Mr. Murray, the sessions will be grouped in groups of five. At the end of each group we will evaluate your emotional state by placing it on the value scale and discuss possible alternatives for improvement.

The man swallowed hard, thinking that this was getting complicated. At first he accepted the demands of the prime minister and member of his party, but now he doubted that this was a good idea.

-Brenda, do you have anything to drink in this office? I could really use a drink.

Dr. Klein smiled at the request. She was too used to attitudes like that. Presumptuous men with high quotas of power, accustomed to dominate the situation, and little inclined to let themselves be guided. And even less so if that counselor was female.

-Mr. Murray, are you sure you wish to participate in this therapy? -he said in a firm tone. Because if not, I would like you to save us both some time.

The politician grumbled under his breath. He wasn't used to being scolded and found he didn't like it, so he decided to take command of the situation and cut the crap. It was time for that doctor to meet the incomparable Michael Murray.

-Brenda, you can call me Michael, and now that we are getting to know each other, let me say that I never thought I would meet a beauty like you. He commented seductively and apparently very used to being seductive.

Brenda took note of what happened, describing a profile that was becoming clearer and clearer to her. Authoritarian, overbearing and womanizing.

-Mr. Mu-rray," she clarified slowly, "I will be your therapist and will be happy to help you out of the trance you are in, as long as you fully understand that this is a strictly professional meeting in which your goodwill is the backbone of any solution. Regarding your dealings with me I would like you to call me Dr. Klein, but if you wish, a plain doctor will not be inconvenient either. Is that all right with you?

He nodded angrily. That woman, besides being smart, was trying to put him in his place and those were qualities he didn't like in a woman. The docile ones, easy smile, and perky ass, were better in his canon of values to highlight.

Brenda smiled at the sight of her patient's total dislocation. In less than five minutes she had shooed his fumes away and tossed them out the window. Michael Murray's background positioned him as a shrewd strategist, a high-level politician, and an unbridled skull, so she thought it best to make him understand the distance between them. She was not in front of one of his many flings, she was his therapist and she had a goal to accomplish. The improvement of whatever his problem was.

-Dr. Klein," the man with incipient gray hair and a raven-black gaze remarked coolly, "I think you have no idea who I am. I don't think you have any idea who I am. Let me make my position clear. Maybe you have been locked up so long among the loonies that you are not very clear about my position and my influence in the political life of this country. He commented threateningly.

Brenda nodded as she drew a smiley face on her notes ☺ . An angry outburst used to be a good way to get information on characters like that.

-Mr. Murray, first of all, I would like to tell you that my patients are not "crazy" but people with problems who, like you, are waiting for the resolution of the most complex situations," the man shifted uncomfortably on the couch, but did not get up and Brenda celebrated the first triumph. Michael, why are you here? -She said, using his first name to placate him.

-The party forces me," he replied, annoyed.

While it was true that her party, the Liberal Democrat Front, had "advised" her to undergo therapy, she noticed by her uncomfortable movements, something that went beyond political pressures.

-It's strange... -He doesn't look like a man who will be convinced or take advice from anyone, and that's why I ask you again, Mr. Murray, why are you here?

Now he was really uncomfortable. Sweat on his forehead, his face was uncrossed and his fists were clenched. Yes, he was on the right track to discover the real reason for his visit.

Why don't you tell me what you want me to answer and we'll save all this pseudo-medicine nonsense that will get us nowhere? -He said, trying to stab at the core of his professional pride.

Brenda did not bother to answer what made no sense to her. Her concern was focused on the search for truths and she would find them, she was the best in her field for a reason.

-I am only looking for the truth. If you are not willing to offer it I think it will be better for both of us if you leave.

The man opened his eyes without understanding her. This woman was not like other women, like the silly little holes he used to conquer to take to bed.

-I said I'm obliged! Did you hear anything I said? And why are you throwing me out? -. He replied angrily.

-I am simply saying that if you want me to help you, you must come clean with me. No therapy based on lies can ever be effective. Our patient-doctor relationship is based on complete trust in each other.

-I don't know her! -he grunted, scrunching his forehead.

-Maybe not directly, but he knows my history and he has been sitting on my couch for half an hour so I consider that I have passed the initial test and it is time to move on to the second level.

-And which one is that? -he commented, challenging the professional.

-The truth. The one that keeps your emotions. And this is when I ask you again, why are you here today? -He said with temperance and absolute resolution.

-Guilt. Damn it. Guilt! I'm guilty...

Dr. Klein leaned her spine against the back of the chair and, crossing her legs, adjusted the fold of her dress. At this very moment the real therapy began.

At a glance

She exhaustedly picked up her laptop and the collection of papers scattered on her desk and kept thinking about the most complicated session of the day. Michael Murray was an exciting case, but one of the most complex he would encounter in his entire career. Getting the man open became maddening, and although he managed to extract some very interesting information, he knew that the man was still hiding a lot in the back of his mind. A high-level politician, interested in the licentious life, it would be nothing new to her if it weren't for the high levels of guilt that plagued him. No, he was not there because of party pressures, as she herself at first came to assume. The man was seeking some kind of redemption that would relieve him of a burden too heavy to carry.

At some point in the therapy he sensed that guilt was intermingled with fear. He was afraid, of whom and why? He was not the kind of man who seemed to scare easily, and what did that fear have to do with the urgent need that moved the prime minister himself? He told her on the phone about a man who wanted to abandon his path of excess, but no one spoke of guilt or fear. What were they hiding?

Brenda stared at the thin brown folder with Michael Murray's name on the cover and thought in concentration.

"Men like Murray are greedy, arrogant, sensual and with a perverse touch, but never fearful or guilty. Boasters of their power yes, but nothing much more serious." She thought intrigued.

-How was your day, honey?

A smiling Connor walked through the door, tossing his backpack full of painter's tools onto the couch.

-Long, very long. And yours?

-He got better and no thanks to you. He replied with mock anger.

Brenda tried to think. The day had been too hard to remember inconsequential details.

-If you mean your fireman," Connor nodded in amusement. Then let me make it clear that if the God of Olympus didn't get your message, it wasn't my fault. He commented with a smile.

-I take it you've seen it?

-She said amused as she picked up her purse from the rack.

-And because of you I almost missed it," he said amused. I almost missed it.

And I'll tell you again, without wanting to be a know-it-all, that it was me! -he pointed to his chest with his hand -the one who called you to tell you about his unsuccessful visit.

-And since I was able to meet him later because of that, let's say I forgive you, a little.

-A little bit? But you'll be... I'd rather not ask how that "art session" went because I fear the worst.

-And you wouldn't be wrong," he replied with a more than satisfying laugh. Let's go have a few beers, we deserve them.

-You have no shame. Me working here nonstop while you were cavorting with a God from the seventh heaven, and you tell me we deserve it?

-Yes, we are both exhausted. He replied, laughing unabashedly.

They both walked out laughing as Brenda turned off the lights.

-All right, I accept, but only one. I have to go home early.

Yes, yes, I know the whole faithful and self-sacrificing wife thing. Let's go get those beers before I fall asleep with the speech.

Connor grabbed her by the shoulders and pulled her out of the building quickly. He knew her too well and if he let her think just a little bit, she would go home and forget about living. At least living in the sense he thought of it, in which life was meant to be lived. With all the passion one was capable of.

Nikola was talking non-stop trying to distract him and Akim did his best not to punch him, and shut him up, before leaving on his bike. His mood was turning from red to green so quickly that even he couldn't stand it. He had a job for which he should be grateful. It was no longer necessary to go around twenty thousand construction sites asking if they had anything for him, he was now part of architect Max Brown's crew and that meant secure work for many years to come, but he was far from happy.

This morning he thought his nonsense of continuing to dream about her was over, but nothing could be further from the truth. As always, as far as his life was concerned, the demon was not only putting in his tail but his whole body. Almost a year seeing her from afar, dreaming of her voice, her perfume, and when he finally believed he had the will to separate from his platonic love, he goes and gets into the very mouth of the wolf.

Now he would not only see her every damn day, but it would be impossible for him not to look for her with his eyes, provoke her with his pokes or try to caress her with his hands. He was totally lost. To ask for another transfer would mean the loss of his job and he could not afford it, and on the other hand there was the small detail of not believing himself capable of leaving her again. That woman had him totally bewitched. It was impossible to get her out of his mind.

-We should have called a couple of girls to change that sour face you're wearing. - Akim's best friend commented as he rested the two beer mugs on the hard wooden table and Akim pressed his forehead with his hand. "Women, no thanks, one is more than enough for me."

Akim drank almost all of his beer in one gulp trying to find a solution he couldn't find. Maybe if he moved to Alaska?

-Are you going to tell me which bug has bitten you? We've got a job and a good one, but you're acting crazy. First you grumble, then you grin, then you curse, then you grin again. What the hell is wrong with you?

-Akim used to be sparing with words and lately he was becoming more and more so.

"Maybe he's overwhelmed. Being a single father is not easy," thought Nikola, who, knowing his friend all too well, tried to divert the conversation in other directions. Akim was the best of friends in the world, but the most closed-minded.

-How about Lola? I understand she's crazy about your bones.

Akim stared at the door, watching the couple that had just entered. He cursed again and again between his teeth, although without looking away from that smile that was engraved in that place they call heart and that he didn't know he possessed. She looked so cheerful, so happy..... What would it feel like to be the reason why the woman you adore wouldn't stop smiling? It was sad, but nothing like that had ever happened to him. Women offered themselves to him and he took them, not much more. None of them interested him. Not even the mother of his son ever made him fall in love.

"Can I be such an asshole?" he thought as he realized that today, after a year of dreaming about her, had been the first time he had spoken to her. No, this was not platonic love, this was imbecility.

He, with his six-foot-five plus, tattooed shoulders and scary hands, was pining for an older, married woman. "May God come down and see," he said to himself and giving Nikola another of his inexplicable smiles.

-Now what? Who are you looking at? -Nikola asked curiously when he saw the sad smile on his friend's face.

-No one. He replied angrily, averting his gaze and taking a huge gulp of beer.

Nikola, whose back was to the door, turned hurriedly to gossip, when he saw them sitting at a table near the exit.

-Isn't that Dr. Klein?

-You can.

-And why are you smiling? - he commented intrigued.

-His anger turned out to be even greater than usual.

-Yes, you do.

-Don't be an asshole," he grumbled as he felt cornered. I wasn't smiling.

-Yes.

-No.

Akim covered his face again with his usual indifference and anger and Nikola, wanting to keep all his teeth in place, preferred to stop asking. If anyone knew about fighting and combat it was Akim, after all, his fists had kept them alive when they left Chechnya.

-So do we call them or not?

-To whom? -Akim tried to concentrate on his friend's conversation.

That smile called out to him again and again like a spring to a thirsty man.

To Lola and her friend -Fuck, man, concentrate!

-No.

-Why not! If you don't come, Lola doesn't come and her friend doesn't come either, and I'm left alone, and as I've told you a thousand times and I remind you, once again..." he spelled out nervously, "I'm very, very, desperate. I've been here for a long time... and I need it.

Akim smiled at his friend's nonsense. They had both spent every hour of the last year working their butts off to get their respective families ahead, and although Nikola had no commitments, his salary was more than necessary for his parents' livelihood.

Lola was a good friend whom he called to meet his needs from time to time, but whom he left at home at the end of the night. He did not wish to create false illusions. The young man drank his last drink and got up to leave.

-Shall we go?

-I am, we get up early tomorrow and I'm tired.

Nikola drained his beer and stood up in a huff.

-All right, all right, but you're not off the hook for the weekend. Akim arched his eyebrow and Nikola smiled cheerfully. From helping me get a couple of babes.

Akim patted her back in understanding as he walked through the door without looking toward the doctor's desk. He had no desire to be found out as a stalker, which was what he had become in the last year.

-And don't you know how to look for them yourself?

Akim followed the joke and left knowing perfectly well who he was leaving behind. One of whom he could neither look at, nor say goodbye to, nor caress, nor kiss....

"I am lost..."

Brenda knew the instant she sat down that a pair of crystalline eyes were focused directly on her, but her reaction was one of utter sadness. That young man had hated her from the first moment he had seen her, and grief and regret washed over her. Her job was to help people with traumas and the worker seemed to have them and although she hardly knew him, she had to admit that her reaction to him in the morning was not the most appropriate. She was not like that, she repeated herself over and over again trying to justify the unjustifiable. Akim was getting on her nerves and she couldn't help it.

-Have I lost you?

-No, it's just that I just realized that I'm not always perfect. He said ironically.

-Why, if you were, wouldn't you have let your dearest friend destroy the building where we work? You could have rented us another place or given us plenty of notice, but, of course, the wonderful Max Brown wouldn't have had time for such trifles.

-Connor...

-Until when we will suffer their martyrdom.

-If you are referring to the construction site, Samir has assured that in two weeks they will have everything ready. He replied, puffing on the foam of his dark beer.

-Two weeks? -Are you sure? But it looks like a nuclear bomb was dropped on us.

-Yes, I thought so too, you see, chaos seems to have an expiration date.

-So, honey, let's toast to our second reason. He lifted the mug and landed it in the air against hers.

-And the first one was?

-This afternoon's great cock.

-Connor!

Brenda smiled somewhat embarrassed at her friend's foul language. She was so controlled, polite and discreet. At least she had been until she met that worker.

-Sorry, I forgot I was in front of the respectable Dr. Klein.

-And don't forget it. He replied cheerfully.

They both laughed with abandon and Connor hugged her with immense affection. Brenda was his friend, his sister, the woman who always raised a hand to defend him. She didn't care about his loose tongue or his sexual condition. She appreciated him just the way he was and that made her his dearest right eye.

-I have to go. He said looking at his wristwatch.

-Some day... some day...

-What is that supposed to mean? -The woman asked curiously.

-Nothing. Come on, if you don't arrive soon, we'll have to put up with your dear architect's protests.

-He doesn't bother." He lied brazenly.

-Whatever you say.

Connor got up and walked beside her to walk her to her car. Someday Brenda should see life through her own eyes and not through Max's, someday....

We are who we are

-You came in very late last night, did something happen?

Max commented without taking his eyes off the newspaper. He liked to read it with his morning coffee in the kitchen, and even though everyone would tell him how old it was, he liked the tradition that went back to his great-grandfather. And if something worked after so many years, then why change it?

-Nothing special.

Brenda poured herself some coffee in a cup as she hurriedly picked up an endless stream of folders, and stuffed them carelessly into the briefcase.

-When you arrived I was asleep.

Brenda picked up a cookie that she held in her teeth as she fumbled for her car keys trying to find an escape route. Max hated it when she went out with Connor, let alone on a weekday.

-A long day. That's all.

-I see.

-And how about Connor? Because you met him, didn't you?

-All right. He really didn't feel like arguing.

-Nothing special?

-For heaven's sake, Max, we went out for a beer. That's all. Yesterday turned out to be a most stressful day for which you are largely to blame. Brenda snorted tiredly and took a long sip of coffee to leave as soon as possible, and she didn't know if it was because of the amount of work that awaited her or because this discussion was proving to be too repetitive, but she wanted to leave.

-I don't know what you mean about guilt. I'm just saying that I arrived late at night, we had barely seen each other, but you preferred to have a drink with Connor. That's all." He said as he folded the newspaper and laid it on the counter.

-That's all? Don't be a liar. You don't like it when we hang out. You hate it when I see Connor and I'm tired of telling you he's my friend. You keep prejudging him for no reason.

-For no reason at all? Despot, tyrant, prissy and constipated are the mildest adjectives with which he usually regales my ears. He is not a good influence on you, and you know it.

-I am not a child. She replied obfuscated for not being able to run away from the same old argument.

-If you say so.

-Yes, I say so. I say it and I affirm it," she replied angrily. And, by the way, while we're on the subject of sincerity, when were you going to tell me about the disaster in my office, when the pigs were flying?

-The pigs... please, Brenda. That dirty phrase sure belongs to him. She shook her head.

-It's one hundred percent mine. And now don't digress. Did you think I wouldn't notice? And how am I supposed to take care of my patients?

-Leave the practice for a while," he said bluntly.

-What? -Not a chance.

-You can afford it.

-And do what? Stay at home?

-I would never ask that of you. I'm not a Cro-Magnon. It's just that now that I'm so busy outside and the practice is under construction, maybe you could dedicate more time to...

-To what?

-To me? he said with a side-to-side smile.

Brenda did not answer. She didn't know if his comments were a joke or a nightmare.

-My life, don't be like that," he said, grabbing her by the shoulders to hold her in a tight embrace. - You're the talk of the town, you're the beautiful wife of a famous architect, I couldn't let you have a cubbyhole as a practice. You understand, don't you?

-Is that what this is all about? The opinion of others?

-Honey, it's all because of other people's opinions. Don't worry, you'll have a practice worthy of a woman of your class," he said as he placed a tender kiss on her head. Don't be angry, you'll see how much a small sacrifice will be worth. You'll be the best psychologist in town, and I'll be the proudest husband.

Brenda accepted the hug, although with very little desire. She would have liked to tell him many things, for example, that she didn't care about others, and that her famous reputation meant nothing if she wasn't able to help those who needed it most. More than once they had argued for similar reasons and Max had simply pointed out the gold watch on her wrist, the Manolo Blahnik on her feet or the convertible parked outside the door.

-I'm late. He commented, releasing his grip.

-And me, I'm in the middle of designing the Crystal Tower.

-They gave it to you!

-Yes, yesterday," he smiled, highlighting his manly features. That's why I was waiting for you to arrive, I was crazy to tell you. With the Bristol play and the start of the Crystal Tower in Paris I won't have a minute to spare.

Brenda felt somewhat apologetic and kissed him on the cheek in apology. She didn't know how, but Max always managed to get that feeling out of her. Guilt.

-Today I arrive early and we celebrate by having dinner somewhere special. How do you see it?

-I'm afraid we must postpone. I leave for Paris early tomorrow morning. We have a meeting I can't miss.

-Will you be away for a long time?

-About three days. -Will you miss me?

-You know I do.

-That's good.

Her husband pulled her into a tight embrace as he gave her a soft, gentle, loving kiss on the lips.

Brenda was rearranging some files when the door opened without knocking.

-I'm sorry, I thought you were out.

Akim apologized petrified on the spot. It was clear that he had not expected to meet her.

-You can come in. And you can talk to me about you again. There's no need for such formality, after all, I imagine we'll be seeing a lot of each other.

-I'm afraid so," he mumbled.

-I'm sorry, you were saying? -He asked as he bent down to rearrange a drawer, leaving Akim with the image of a pair of pants that fit perfectly on each of his buttocks.

-I'm going to die...

Brenda was willing to be a better person than she had been the day before. She would treat that worker with the absolute politeness she was accustomed to, but it would be helpful if he would be able to speak a little louder since she wasn't hearing anything he was saying.

-I'm coming for the screen," she said, trying to turn her face away from her beautiful buttocks and towards the hideous, badly painted wood.

-Yes, please. She commented amused, getting a smile out of him.

-Your friend, the painter...

Brenda sat up and the silk shirt moved just enough to show a small embroidered detail of the bra. It wasn't much, to tell the truth, it was almost nothing, but more than enough for a man as interested as he was.

-My friend the painter?

Brenda helped him trying to understand the unfinished sentence. It was not that this man could be considered a man of few words, he was almost mute, she thought strangely.

Akim cursed himself and his stupid throat that went dry at the mere glimpse of a tiny bit of white lace. He was coming off like a brainless idiot.

-He found another office," he replied quickly before getting stuck again.

He reached over to the furniture to grab it and lift it up with his hands and get it out of there as soon as possible. He didn't want to look even more stupid than he already felt.

-Another site? -Where?

-At the end of the hallway," Akim replied, carrying the wood on his back and blocking his view of Dr. Klein. That woman upset his temper and something else that wasn't exactly temper. His body was responding like a lapdog and he preferred to get out of there as soon as possible or the physical changes would be more obvious.

-I don't understand, yesterday there was no room and today we have plenty? And you don't know if...?

-Doctor, this thing is heavy, could you let me come in and sort it out with your friend? -The worker spoke agitated and Brenda was embarrassed by his lack of tact. Surely that thing was heavy and very heavy.

-Excuse me, excuse me... I follow you.

-That's all I need.... -the man stammered in annoyance.

-You were saying something?

-No.

Akim carried the wooden thing on his shoulders closely followed by Dr. Klein. Too close he thought as he smelled the sweet scent of her exquisite perfume. He had never been with any woman who smelled like her, dressed like her, talked like her, looked like her....

He was grateful that the screen prevented him from seeing the delicate swaying of her hips as she walked, but his imagination, which had been flying out of control lately, decided to picture it without asking permission. Her arms tightened their grip on the wood. She had to finish that task as soon as possible and return to her world of dust, cement and paint.

A world where a delicate doctor with luscious curves was the most evil, selfish and shallow witch of them all. It was either that or recognize that in his first judgment of her he had been wrong and admit that Brenda was as delicious on the outside as she was on the inside.

-I am leaving.

The worker walked out in a more than frightened manner, leaving the piece of wood almost at the entrance of the new studio and Connor watched him in amazement.

-What have you done to her? -She asked her friend as she walked through the door of her new studio.

-I can't stand it. What about you? What is this place?

He asked, directing his gaze to the wide space.

-It turns out that this morning Akim came to see me and offered it to me.

-It's pretty good.

Brenda looked around the place, amazed that it was still standing. The walls were intact, the large window looked decent enough and the natural light was enviable. Undoubtedly a well-hidden treasure in the midst of the hecatomb.

-How was it saved?

-Akim said to leave it until the end of the work, so I will have a place to work without bothering you in your practice.

-And you say he offered it to you?

Yes, apparently he's the day-to-day manager. Isn't he great?

-Yes, yes it is, but...

Connor waited for her comment, but Brenda declined to continue. There was no point in looking for a fifth foot in the cat.

-I won't bother you anymore, honey. He said giving her a loud kiss on her cheeks.

-You never bother me. He said smiling.

She glanced at the watch on her wrist and stormed out the door. I'd better go before Murray gets here.

-Michael Murray, the politician?

-Same.

-Honey, be careful. Politicians are like a mafia.

-Don't be silly," he replied, his voice rising as he ran down the hall to his office.

We have come up against politics

-Mr. Murray.

-Brenda.

-I thought we had agreed on certain rules. She commented seriously, but far from feeling angry.

-My dear, we both know I'm not going to hit on you. You are as safe by my side as with a pet kitten.

Brenda adjusted her glasses on the bridge of her nose, not quite knowing how to respond to such a comment. As a professional she was grateful, but as a woman, that was something else. "Am I so bad physically that I don't even attract a party animal by nature? The truth is that I don't consider myself so old, maybe mature, but not old at all. And I don't look bad at all, what's more, many men might even see me as pretty..." She thought pursing her lips and raising her eyebrows. Murray leaned back on the couch unbidden and began to speak, making her forget her upended feminine pride.

-I'm here because I don't know where to turn.

-I thought we were here to clarify your behavior and try to make you feel better about yourself, weren't we? -He said with a touch of sarcasm and unaccustomed confidence.

-Yes, that too, if I have any hope," he replied with little grace. You see, Brenda? -He looked at her as if asking permission to call her by name and she agreed with an affirmative gesture. A little over a month ago I got involved with a woman I shouldn't have.

-I thought he was married.

-But not castrated. You know, we are men and we have our needs.

Brenda wrote in her notebook: Macho asshole. Treatment: Hit him over the head with a mallet. ☹

-And does being with other women make you feel guilty?

-Not at all.

The patient's sincerity surprised the doctor and she said: "Remorse, zero. Treatment: exchange sledgehammer for kicks ;-)

Brenda smiled as she wrote down her nonsensical notes. Many of her colleagues might not agree with the peculiar style of her diagnoses, but they served her well. At the end of therapy and in the solitude of her office, those little written jokes often gave her another perspective on more intricate cases.

-Michael, why are we in these therapy sessions?

-Why am I paying you?

-I touched. He replied smiling.

The man loosened the knot of his tie to lie more comfortably on the couch. He crossed his legs and took a deep breath. Brenda knew from his gestures that he was going to start to come clean and that made her very excited.

He still did not understand why the politician and his party had called upon his services. Murray, at no time did he show any desire to be a sheep returning to the fold, so what exactly brought him to his practice? He waited without speaking. Murray was taking his time and she allowed him to. Opening up to a stranger is not always an easy task and she understood that perfectly well. Not for nothing was she one of the best in her profession.

-Brenda, I am going to tell you a story and I hope you will listen to me. At first I refused to come, today, however, I am absolutely sure that you were the only person who can help us.

-Help us?

-To my wife and me.

Brenda adjusted her glasses on the bridge of her nose to write enthusiastically: Concerned about her partner's well-being. Therapy: Possible joint therapy (finger up).

-Do you want to save your marriage?

-My marriage has nothing to do with it. I will never be separated from Lorelaine.

-Never is a very long word.

-It is the reality.

-So, what should I help you with?

-To save her.

Brenda uncrossed her legs to sit up straighter on her chair.

-From grief, pain, sadness?

-No. From death.

Dr. Klein's eyes widened as her mouth closed from side to side. For a few seconds she felt as out of sorts as ever, but instantly she remembered the story of one of her patients, and the ongoing dramatization of her life, so she took a breath and affirmed professionally.

-I am sure that if the two of you work together the possibilities are great. I understand your feelings and admire your concern, but even though infidelities can be painful, they don't cause anyone's death. At least not physically.

-This one is.

Brenda held on to her notebook and dug her nails into the armrests for balance.

-Even though she was afraid of the confession, Brenda knew she would go all the way.

Was she curious? Very much so, caring? Even more so.

She leaned the notebook on the desk and folded her hands under her chin, ready to listen to every detail of the story. The politician looked at a fixed point on the ceiling concentrated in his thoughts and began to narrate as if it were a movie.

-It all started a little over a month and a half ago....

Confessions

-... it was one party among many. A yacht, good alcohol and good company to enjoy it with.

Brenda nodded in disgust. Those little parties where drugs and young models were offered as an open bar were known throughout high society.

-Nothing out of the ordinary," he continued unchanged. Just a spree to distract me from my obligations. Nothing important. You know, life in politics can be too stressful, and a few drinks now and then won't kill anyone.

Murray crossed his arms over his chest and Brenda analyzed his every move before writing in his notebook: Unnecessary justifications. Treatment: Observe guilty behaviors.

-I was with a friend having a glass of champagne when a beautiful model approached me," he continued, totally focused, not paying attention to the doctor and her notes. Normally the guests expect us to choose, but Roxane did not.

"Shall we choose?" Brenda shifted uncomfortably in her seat. The way he spoke of women as mere commercial commodities churned her insides. She was incapable of being able to count the number of women beaten or discarded by men she had helped. Women treated as mere articles of use and enjoyment. Many hours of her work were dedicated to collaborating with non-profit associations in order to reinstate in these women the confidence and self-esteem damaged by men like Michael Murray who saw them as mere pieces of meat. Brenda felt that her moral duty and social responsibility obliged her to collaborate with their recovery, but ethical ethics were mixed with a deep feeling of wanting to kick that guy out of her office.

She restrained herself from expressing any thoughts by drawing on her years of professionalism. That, and a sharp bite on her thumbnail that despite being a gesture Max hated, helped her keep her mouth shut in somewhat inappropriate situations. She may not have been there to judge but to listen, but her high level of professionalism did not prevent her from expressing on paper her most sincere repulses. Irritating macho asshole (angry face). Treatment: Kick in the balls. Several. Brenda smiled as the word 'several' stood out.

-I was flattered," he continued, speaking matter-of-factly. When a beauty with long legs, a black micro bikini, and a clump of silky hair as red as fire approaches you, it is impossible not to react. At first I was paralyzed. A woman like that, attracted to me, without any interest, threw me off.

"No interest? Doesn't he know he's one of the most influential people in the country? Really!" The doctor snorted and pointed out: dumb as hell. Treatment: No solution.

-We talked for a long time and although it was not as pleasant as I would have liked, it was enough for what we were looking for. You know, he was interested in my activities in politics, he gave his opinion on some projects proclaimed by the party, he even seemed to me almost intelligent.

Dr. Klein stirred in her seat looking at Grandma's old teapot. "Too far." She thought smiling.

-She was looking for a celebrity and I was looking for a good fuck, but you know, it's necessary to cover the file.

-File? -he said aloud without meaning to.

-Yes, you smile at her, pretend to be interested in her life and the fuck is assured.

Brenda continued to search with her eyes when she stopped on her own writing pen.

"Works for me." He thought about sticking it in his forehead and smashing that atrophied brain but his professionalism wouldn't allow it. "Damn deontology." She thought saddened.

-Normally I care very little about their conversations. You know what I mean. Men are more about asses and nice tits, but this time I made a mistake.

"Connor will bring me cake." She thought as she imagined the front page of the next day's newspapers: Famous doctor freaks out in front of her patient's wretched male chauvinist prick. Rumor has it she found her freaking out over him pummeling him with her grandmother's old teapot. "That doesn't sound so bad," she said to herself amused.

-I know I may hurt your puritanical ears, but I have to tell everything so that someone can understand me. He said as if he could read her mind.

"Puritan ears? But it will be wretched."

-Don't worry about the health of my ears. He replied gruffly.

Her words resonated so confidently and professionally that Murray accepted her intervention.

-We drank without worries. The usual at these events. You can imagine. We talked, laughed and went to a cabin. I wanted to start a little softer but that woman was pure fire. If wearing a bikini was too much to hope for, you can't imagine the way she drove me crazy when she took it off. Sensuality was pouring out of her body like day over night. Delicious, exquisite. A feast for the eyes.

Brenda knew she should listen, but the image of this man valuing only a body was making her sick. She knew perfectly well that not all men were like that, although at this moment she felt revulsion welling up in her veins uncontrollably and without reasoning. Men like Murray were soiling their own gender.

-I plunged into his body without rest. My reason was lost. My body transported me to another place. I hadn't done it like that for a long time. Brenda heard those words and something inside her stirred. To feel her so willing, so devoted..... Her soft skin, her perfect breasts.... My blood boiled and made me feel alive. I usually have varied sex, but with her my lust was triggered and to tell the truth it doesn't always happen to me. I like to fuck, although that doesn't mean that the woman in front of me always arouses me. I'm not sure you can understand me, you know, we men are... ahem, different from you.

Brenda closed her eyes, avoiding answering him. It was not relevant to have a discussion at that moment about the fervent desires of a man and a woman or their possible differences. The asshole thought that women didn't feel the same desires or needs as a man and she wasn't willing to clarify that for him. She sighed resignedly. Of course she understood him and perhaps more than he could imagine. The man, oblivious to her thoughts, continued to talk as if he still enjoyed the woman.

-I was indelicate and she didn't seem to mind. My imagination ran wild and I couldn't contain myself.

-Did you hit her? -She asked scared, forgetting all formalities between them.

-No for God's sake, I'm not one of those, but I unloaded on her body for at least a week. I did everything I could think of and she was willing. We left nothing to the imagination, at least not to mine.

Brenda swallowed and closed her eyes hoping the session would end soon. Murray disgusted her. He was an egotist only capable of thinking of himself and no one else.

-Exhausted by the effort, I realized that it was late and I had to go home. I had such a good time, it was such a good fuck, that it was there that I made the worst of my mistakes.

Brenda listened expectantly and Murray lowered his voice as if that way he could turn back time.

-I promised to see her the next day. He said apologetically.

The doctor understood the situation instantly. Men like Murray were not looking for a commitment, let alone a relationship. One good night was more than enough to send them home satisfied. Nothing else would fit in their heads.

-And you called her.

-Yes.

-You've never done it with anyone else?

-No.

-And that surprised you?

-At the time a little, but I just wanted to enjoy her a little more," he sighed regretfully. I called her and that same afternoon we met at a hotel near the party headquarters. They are very discreet there. If you were a man you would understand me. It was spectacular. We did it all afternoon. We fucked non-stop. I still don't know how I didn't have a heart attack," he said, remembering the moment. That woman is the best. She doesn't care how you put her or where you put her, she always enjoys it. They should all be like her.

-What did you say?

Brenda counted one two three and took a deep breath as her teacher Yogi taught her trying not to make the next day's papers.

-Yes, well, erase that if you want to," he said parsimoniously. The important thing is the other thing.

Brenda kept counting one, two, three, or the session would end like the rosary of the dawn.

The man settled back on the couch and she waited for the pause to end, but Murray seemed to be searching for the words that wouldn't come out. So far his account had been frank and direct. Now his countenance was changing to make room for what?

-What happened next, Michael? What happened in that hotel?

-After a few hours, and even though I was more than satisfied, I wanted to leave. We had already done everything and I had no reason to stay. I got dressed and said goodbye," he said, shuffling his thick hair with his fingers. I'm a married man. What did I expect!

"At good times he remembers." Brenda preferred to ignore his excessive moralistic outburst and continue listening.

-It may have been a good fuck, but it's not the first and it won't be the last. I would never leave my wife. I'd be a fool to even think about it.

-But he asked you...

-Yes. He thought that repeating with her meant something. She imagined we were starting a relationship.

Murray closed his eyes bitterly to speak in a muffled voice.

-You may not understand me and it may be a little confusing. I love my wife. This has nothing to do with feelings. We men are different from you. Sex for us is not synonymous with anything.

-Michael, we're not here for a discussion about men or women," she said, tired of hearing that women were little more than a container for emptying needy men. Focus on your issues. Because I still don't understand the situation that has brought you to me. I see macho behaviors, maybe even a little misogynistic, but...

-Misogynous? Not at all. I love women! And the prettier the better. He said smiling while the doctor shook her head.

-As I was saying, but you have no intention of changing. None of your behaviors show it, in fact, they even amuse you, so, Michael, what are you looking for? That girl marked you to such an extent that you need to tell me. Why?

-She didn't mark me. A good fuck is still a fuck. That's not the problem.

-So?

-I left her at the hotel. I thought everything was settled between us. We hugged, I gave her a couple of kisses, left her a voucher to pick up a beautiful Louis Vuitton bag in store and thanked her for her dedication.

-I understand.

-Well, she didn't understand anything! -he said, growling. Ever since that darn afternoon she hasn't stopped harassing me. She started calling me several times a day. The first time I answered her, then I asked my secretary not to put her calls through," he snorted tiredly. When I refused to answer him at the office, the calls continued on the home phone.

Murray took off his tie as if she was choking him and tossed it in the air hanging it straight up on the metal coat rack.

-If Lorelaine answers the landline, she listens for a while and then hangs up, if I answer, she tells me how much she loves me and then hangs up. No matter where I go, she seems to know my schedule in detail.

-It sounds a bit dangerous.

-I'm not done yet," Brenda's eyes widened in fright. I made an excuse to Lorelaine and we disconnected the landline. I thought she would give up with that detail....

-But it wasn't.

-On the contrary. That upset her so much that she went on a rampage with my car. When I went to the garage at the end of the day, I found it scratched. The bitch wrote the word pig in capital letters on the side with a coin. I had it painted. Nobody asked many questions, in the party they thought it was a political opposition issue, but I know it was not. I am sure it is Roxane.

-You have no proof.

-It was her. I assure you.

-You may be spinning facts that are not really connected, you see, many times our brain plays tricks on us when analyzing....

-It's her! I'm sure it is. A week ago she sent me a USB key with romantic songs on it apologizing for the car. She said she was hurt but forgave me because she loves me....

-Have you reported it?

-No. If this gets to the press, my political career will be over and I could...

-Could I?

-Lorelaine. It is not the same thing to accept a way of life as it is to endure your husband's alleged infidelity in the press and on television.

"Supposed to be? No one beats a hard face." He thought as he shook his head.

Murray squeezed his forehead, burdened by a decision he knew he had to make.

-That woman will continue to threaten you as long as she has the chance to do so.

-I know, I know! But how do I do it without hurting her? My wife...

-If you tell her first, you will eliminate the possibility of a threat. That woman will be left with no tools to use against you. It may be for the best and you may be able to stop her.

-You think I should talk to Lorelaine and tell her everything? Are you crazy? And for this I pay you?

-I'm actually paid by the game, and yes, that's what I think. I think you should protect Lorelaine from your own actions and their horrible consequences. It is clear that woman is hoping to have a relationship with you, if she finds out that your wife knows your history, and still decides to forgive you, then Roxane will be forced to give up.

-That's as long as my wife forgives me, but what if she doesn't? What if she's not willing to forgive me? We're a family, we have children. Fuck!

Murray stirred on the couch as he pounded the leather with his clenched fist.

-At the beginning of the consultation you said you feared for her safety, if you don't come clean with her you will not be able to protect her from the press or from Roxane herself.

Dr. Klein's phone, though silent, vibrated insistently, and for a moment it frightened her. No one interrupted her when she was in consultation unless it was urgent. Let alone insist over and over again.

-If you'll excuse me," she said as she looked at the screen displaying an unknown number, "Hello? Yes? Who is this? - The call was cut off immediately and she shook her head trying to calm down. Roxane's story was upsetting her too much.

Murray finished his session and left while Brenda tried to finish her report. Was it possible that part of the politician's fears were due to guilt and that led him to a paranoid attitude of unfounded persecution? It was possible. Yes, it was.

She wrote it down as part of her diagnosis and closed her diary when the cell phone rang again without answering. "Damn it, who is it, why isn't he answering?".

Personalized visits

Akim watched her from afar, as he always did. He expected her to turn, to catch his presence, to say something that would lead him to nourish some of his desperate hopes, but again she left without looking back.

He cursed, throwing the last of the day's debris into the dumpster. Maybe someday he would stop thinking about her and forget her. He smiled half-heartedly. Even he couldn't buy such a lie. He walked thinking about her, as always.

"I'm so in love that the whole city could scream at me saying you don't love me and I'd still love you. You fill my darkest voids, clear up my most dreaded feelings and smile with friendship to a heart that begs just a little bit more..."

After a day full of work, the last thing Brenda expected was to receive a desperate call from Michael Murray. The man had begged her to come over to his house and she couldn't refuse. She didn't make private visits but the morning session had left her somewhat confused and now such a burdensome request proved to be an impossible temptation to refuse. She rushed out, but something made her stop. There it was again. That strange, unexplained shiver. She shook her head and reached into her purse for the keys to the convertible.

As she got into the car she remembered that her husband was not at home and cursing under her breath, she pressed her friend Rachel's name on the speakerphone.

-Hello sweet, how are you?

-Good, good. I'm fine. Rachel, I wanted to ask you a favor. Could you put some food in Bonbon? Max is out of town and I have an emergency case.

-No problem, I'll be right over.

-Thank you Rachel, you don't know how much I appreciate it.

-Don't be silly, we are friends for a reason.

Brenda thanked him immensely. She adored that cat.

-Sweet, don't forget you promised to help me find the super cool caterer for George. The cream de la cream will be there.

George Carrington was her husband, Max's best friend and a partner in the architectural firm. Yes, that would be a party in style.

-Of course. Count me in.

-Great!

-Rachel, I'll call you later. I'm arriving at my destination.

-You don't worry, I'll take care of the hottie.

-Thank you very much. I'll talk to you later.

-Chaito sweet.

Brenda cut the call short as she stopped at a red light with a smile on her face. Many considered Rachel to be a flower woman, but she had a unique and wonderful background that few knew about. George, it turned out, was one of her discoverers and the two formed a somewhat peculiar but very happy couple.

Dr. Klein parked right in front of a villa completely surrounded by a large fence that rose over two meters high and prevented her from observing the magnificence of the interior. He rang the camera phone and waited. A thick male voice asked his name and instantly the huge metal door swung wide open. After parking in front of the entrance, the door to the house opened and a tall, very thin man dressed in an impeccable uniform escorted her into the main room. If at first she thought the place was wonderful, what she saw once inside simply became spectacular. Brenda was used to Max's elegant designs, but those rooms were spectacular. Nothing escaped absolute perfection. Colors, structures and materials combined with exquisite taste. Spacious cream-colored armchairs resting on a large dark brown long-pile carpet together with colorful paintings in pastel tones harmonized the place in a delicate and suggestive way. The modern library in mahogany tones and full of historical books topped off a simply perfect room.

-Dr. Klein, it's a pleasure to meet you," said a very proper woman, "but as I told Michael, you needn't have bothered.

Elegant as can be, wearing a perfect silk shirt with pinned pants and sporting a high ponytail, the lady of the house approached to greet her with both hands.

Brenda knew as soon as she met his gaze. That woman was in pain, and even if she didn't believe it, they had been right to call her. Her body showed no sign of weakness, but it was her eyes and the dark shadow under her gaze that told him she had not rested for some time.

-I assure you I'm perfectly all right," he said emphatically, "but you know how melodramatic men are. By the way, tea or coffee?

-It's no trouble at all for me, in fact, I'd be delighted to try that wonderful coffee.

Lorelaine shook her head with a feigned smile. She hoped to see Brenda Klein out of her house as soon as possible. Her weaknesses were hers alone, she had no desire to air any dirty laundry in front of strangers and even less so if the stranger was a shrink doctor. When she heard the whole story she wanted to kill Michael with her bare hands, how dare she sabotage what they had worked so hard to achieve? Position, friends, income, everything hung in the balance because of his loose pants. Headless bastard, she thought obfuscatingly.

Angry on the inside, but with the best of her smiles on the outside, she pointed to the huge leather sofa specially set up for visitors. Answering the silent request of the mistress of the house, the butler left in search of two coffees.

-You see, Brenda, may I call you that?

-Please. She replied politely, putting her bag aside.

-Life is a hard road to make a place for yourself. It's not easy. I learned that lesson many years ago. I am an adult woman who understands perfectly well the current situations, I don't need any... specialist. I hope you don't take this the wrong way, I know how to fend for myself without the need for self-improvement talks or homologous therapies.

The woman instantly fell silent when she felt the butler's presence. The man in black clothes and white gloves placed the silver tray with the two cups of coffee on the glass coffee table, and left with the same silence that accompanied his entrance. The mistress of the house waited for the employee to disappear from the room before continuing her most revealing speech while Dr. Klein listened attentively.

Politics is a long-distance race in which both the person involved and his companions are part of the great game of promotion. There are many years and many campaigns that I have played hand in hand with Michael. This may be his life, but it's our race, and I'm not going to lose it because of some stupid misstep. I don't know if he understands me.

He said as he pointed to the sugar cubes with tweezers.

-Two please. Brenca replied, studying his every gesture.

-Politics can often be a quagmire, but what ascent to power is not? Longtime friends will judge you like the strictest of judges, party colleagues will wait for your downfall like rapacious men waiting to find a power hole. The woman took a sip of her coffee with total tranquility as Brenda studied her attentively. I hope my words don't scare you, I imagine you are used to sincerity.

-I am, although it doesn't stop overwhelming me whenever I meet her.

The woman smiled half-heartedly as she sipped delicately from her coffee cup.

-I'm sorry to disappoint you, but there are too many interests at stake in a marriage not to evaluate them all before committing inappropriate actions. As I have told you before, this marriage is an investment in which I have been invested for many years. I am not willing to give up any of my accomplishments.

-Economic power?

-That I have earned by working from the shadows, Dr. Klein. I've been there for Michael at his worst moments, I'm not going to give up now with inadequate answers.

-And could those inappropriate responses become pain, suffering or guilt?

The woman smiled with some sound and Brenda sipped her coffee as she felt she was being discovered. He was analyzing her without her wanting it.

-I see that your professional interest is getting the better of you, Dr. Klein. Let's just say these are answers I don't allow myself to give away lightly. Tell me, Brenda, are you married?

-Yes.

-And isn't that what marriage is all about? To be their support in difficult times? To understand the incomprehensible and support the irreversible? -he commented sarcastically.

Although anger tried to surface, the woman continued to control her every gesture. A perfect manipulator of feelings.

-Being in a couple does not turn us into programmed machines. Her anger would be a logical and perfectly human feeling, and would have nothing to do with her duty as a wife. Feeling the weight of betrayal is rarely related to what is more or less convenient," she replied, waiting for an answer that she did not receive. We women tend to become the refuge of our partners, completely forgetting our own refuge. Understanding our needs or suffering for our mistakes does not make us less perfect but more bodily. We were taught to accompany, but how many of us have learned to pilot.

Dr. Klein tried to get her to talk, wanted to discover her concerns, her feelings. She wanted her to open up to her, admitting to being a perfect imperfect woman, but to no avail. Lorelaine, still locked in her shell of a loyal matrimonial companion.

-Brenda, I appreciate your visit, but as I said before, it wasn't necessary," he answered trying to put the visit to rest. I don't need psychological help to bring down a cheap prostitute," he said astonishing Brenda with his vocabulary so out of character. Michael may be the visible face, but I don't think you've understood correctly. I'm the driving force behind it, I'm not going to let anyone stand in my way!

The wife's blunt words of hatred told the doctor that this woman was more damaged than she wanted to show. She was hurt by the deception, but mostly by the hateful place her husband had placed her in. Friends, party colleagues, all would see her as weak and helpless, and she did not consider herself worthy of such undesirable virtues.

The double door to the salon opened to reveal a butler with a slightly disgruntled face.

-Mrs. Murray, I am sorry to interrupt you, there is a messenger at the door with a package for you. He says he has been paid to deliver it by hand and refuses to do anything but see you in person.

-Don't worry Thomas, you can tell him to come in.

-As you order, ma'am.

The helpful clerk waved in acceptance and headed toward the entrance gate to enter with a young boy wearing a cap bigger than his head who kept jumping nervously on his legs.

-I was told to give you this box.

-Who sent you?

The landlady spoke with confidence, but the young man, no more than fifteen years old, hesitated to speak.

-I can't say.

The butler was about to act when the lady stopped him with an authoritative gesture.

-Have you been paid to deliver it with no questions asked?

-Twenty bucks," the boy shook his head affirming his words, "Can I go?

-Yes, you can.

-But madam... -The butler was about to protest, but was again silenced by a gesture from the lady of the house.

The young man left so quickly that Brenda thought she saw him lose his pants along the way.

-Madam, you shouldn't open it," commented the employee. If you allow me, I can call the gentleman for you and tell him what happened. I'm sure he will know what we should do.

-Thomas, I don't need my husband or anyone else to know what I should do. He said staring at Brenda.

-But we don't know its contents," he replied uncomfortably.

-Please, Thomas, you don't think it's a bomb, do you?

The lady commented bored while Brenda observed the situation without expressing any opinion. It was clear that this was not a typical mailing from the post office, but she didn't think it was dangerous either.

Lorelaine walked to a small office next to the living room carrying the cardboard box in her own hands. Both Dr. Klein and the butler were watching her from the other room, but not daring to accompany her, after all, they had not been invited either.

Shortly after opening the shipment, the woman uttered a scream so piercing that it sent them running to the desk with or without an invitation. When they entered the small room, both Thomas and the doctor were petrified by the image.

The owner of the house screamed again and again in horror, looking down at the floor. Brenda was the first to react to the macabre image. Something that appeared to be a replica of Lorelaine's head lay on the floor with open eyes, disheveled hair and stains of something that looked like blood. The head of a silicone-like material had been made to perfection. If Dr. Klein did not have the real Mrs. Murray in front of her, she would have believed perfectly and without hesitation that the head bleeding from the floor was undoubtedly Lorelaine's.

-Thomas... call the gentleman," said Dr. Klein, trying to control her nerves, but the employee still did not move. The man was barely able to breathe. Thomas, now!

The gray-haired man reacted to the doctor's scream and ran away as Dr. Klein hugged the lady of the house by the shoulders in an attempt to calm her down as she carried her into the living room, leaving the hideous souvenir bleeding on the office floor.

-Michael is on his way. You'd better sit down. He said as he guided a mute Mrs. Murray to the couch.

-Thomas. Brenda spoke with confidence.

-The master is on his way," he replied hastily and nervously.

-Good. Now could you ask for a lime tea to be prepared for the lady?

-Yes, doctor," he said, his voice still trembling.

-Thank you.

The woman trembling in the seat seemed to react and looked up to counter Brenda's command.

-Thomas, make it something stronger.

-Of course, ma'am.

The man was about to leave when the doctor spoke for the second time.

-Thomas.

-Doctor?

-Make it two.

Brenda swallowed and the butler nodded in understanding. If it wasn't working hours he'd have a double scotch or something like that too.

Michael Murray ran into the house and disappeared before everyone's eyes on his way to the office. Brenda and Lorelaine watched him run into the office and then curse over and over again at the top of their voices. He had been warned by Thomas and had run as fast as the throttle of his Jaguar would allow. Fear, along with rage, boiled fiercely from his gut.

No more than five minutes had passed when the doorbell rang loud and clear and an angry Murray shouted into the room where they were standing.

-Thomas! Damn it, Thomas! Open up right now! That must be Inspector Gutierrez. I called him on my way out," he said red with rage as he approached his wife sitting next to Dr. Klein. Honey, are you all right?

-Yes.

The woman was sparing with her words and Murray seemed to accept them.

-Brenda?

-I'm fine, thank you.

The doctor was waiting to begin with her questions when a man in a slightly worn suit bought at a department store sale entered with a determined step, accompanied by the faithful Thomas.

-Mr. Murray, Mrs. Murray. The man said in a deep voice.

-Inspector Gutierrez, come this way.

-Michael, I really don't think all this is necessary. It's just a simple practical joke by some stupid person." The woman said with her voice cracking as she tried to regain her cold demeanor.

The man looked at his wife, but she did not answer him. Michael was furious. He simply walked the inspector into the office and both women followed them without asking permission. The detective touched the head of the floor with a pencil as he thought silently.

-Michael, I insist that there is no need to have any detectives in the house. It's a simple practical joke, and I'm sure that, like me, you don't want the press to show up here in an uproar over such stupidity, don't you think?

Mrs. Murray was talking nonstop trying to convince her husband of the consequences of such a scandal when the detective asked squatting next to the mock amputated head.

-Have you received any more threats?

-Threats? What nonsense, of course not. Lorelaine replied angrily and hoped that the detective would get out of there as soon as possible.

-Yes.

-How is anyone doing? -The detective asked without paying attention to Mrs. Murray who was walking like a locked wolf.

-No, they were just notes on paper. Murray said in a low tone.

-Do you have them here? I'm going to need to see them.

-They are in the party's office, I will send them to you first thing in the morning.

The detective accepted her reply as he looked curiously at the image on the floor and then stopped at Mrs. Murray's face, which twitched uncomfortably.

-Whoever did it seems to know her pretty well. Do you have any suspects?

The lady was about to answer with her usual poised speech when her husband held her by the arm so that he would be the one to answer.

-Yes. A woman. She's been harassing me for some time.

-I understand. The detective stood up and looked around as if looking for someone.

-Charly? -Charly!

The furious shout that echoed through the walls caused a young man, who until now no one had noticed his presence, to run to his boss's side while swallowing the remains of a delicious profiterol filled with cream that the butler had brought earlier to accompany the lady's and her guest's coffees.

-They are delicious... -he commented as best he could with his mouth full while his boss shook his head.

-Have this piece of wax sent to the lab to look for fingerprints or anything that might lead us to its creator.

The young man nodded behind his thick, dark-rimmed glasses. He went to a corner to make the corresponding calls, but not before hiding another profiterol in one of his jacket pockets.

-Charly! -. The boy raised his head in fright when he was caught. He is looking for some information about Miss... -The detective looked at Mr. Murray who answered instantly.

-Roxane... Roxane Boucher.

The detective looked at his apprentice detective who stated confidently as he repeated.

-Roxana Boucher, I got it.

Murray's wife huffed in annoyance and walked toward the living room. Dr. Klein accompanied her, followed closely by the footsteps of a husband as angry as his wife.

-Honey, you must understand. This cannot go on. We must stop it.

The politician tried to justify himself when uncontrolled and totally unpredictable shouting erupted from the mouth of the always, very calm, Mrs. Murray.

-You couldn't! You couldn't! -And what exactly couldn't you Michael? Keep your pants on or run after a whore? Tell me, Michael! Answer me!

The woman struck again and again at her husband's chest, but he did not move. He accepted each blow, each insult with the utmost dignity until she calmed down. He tried to hug her, but the woman broke away, walked to the bar and poured herself a drink. She twirled the glass in her hand and when everyone thought she would throw it at her husband, she drank the contents in one gulp.

-Because of you, tomorrow we'll be on everyone's lips..." he said with recovered serenity. -Our friends, our neighbors... everyone will know about your damned stupidity. Everyone will talk about me with pity! With pity for me, for me.... -she stammered feebly.

The woman poured herself another drink and drank it, but this time she threw the glass hard on the hearthstone.

-How could you be such an asshole?

The woman fell silent on the couch and her husband wrapped his arms around her shoulders knowing that this time she would not be rejected. She, who at first tensed, then accepted her husband's comfort, and let her face fall on her chest hiding her heartbreaking cry.

Dr. Klein, who was observing the situation from a distance, did not want to intervene, although she was able to extract some interesting information. She searched for her bag, lost in the hustle and bustle, and tried to say goodbye.

-I'd better get going," she said as soon as she found her precious short-handled Gucci.

-Nobody leaves here until I say so.

-I beg your pardon? - Dr. Klein replied angrily.

-I say that no one leaves until I have questioned them all. And, by the way, we haven't been introduced. The detective said, holding out his arm.

-I am Dr. Klein, Brenda Klein.

-Klein... mm, is that the one from the father bomb case?

-I am," he confessed with some pride.

-Well, I'll start with you....

After two long hours of questions, and a totally wasted day, Brenda decided to go to her office to pick up some studio material so she could move some cases forward at home. With a bathtub full of hot water and lots and lots of suds.

As she opened the office doorway she tried to ignore the growing mess of the work, after all it would only be a couple of weeks. She dodged a large canister of something resembling river sand and opened her office to be perplexed.

His office, his sanctuary, and so far the only halfway decent place, was in complete chaos. Papers lying all over the place, broken drawers on the floor and files, hundreds of files, jumbled all over the room.

-Connor! Connor!

She shouted in desperation as she tried to get inside without stepping on anything important.

-Connor!

-You don't need to shout. There's no one here. They've all gone.

Akim appeared in blue jeans and a breathtaking black cotton T-shirt. Brenda watched him curiously as it was the first time she had seen him without that hideous paint-stained jumpsuit or at least the first time she had looked at him with those eyes.

The young man was more pleasant than he had first appeared to her, indeed, he would be a most interesting man if he were not so dry, curt and ill-tempered. He had eyes as crystalline as the summer sky itself, hair as black as the darkest night, and a sturdy, not overly so, hiccupping body. Yes, you could say he was a handsome young man, a young man..... Brenda chided herself for her hormonal thoughts and began to check the damage without another glance at the young man in blue topaz.

-What the hell... -Akim commented as he surveyed the state of the office, "What the hell happened? It's as if someone has been looking for something.

Brenda raised her head at the bricklayer's words.

-Searching. It's that.... -The doctor stammered thoughtfully.

Akim watched her with narrowed eyes, highlighting her wide bushy eyebrows that were slightly darker than her hair.

"They're perfect, do you outline them?"

-What are you talking about? And why are you looking at me like that? You don't think that I...

Brenda cursed to herself for being caught in full scrutiny and reacted the only way she knew how to with that man. Too bad.

-Stop this nonsense, I think I'm getting tired of your continuous grumbling like a martyr man. I didn't say anything. You are a very handsome man and I can tell you are a hard worker, I don't see why you always have to be on the defensive.

Akim's eyes widened like saucers. The distinguished and well-educated Dr. Klein was losing her temper with him. The smile came as naturally as it did spontaneously. He could feel offended, even mistreated, but on the contrary, he felt grateful. No way, he was delighted.

"Did she say I'm a handsome man? Yes, yes he did. No! He said handsome. That's more than handsome, isn't it?"

I shouldn't be happy with such a superficial comment, but I was very, very happy, to tell you the truth, too happy. God, no, I was overjoyed!

-Now please help me and check if you find anything strange in Connor's study while I call Detective Gutierrez," she said as she rummaged in her purse for the card he had offered her before leaving.

-Detective? -You think it's a robbery?

-Yes, I do.

Akim nodded in agreement as he left on his way to Connor's office.

The inspector's greeting on the other end of the line distracted her from her doubtful thoughts.

-Are you saying that files have been stolen from you?

-I'm not sure, I just got here and saw the mess, from what little I could verify, I'm sure I'm missing one.

-Let me guess," he commented to the other side, "Michael Murray?

-Yes.

-I'm on my way there.

-I hope so.

-Is she alone?

-No.

-Well, nobody move until....

-Until you arrive. She cut off amused.

-Exactly. We seem to be getting along, Dr. Klein," he remarked amused.

-It seems so... it seems so...

It's you

-I've been all over the building and the only damage is my crew's own.

Akim commented with an uncharacteristic joy as he entered the doctor's office, believing her to be unaccompanied.

-And you are?

-Akim Dudaev. He said, his smile fading.

-Russian?

Akim did not answer, he did not know the man and did not wish to meet him.

-I didn't catch his name. He replied with his usual low tone.

-Inspector Gutierrez. And why do you say you are in the building?

-I didn't say.

Akim began to tense his arm muscles in discomfort and Brenda felt compelled to defend him, even though no one was asking her to.

-Akim is part of the renovation crew.

-That doesn't explain why he's still here. I don't see any other employees around. He said, looking around the room.

-I stayed to finish the electrical installation. I imagined that the doctor would be happy to be able to use the light without having to endure more outages.

The man ducked his head in annoyance at himself for looking like a real nincompoop, and Brenda smiled in delight. He didn't hate her so much after all. That man was all front and she was pleased to find out. Akim looked up and collided squarely with those little chocolate eyes and full lips saying thank you, but in complete silence so that no one but him would notice. The man closed his eyes in acceptance and deep joy. Feeling that intimacy with her was so much more than he dreamed.

-I need you to tally up all the reports to see if only Murray's or someone else's are missing. Are you seeing any other politicians?

-This is information I cannot give you.

-Dr. Klein, I don't think you know the risk you are taking.

-Risk? - Akim asked nervously.

-Yes. The inspector said firmly.

-No, not at all. I'm perfectly fine and nothing will happen to...

A thunderous crash and shattering of glass echoed throughout the floor and the three ran to the front door to see what had happened.

-Charly! Are you all right?

The young man rearranged his glasses and shook out the rest of the shattered glass that had hit him in its entirety.

-I'm fine. She stammered in reply, "although I'm afraid he's not.

A rat had been thrown through the door shattering glass and bloodying the entrance.

-What the hell is this?" Akim spoke in bewilderment.

-I'm afraid he's a dead rat now.

-And who the hell would break a glass portal by throwing a dead rat?

-The correct question would be, for whom? - The inspector commented, staring at Dr. Klein, who could not get over her astonishment.

The assistant, who at first seemed a bit nervous, managed to recover as if by magic and spoke into the inspector's ear. He nodded and turned his full attention to Dr. Klein.

-Doctor, after recent events, I feel obliged to ask you to come with me.

-What?

-Don't you dare touch her. Akim replied more vehemently than expected and the inspector narrowed his eyes.

-Goliath, I did not express myself well. I don't have staff to protect you and at the Murray's house you said you were alone, didn't you doctor?

Brenda nodded, unable to hide the disgust she still felt at the sight of that disgusting mangled bug on the door.

-I'm afraid I can't risk it. First Murray and now this. I can't say for sure, but we may be looking at the same case.

-That is impossible.

-Murray? What case? -Akim asked, but no one answered him, except Charly who took pity on the poor man and briefly summarized the situation. Akim was perplexed and cursed between his teeth.

-I'm not going to take any risks. She will be protected at the police station.

-I'm not going to stay in a cell just to be protected. That's stupid.

-Stupidity or not, he's coming with me. I won't risk his life because he wants to spend the night at home without protection.

Charly nodded as he began the situation report on his tablet.

-I'm not going anywhere. If you want to imprison me you will have to do it by force.

-If that's what he wants. The inspector smiled at the frightened look on his face.

-You are not going to handcuff her, it won't be necessary. I will go with her. Akim, who had not spoken so far, stepped forward to speak with confidence.

-I'm sorry "little boy", but I don't think this is the place for someone like you. I don't want to have two to take care of. The inspector commented amused, and the assistant let out a small, light laugh, when Akim, without warning, lifted the man by the neck to slam him against the half-broken door.

-Do you want me to show you how this little guy fights back? -Brenda emitted a slight groan between fear and admiration when in less than a second the worker lifted and slammed the inspector against the shattered window. Akim's crystalline eyes glittered with anger, but the inspector didn't flinch, on the contrary, he laughed enthusiastically as he tapped the man's shoulder to get him to let go.

-Charly! You should train with this Russian. He sure knows how to get something good out of those little scarecrow arms.

The eavesdropping scholar's eyes widened in astonishment at the comment as Akim released the inspector and set him back on his feet.

The man turned to Dr. Klein who was unable to reason what was going on there.

-I don't like...

In the doorway, a filthy rat was embedded among shattered glass, next to it a worker was lifting the inspector by the scruff of the neck, while an assistant with zero percent muscle and paper bones was stroking his biceps with sorrow in his eyes.

The inspector took pity on her and considered letting her go home with the Russian. Something about him did not quite agree with her, but he had no choice but to let her go. He could not take her away against her will. With a throatiness in his voice he spoke with absolute coldness and in a low voice so that only the bricklayer could hear him.

-I don't like you, you're hiding something and I don't like people who hide things, but my instinct tells me you'll take care of her.

-I would kill for her. He answered without thinking and the inspector narrowed his eyes trying to decipher something more than words.

Akim smiled unwillingly on the side. After all, that inspector was not such an idiot as he first imagined. Of course he hid many secrets, but he would never confess them to a guy like that, and much less if one of his embarrassments was to be madly in love with a certain doctor who left him breathless just by looking at her.

-Dr. Klein, I leave you in good hands. I will see you tomorrow morning. If there are any problems," he said, looking at Akim, "please call me urgently.

The inspector left, accompanied by Charly who walked beside him, concentrating on the case. The therapist felt nervous about the situation. She had to go home with a man she hardly knew and who made her nervous. Maybe it was his aloofness or that crystalline gaze. It didn't matter. Whatever it was, she trembled to feel him near.

"I'd better get rid of it as soon as possible."

-Akim, I thank you for your help. You have freed me from the inspector and I am indebted to you, but it is no longer necessary for you to act.

The worker narrowed his eyes as if trying to understand her as he crossed his arms at chest level.

-What performance are you referring to exactly?

Akim's eyebrows arched upward questioningly and Brenda averted her gaze. That look would definitely make anyone in her place nervous.

-I imagine you have commitments and don't want to waste your time with me. I thank you, but I am fully capable of taking care of myself.

Brenda turned around satisfied with her performance and with a mad desire to run out of there. Akim's presence alone made her nervous in an unfamiliar way. She was used to dealing with all kinds of people, everything but that of a man who seemed to undress her with his gaze, but not in a physical sense. His scrutiny went far beyond that. He crossed all her barriers of politeness and courtesy. He reached where no one knew her and she didn't like that. Her fears, regrets or anger were his and his alone.

She walked toward the car thinking she had dodged it when his deep, accented voice startled her to the side.

-I happen to have given my word to take care of you and that's what I intend to do," he said as he snatched the car keys from her hand and pointed politely to the passenger door. You'll be a good girl and show me the way," he said mischievously with a wink.

Brenda's eyes looked like two fried eggs. "Good girl? Good girl? But who the hell did she think she was?"

He pulled himself together from his astonishment and responded with total sarcasm and very little sympathy.

-Que-ri-do, I don't think you remember exactly who I am, please allow me to refresh you on the situation.

-Yes, yes, I know all that stuff about the famous Dr. Klein and her social status, you can save it. Now sit in the damn car, point me in the right direction and do me a favor and be quiet. I'm not in the mood to listen to our profound social differences," he said seriously as he opened the car door. It wasn't part of my plans to spend an evening at your house, but here I am.

"Liar." He thought amused. He wasn't angry at all, far from it, but he didn't want to see that good family lady side reappear among them. He adored Brenda, the supportive and gentle one. He hated the polite, stuffy doctor.

Dr. Klein sat in the passenger seat of her own car dropping down in a huff. She grumbled at the top of her voice looking for a fight. No one treated her like that, let alone with such manners. "Who the hell does he think he is! He always manages to bring out the worst in me. And I'm not like that!

-I've had too complicated a day to argue with a child," he commented, remembering his annoyed reaction to the inspector.

Akim started the car and his reaction was very different with her. The man smirked sideways as he settled into the seat to look her straight in the eyes making her tremble and not exactly with fear.

-Are you provoking me, doc-to-ra? Do you want me to show you what a kid like me can do? Because if so, we should go somewhere else. Is that what you're looking for?

"Shit..."

Hot flashes began to rise throughout his body. No, this was not the expected reaction. He deserved it. He had played with fire and was getting burned, or so it seemed to him from the heat rising from his feet to the tips of his hair. He swallowed, trying to answer. He only needed one clever sentence, just one to dumb him down. but which one! He could hardly think. Her wide arms crossed and straining over that hard torso didn't let her be very rational.

-Well, I see from your silence," he said amused when he noticed her heated up, "that we're going straight to your house. Are you going to tell me which way?

-Straight on the main road to the Stonebridge exit. Urbanización la Alameda. He said in a rush.

-The most expensive in the district, of course....

-I beg your pardon?

-Nothing, I didn't say anything. He said trying to take his mind off the luxury of the residential neighborhood, one of the thousand reasons that separated him from her.

Akim accelerated furiously and Brenda was amazed at his sudden change in mood. From mischievous and sassy to angry and taciturn, and all in less than a minute. What exactly was wrong with him? Why bother with the neighborhood where he lived?

"I think someone needs to pay an urgent visit to my office." She said to herself amused and catching Akim's attention.

-Why are you smiling?

-Nothing important. Patient nonsense.

The man accepted the reply to concentrate on the road while Dr. Klein preferred to watch the nightfall through the window. She didn't like taking orders from anyone and hated having to obey the inspector's stupid imposition, but it had been the only way to get out of spending a whole night at the police station, and she had Akim to thank for that. After all, he didn't feel like wasting his time with her either. He had made that quite clear.

"The poor guy may even have had plans with some girl and he has to take me home like a little girl. As soon as I get home I'll release him from his engagement and let him go." She thought somewhat disgusted with the idea.

She slyly watched him out of the corner of her eye. He was wearing a black T-shirt, which, although from a department store, fit him like a glove on that most defined body. "Will you do any sports or will you be a natural? If so what an envy because I kill myself three times a week with zumba and weights and I still have this michelin here that I hope you haven't seen and ....."

-Brenda!

-Yes?

-It said which house number. Are you all right?

-Perfectly. Twenty-sixth.

-Good.

Akim parked in the driveway without taking her eyes off the huge two-story villa with seemingly endless windows. The delicate columns of the portal and the small details of the carved walls of the porch pointed directly to her husband's undisputed touch. The perfect and exquisite architect Max Brown.

The doctor quickly got out of the car and he stood watching her for a few minutes. That woman was so delicate, so determined and yet so feminine that she could lift the spirits of any man, including his own, although he doubted she knew it. He scratched the back of his head in confusion. He had never been particularly attracted to any woman, let alone an older, married one, but Brenda was so much more. Her smile and momentum enveloped you with no chance of release. At first you thought her unfriendly and stuffy, and no, she wore a mask, one that helped her do her duty in front of patients, but as soon as she relaxed, the mask would fall off brazenly leaving a bold, spunky woman in full view. A strength unique to her kind. When he made her angry, the hidden Brenda would poke her nose out and was deliciously adorable.

A woman with long hair, and a somewhat strange way of speaking, came running up to her and Akim jumped out of the car fearing the worst. If it was the crazy rat death she would hang her there and then rather than allow her to harm her doctor.

Akim ran towards Brenda with a desperate intention to protect her when the woman hugged her tightly and then started ranting in a very, very, strange accent. Did she have a potato in her mouth or did she speak like that naturally?

-Sweet! You've got me super scared to death. total dihedral!

"They may have a lot of money, but these people are not quite right in the head." He thought amused.

-What a scare! The police called me. They were looking for you. How scary sweet!

-I'm fine. She said freeing herself from his tight embrace so as not to drown.

-I was so scared that I almost did something crazy and started cooking. Can you imagine me cooking and getting my pretty hands dirty?

Akim's eyes widened in amazement at such a specimen while Brenda was amused by the spectacle.

-I called you on the Iphone about a thousand times and nothing. He said with a slight hint of annoyance.

-I ran out of battery.

At that moment Akim approached the two women who seemed not to be silent to interrupt them.

-I think we should go inside.

Rachel for the first time became aware of the escort's presence and indiscreetly looked him up and down to ask her friend without the slightest qualms.

-Since when have you had a chauffeur?

Rachel looked back at the man who stirred nervously as he felt watched like a chicken in a delicatessen.

-I am not a chauffeur. He replied annoyed.

-Ah, I thought Max wouldn't have someone looking like that working next to his wife.

-Rachel!

-What? You're not going to tell me that goes with us. And where's that accent from? - The woman asked bluntly and Brenda wanted to bury herself right there. She adored her friend, but she could often be the most frivolous woman on the planet.

-Akim has been kind enough to join me. He works on Max's team.

-Are you an architect? -she asked in horror.

-I'm from the gang. He answered between his teeth so as not to send the woman straight to the septic tank or as they would say in his neighborhood, to hell.

-Cuadrilla? Those are the ones who paint and carry dust, aren't they? I was saying that the studio could not have fallen...

-Rachel, why don't we go inside the house and talk more quietly? -She said as she pushed her friend by the arm so that she wouldn't finish her clarifications.

-Yes, sweet you have to tell me everything. And by the way, call Max urgently because he was very crazy.

-Did you call Max?

-Of course, my nerves were super frozen with fear.

-Let's go inside, I need a coffee," said the doctor, pushing Rachel through the doorway from behind. Akim, I thank you for all your attention, if you want to leave you can do it without regrets. As you can see, I am already accompanied.

The doctor commented exhausted. The day was turning out to be longer than usual.

-I'm staying.

-Is she staying? -Rachel asked, peeking her head out of the main porch.

-It seems so.

Rachel walked into the doorway on her friend's arm as the man walked a few steps behind. The doctor's friend symbolized everything he hated about high society. She really was a frivolous stiff.

-So you're from another country? He asked turning to face him and with a tone that he didn't like one bit.

- I'm a fucking immigrant out of necessity, a young father out of idiocy, and a beggar because of the bank. Happy?

Rachel fanned herself heatedly and Brenda didn't say a word. Akim was well within his rights to put her in her place.

"By the way had he said father? So there was a Mrs. Dudaev?" He couldn't explain it, but something different and strange stirred in his guts. Something more like an indigestible broccoli dinner than a brownie and ice cream snack.

The women talked incessantly while Akim looked around the living room of the house. There was more living space there than the sum of all the houses he had lived in all his life, and there had been several. Six to be more exact. First in the little house in front of the stream where he was born, the other one made of wood that he shared with Juliana, then the three refugee tents, and, finally, the current one, which was on the outskirts, very, very, very far away.

"What about the furniture? That couch costs like my entire salary for a year." He mumbled to himself.

She looked into the kitchen and saw the women talking nonstop. Dr. Klein had taken off her shoes and was walking toward the refrigerator totally unconventional. At times she spoke earnestly, at others she smiled with a freshness that left him spellbound. Seeing Brenda move about his home with such ease awakened in him feelings of possession that he never knew he had. If he adored her before, when he admired her from a distance, how could he not die of love? Now that she was relaxed, with her long hair in a ponytail, her lovely bare feet and that scent of hers that filled the whole room, she was beautiful.

Akim imagined what it would be like to feel her in his arms in a home just for them. He would kiss her until she was breathless and then caress that softness of skin flushed by the passion he himself would offer her every single day. And her eyes. Those fiery little chocolate eyes, shining with rapt attention and begging for more as he would possess her again and again without rest. Now that would be a perfect life. He remembered her impertinence in the car and smiled mischievously. He had said it without thinking, but she was provoking him and he wasn't able to resist. He had warned her of what he would be capable of doing to her if she accused him of being inexperienced and the very poised Dr. Klein had suffocated like a virginal young girl making her cheeks redden intensely and he wanted to kiss them to placate them with the moisture of her lips.

The sound of a phone ringing and Max's name made him explode with rage and go crazy with jealousy. He looked out the window trying not to pay attention to the conversation, but he couldn't. Where was Don Perfect supposed to be? Didn't he know she was in danger? He snorted as he took a sip from the bottle of beer he had been offered. If she were mine I would never leave her, he thought, disturbed by envy.

-So you say you work on Max's crew? -Rachel crept up behind her, taking advantage of the fact that her friend was talking to her husband and avoiding her overhearing the conversation.

-Yes.

-Then you'll meet his partner, George Carrington? He is my husband.

-No.

Akim took another sip without looking away from the garden. Of course he knew her husband, but he didn't want to explain to that hateful woman that men like him didn't deal with the bosses. Her elevator went no higher than the second floor, the one where the tools and coveralls were delivered. Her husband or that Max guy moved around on the fifteenth floor. The one with a private entrance and elevators with champagne-colored carpets.

-At this moment Brenda is talking to Max and I imagine he will ask you to leave his house as soon as possible. My friend doesn't need your company, you can leave quietly, I will say goodbye on your behalf. If you wish, I can ask for a car to take you to your little house, wherever you live.

Rachel commented with a certain tone of contempt that made Akim turn to set her on fire with his gaze.

-I promised I would look after her tonight, and I don't intend to leave her alone. And I don't care what you or anyone else wants.

-But how insolent! You're not needed at all. I'm sure Max will be back soon and take care of everything. We don't know you and we don't even know where you come from. I'm sure there are little things in this house that cost more than your own life. Who's to say you're not a thief or a serial killer?

-If it were, you'd be dead by now.... -He muttered under his breath just as Brenda appeared in the room. "Fucking poisonous harpy." He thought furiously.

-And, sweet, what did Max say? -she asked with a victorious smile.

-Nothing special. I didn't tell you half of it...

-How!

-Go home, I'll call you tomorrow, I promise.

-I'm staying with you.

-Rachel, please... I'll be fine.

-If you say so... -She answered with surrender. Will you walk me to the door? -She said almost as an order to Akim. We'll go out together.

Rachel spoke confidently trying to throw him out of the house and he instantly tensed up.

-You're leaving? I was thinking of ordering pizza for dinner. I understand, you have commitments and you don't have to waste your time with me.

-I said I was staying and I'm not going anywhere," he replied to make his intentions clear to the snake.

-Well then, we order pizza and try to get some rest because tomorrow the inspector will be waiting for us at the police station first thing in the morning.

-But Brenda... -Rachel lowered her voice so that only her friend could hear her, "You're not going to let this guy stay the night here? We don't know what suburb he comes from, look at him, he even looks like one of those foreigners. Haven't you heard his accent? Maybe if we try to track Connor down and tell him....

-Rachel, please don't call anyone else..." Brenda practically pushed her friend out the door. -Brenda practically pushed her friend out the front door. It's late and you're expected for dinner, I'll be fine.

-Okay, okay, okay, but sleep with your cell phone under your pillow or scream loudly, I'll leave my bedroom window open.

Rachel lived two houses down from his, so he thought her capable of doing what she said.

-I love you. Now go quietly. Nothing will happen to me.

At that moment Bombón appeared wagging her tail and snaking between Akim's feet who bent down to pick her up in his arms and caress her while she purred delightedly.

Rachel and Brenda watched in the distance in some surprise. Bonbon was not what you might call a docile cat with strangers.

-Go quietly. Nothing will happen to me. She said in a low voice.

-Okay, fine, but I'll come first thing in the morning.

-It is not necessary.

-Sweet, you're very good, but with that riffraff in the house you never know. Look at her hands. They're cracked and calloused. She commented in horror.

-That's called working.

Rachel clutched her chest in obfuscation as she walked away grumbling.

-If they leave that sandpaper skin on your hands they should call it slavery.

Brenda shook her head and closed the door ready to phone the pizzeria to bring her a family size. She was starving.

I could...

Akim was sure that there was no one with more bad luck than his. If only she was the selfish ogre he imagined at the beginning, everything would be much easier, but no, he couldn't be that lucky. Brenda wasn't a snake like her friend, no, she was sweet, polite, caring, intelligent, beautiful... God, she was damn perfect.

They ordered a couple of pizzas and waited for them sitting on the high benches in the kitchen. The woman opened two bottles of the best Irish beer, and even though she didn't drink it like he did, she behaved like the perfect hostess. Gentle, kind, cordial and with a permanent smile on her face. Perfect and exquisite, that's how she was. At least in his eyes, she was.

Akim could not take his eyes off the woman. He was enraptured. She was talking while he was falling a little more in love every minute. The woman in front of him was not the Dr. Klein he knew from the office. This was Brenda, a sweetheart who spoke to him as an equal.

Akim sipped his beer as he watched her poke his slice of pizza with a fork and smiled as he imagined the comments his son Lucien would make at such a perfect, polite image.

Brenda talked non-stop avoiding the dead spaces and he, sparing with his words, was having a lot of fun with the situation. She had also subtly dropped her age and Akim smiled again at the thought that if that were the only stumbling block separating them, she wouldn't be sitting across from him right now so calmly and with so many clothes on.

"If only it were just that..." He thought saddened.

When he finished his dinner and with a typical caveman instinct, he stretched to emphasize his physique. He knew it was silly and that he was far from being able to provoke a woman like that, but he couldn't help it. The desire to conquer her was boiling inside him.

-Light chocolate mousse?

-Does it exist? -he commented amused.

-I hope so, because if not, the hour of zumba and weights in the gym will be worthless.

Brenda guffawed openly as she made her way to the fridge and Akim followed her bare feet and imagined for a moment what it would be like to caress that woman's bare skin.

Dessert continued like the rest of the dinner, in total complicity and Brenda was happy to have accepted Akim's company. She had her misgivings at first, but scolded herself for having been so predictable. It was unbecoming of a professional of her stature to prejudge so viciously. She thought him sullen and ill-mannered, but Akim was not only attentive but behaved like a complete gentleman.

-I may sometimes get caught up in my world of stressed out patients, but that doesn't mean I don't know how to say thank you when someone deserves it, and I want you to know that I really appreciate you being here with me.

Brenda spoke with complete sincerity and Akim had to hold onto the bench to keep from launching himself at her and eating her up with kisses. There she was, his distinguished and proper Dr. Klein, with a beaming smile on her lips, offering him her gratitude and something akin to an apology. She took a deep breath and tried to calm herself from approaching those full lips, biting them until they lost their breath together and let fate decide their future.

-Thank you. He replied in a low, husky voice.

-Thank you? -Brenda didn't understand the answer, maybe he hadn't understood her, she was the one who gave them, why was he doing it?

Dr. Klein looked at him in confusion and Akim came back to earth thinking at full speed, "What did I say? God, I don't even remember. I'm definitely an imbecile."

-You're the one who saved me from a night at the police station, why are you thanking me?

"Why are you divine, precious, perfect and I a foolish fool of love?"

Akim did not answer. He couldn't think of anything and Brenda preferred to cut the subject short with the typical sappy question.

-Coffee?

-Please... -He sighed in relief.

-So you were born in Russia?

-No.

-I thought you told the inspector. She said confused.

-It's what he assumed," he said with a slight grimace.

-And you didn't bother to clarify it.

The man raised his shoulders to show the inspector's lack of interest.

-And so? -The woman's curiosity overcame her discretion.

-Chechnya.

-Refugee?

-Immigrant by necessity seems more accurate to me.

-Totally understandable. She said with conviction.

Brenda knew the stories coming through the media and could imagine their suffering. She was strongly in favor of humanitarian collaboration with migrants and refugees of any nationality.

-And are you alone or do you have a family?

Akim stirred the sugar cube in the coffee more intensely and Brenda regretted her curiosity. She had made him uncomfortable.

-I'm sorry, I didn't mean to...

-It's okay, it's just that I don't usually talk about it. I live with my father and son.

-Are you married? - There it was again, broccoli indigestion.

-Father and son, I did not mention any woman.

-I'm sorry," he said with a sense of regret.

-Why?

-Aren't you a widower?

-I was never married, but if I had been, I doubt Juliana would be dead. She likes living life too much.

His voice sounded harsher than intended and he cursed himself for being such a brute. Brenda fell silent behind her coffee and he felt awkward for pushing her away. He knew it was crazy, stupid, foolish, foolish, but he couldn't call that evening over, not yet. Brenda's company was refreshment for the thirsty. Gorgeous on the outside and enchanting on the inside, what mortal would not be enchanted by what he had never known? Beauty, intelligence and distinction wrapped in a wonderful woman's body. No, he could not call it a night, much less because of the rudeness of his words to his frivolous ex.

-She abandoned us," he commented, trying to regain her attention. Lucien was a delicate baby and she was not willing to lose her beauty and youth caring for him.

Brenda shook her head and closed her eyes in incomprehension.

-She got pregnant and blamed it on me. I asked her to try for the baby, but it didn't work out. She worked in a department store and managed to get the distinguished position of the boss's mistress. He bought her a modest car and rented her an apartment, that was enough to leave us. Lucien needed medical treatment and we decided to seek asylum in a country with better possibilities. My father, a widower, decided to join us. I have no siblings and the three of us learned to be a family and take care of each other.

-Didn't the child's mother try to...? I mean, when she found out that you were taking him out of the country, didn't she regret it?

Akim sighed before telling him something he had never expressed to anyone, not even his best friend Nikola.

-I tried. I looked for her so that we could forget everything. To start from scratch, but...

-She didn't want to. Brenda knew of many cases like hers.

-I wish it were just that. He laughed at me. He told me I was crazy, that I was deluded if I thought he would give up his well-to-do life for a sick brat and a poor devil with no future.

-You loved her... -Brenda commented without thinking as she noticed the sadness in his voice.

-We were never more than a weekend fling. He clarified embarrassed.

-I'm sorry, from your tone I thought....

-I did it for the child, he didn't deserve to be the mere fruit of carelessness.

Akim fell silent and Brenda did not ask again.

-I'd better show you to your room.

The doctor didn't know how to pick up the conversation after that. She was very used to patient confessions, but these turned out to be a bit strange. Akim reached out and unthinkingly clasped her hand on the counter. He didn't know what had made him do that, perhaps the fear of knowing that he would never have her like that again. Whether it was out of daring or fear, it didn't matter. His calloused hand wrapped around hers, holding her hand.

-Not yet... -The man pleaded, trying to find some understanding in his request.

He pleaded with his eyes and smiled as he felt how she had understood him as if she had known him forever. She saw where no one else ever looked. Their still joined hands vibrated as if an electric current was tingling through their fingers. Akim watched her hoping to know if she had felt the same, Brenda didn't speak. She simply stared at him as if silence could explain the inexplicable. She slowly released him and he accepted her abandonment. They both walked to the living room and Akim accepted a drink as he sat on the couch. He was tense. Never in his right mind would he have done such a thing as begging a woman to stay a few more minutes by his side, but she wasn't just any woman, she was Brenda, his Brin. For heaven's sake, how could something like this be happening to him when he didn't even know the taste of her lips?

They talked for a long time, but it was when she yawned that he knew he could no longer hold her. He had to let her go and end the best night of his life.

-You're tired... - he commented gently.

-Not at all. Brenda tried to hide another yawn, but she couldn't. "I'll be with you until you finish. I'll be with you until you finish it. She said, looking at the cup between her fingers.

Akim finished it in one gulp and asked with ill-concealed sadness.

-I can sleep on the couch.

-It is not necessary. The guest room is small but the mattress is very comfortable.

The man followed her up the stairs without missing any detail of the house. Every piece of furniture or decoration that was found showed her husband's skills as a designer. Brenda kindly showed him the room and left, closing the door.

"And what did you expect, that she would stay with you?" he thought as he sat on the bed trying to calm feelings that were weighing him down more and more.

-For heaven's sake! But even the guest mattress is better than mine.

He hit the cushion pretending to accommodate it when in truth all he intended to do was to calm his insatiable rage provoked by an unbridgeable class difference. At first he thought his discomfort stemmed from his material possessions, then he had to accept even more powerful reasons. Women like Brenda were not and would never be within the reach of someone like him. They didn't deign to waste their time on men in department store T-shirts and flea market jeans. The unfortunates of life had to settle for women with squeaky voices and scant speech.

He took off his shirt and lying back on his fluffy bed he imagined her. What would she do at this moment? Would she think of him as he did of her? No, he smiled mischievously, surely not.

She would not dream of hands caressing him until he lost his mind. She would not open the buttons of his jeans and caress his manhood imagining that it was her fingers tightening on a skin taut and hardened by desire.

Akim stretched his head back as he took a deep breath savoring the last vestiges of her perfume in the room. Jasmine, vanilla and that sweetness of the very chocolate in her gaze. All blended into one to become pure feminine essence. Hers and hers alone.

She gently slipped her long fingers inside his tight boxer shorts as she murmured his name like a mantra of passion. She caressed him, leading him into a world where he was king and she was queen. The feminine smile invited him to bite her while he, eager to satisfy her darkest pleasures, became her most devoted servant.

The calloused hand pressed hard on the smoothness of his erection and he moaned as he felt that dream as real. He trembled anxiously to feel saved and her kisses became one by one his only elixir of life.

-Yes... -He whispered in agitation.

In a parallel universe Brenda kissed him passionately, even with a touch of desperation that drove him crazy with excitement. Impatient to feel alive he squeezed his increasingly tense body even tighter. He imagined that her mouth ran over him with insatiable kisses until it reached the most yearning part of his body while he looked at a silky hair that was lost in his nervous crotch. The man shivered as he imagined those full lips, caressing him and encircling him to cover him completely, and sucking in his purest essence.

-Yes... -he murmured, closing his eyes so as not to wake up.

This was his dream, and like every night for the past year, his one and only muse would caress him in the darkness of his room, whispering words of deep desire learned just for him.

His chest was rising and falling upset and his reasoning was begging him not to wake up. She was there with him, she enveloped him and pressed into him again and again begging for a satisfaction that he would offer her along with heaven.

-Yes... yes... -He said in a hoarse voice answering her sweet imaginary pleas. Yes, Brin.... Yes.

The hard body tensed in the face of ever increasing pressure and an unbearably intense movement covered it completely. Hips rose desperately in the emptiness of the night trying to reach her while his expert fingers pressed once, twice, three times more until he got his body to stir intensely to then fall limp on a mattress that sheltered him in the sorrow of loneliness. She was not there.

Akim calmed his breathing, but without moving. Her hand, still inside his boxers and resting on his now sleeping manhood, brought him back to a reality he always hated to admit. He was not satiated at all, he still desired her with the same intensity as in the previous moments. Her eyes still haunted him in the depths of his memories and her perfume continued to be etched in his desires. He reached out for a towel Brenda had left for him, when a desperate scream cut through the air. He was only able to run like a demon-ridden soul down the stairs and pray that she was all right.

"Please, God, she didn't..."

He buttoned a belt loop on his jeans to keep them from falling off as he ran down the stairs like an uncontrolled demon. Without her there was no hope.

A matter of jealousy

Akim was running with the speed of a thousand demons as panic boiled through his veins.

"How could I have been so stupid!" he said to himself in despair. He was at home, he had to take care of her and not dream of impossible alternate realities. If anything happened to her because of his inattention he would never forgive himself. Brenda screamed with even greater desperation and the hallway became an endless run. She had to be by his side. It mattered little to her whether the threat was a six-foot man or a ruthless woman. Whoever it was she should prepare herself for his fury, because she didn't intend to stop until she saw him pleading for his own life. With a by no means easy childhood, and in a godforsaken land, life had taught her to protect herself, and by all that was holy she would not be in any danger. Not as long as he was around.

Akim entered the room, barefoot, half-dressed and agitated, when he found a hysterical Brenda crying non-stop. His hate-filled eyes searched uncontrollably for the cause of his suffering, but he could not find him. In the room there was only her and that little thing she was cradling in her arms, trying to protect from the inevitable. Tears streamed down his face and he felt like dying when he understood who it was.

-We have to take him to a veterinarian," she sobbed as she looked at him. Bring the car around.

The man reached over and squeezed her shoulders trying to bring her back to reality. Bonbon's neck was broken and her eyes were closed. There was little they could do for the little cat.

-We can save her... -he said as he pressed the little furry bundle against his chest. Don't just stand there! We have to save her...

Akim would have made a pact with the devil himself if he could give life to the little furball and stop its suffering, but despite having direct communication with the hot hell, the sweet little animal was already dreaming of other, more heavenly arms.

-Brenda...

-Please Akim... please... Help me...

The man felt that heart he had thought dead for decades was shattering into tiny specks of dust. He had to help her. How? He knew nothing of comfort. He had never been given any. He closed his eyes and expressed what was typical and socially stipulated, but not because he felt it, but because it was the only thing he was able to express in words.

-I'm sorry... I'm so sorry," he said, patting her shoulders.

Brenda raised her eyes and her gaze was no longer pure and intense chocolate, the tears had turned them into a muddy, sad and soulless mud, and he felt himself dying. Maddened at not being able to heal his wound he hugged her tightly. Brenda rested her face and small body on his broad chest and he enveloped them both with his warmth. She was so cold on the outside and so broken on the inside that she wanted to howl like a caged wolf seeking revenge, but what good would it do, who or where to look? Damn life, she didn't deserve it. She didn't. Only a few hours before she had enjoyed telling how happy she was to collaborate with the group of abused women. At no time did she speak with vanity, on the contrary, she showed pride in the courage of those women who wanted to continue in spite of all their despair.

"My advice is just a bridge to a better way. Their own bravery leads them to rebuild their cobblestone paths," she said proudly. Damn it, no, she didn't deserve it. People with hearts as big as Brenda's were the ones who gave meaning in life to people as wretched as he was.

"Fuck..."

After a long, long time and many tears, he was able to convince her to put the little one in a shoebox and bury him in the huge garden. Brenda nodded. She never stopped crying. She no longer screamed, but she didn't speak either, she just cried silently trying to look strong while Akim, with the greatest of care, placed the little ball of fur in its little box and covered it with the black earth. "Death," he thought saddened. How many times he had dealt with it in the refugee camp, but every time he had lost.

He gently embraced her around the waist and tried to guide her to the kitchen when the woman in a totally unforeseen act hugged him tightly and began to cry inconsolably on his bare chest. Akim squeezed her with all the strength he could muster. He wanted to offer her the comfort she needed, he wanted to tell her a thousand and one words of affection, but nothing came out of his throat. She was dry with grief. He embraced her with the greatest of affection hoping that his strong arms would be able to express all that his heart was silent. In a way almost imperceptible to her, he brought his lips close over her head and caressed the softness of her hair with a delicate kiss that had little of sensuality and lust. Care, protection, tenderness, love? Yes, all these were the feelings represented in a soft kiss that barely touched her but that she felt like a current of life, and that she needed.

-Brin, we have to go inside, it's getting chilly and you're freezing. He said as he noticed for the first time that she was wearing pajamas with shorts and a tank top. She looked adorable.

Brenda didn't flinch and walked slowly towards the house, letting herself be guided at all times by Akim's expert hand holding her by the waist. He was a wreck. Bonbon was everything. Her pet had been with her for fifteen years, the same as her marriage to Max. He would always threaten not to let him in and she would scold him, telling him not to talk like that, the little guy could understand. Max laughed and squeezed his little ball of fur as he purred delightedly with his master's caresses.

-I found it in the kitchen, it will do you good. The woman stretched out her hand and accepted the cup of linden tea with barely any strength. My father is the expert in the kitchen so I am not responsible for its consequences. Akim joked trying to make her smile, but his intentions fell on deaf ears.

The doctor simply ducked her head and drank.

He sat beside her in complete silence. He understood her pain and did not wish to burden her. He knew what it meant to be speechless. It always happened to him. Parsimonious people called him, but introverted would be the more accurate word. When Brenda could, she would speak, in the meantime, he would be waiting like a faithful servant waiting to be called.

-Why would anyone do such a thing? -He asked after an hour of complete silence. Bonbon was a little guy who only brought smiles.

Tears welled up again as she asked him, and he could no longer hold back. He glued his body next to hers on the sofa and dried with his rough hands the face wet from crying.

-It could have been an accident. He commented unconfidently.

-They left a note.

-What note?

Dr. Klein did not answer and Akim asked again, but this time with more emphasis.

-Brenda, what note? I need you to show it to me. He spoke gently, she did not answer. She was in her world of pain and did not return.

-Brenda, please car.... -she stopped as she realized what she was going to say. Brenda what note?

The woman removed the blanket from her body as if awakening from her world and left her left fist, which, clenched tightly, held a crumpled piece of paper.

-Can I have it? -He spoke as gently as he could, even though he was trembling with the rage that roared from his gut. Who was the wretch? She would kill him with her hands if she had him in front of her.

Akim knew perfectly well that calmness was not one of her virtues, seeing her in her pajamas and with the dead kitten in her arms had overcome him beyond belief.

-Would you please give it to me...?

The man's voice sounded as tender as when he was talking to his young son and Brenda brought her fist almost to his face, opened it and handed him the crumpled note without speaking.

> You fucking bitch, you'll pay
> for taking away what I want. My
> first warning.
> Enjoy it...

-I'll call the inspector," he growled fiercely.

Akim got up from the couch determined but Brenda's grip on his elbow left him static in place.

-Don't do it.

The woman's eyes were puffy and her nose was red from crying. Akim wished with all his heart that he could embrace her and offer her at least a little comfort, but as always, the clouds of his social status brought him back to a reality that night he disowned more than ever. This was not his home and she was not his wife. It didn't matter that she wore soft cotton pajamas with suspenders and shorts, or that her soft fingers gently squeezed his arm or that her little brown eyes were irritated from crying, he was not and would never be the man to comfort her in her sad moments.

-Brenda... -. The hoarse voice showed more tenderness than I would have liked to express. Please...

-I can't. That man will insist on taking me to the police station and I can't do it anymore, I don't have the strength. Not tonight. I'm too tired... Why would that woman do such a thing? What could she achieve with such cruelty?

Brenda began to cry again and found it impossible to contain the depth of her feelings. He just did it. He reached over and without a second thought, hugged her to his chest again. With the greatest of care, he lifted her up and placed her on his lap and cradled her with the sweetest of tenderness. She needed him and he could no longer contain himself. Let the world, formalities and matrimonial rights all go to hell. She wept on his naked torso without consolation and he stroked her long hair saying with caresses what her throat and reason would not allow her. He lowered his head and breathed in a perfume that he would never be able to erase. Vanilla, jasmine and his Brin, unique and unmistakable scent of his precious Dr. Klein....

Time was passing too fast and he was only able to listen to the hands of an imaginary clock that would soon order him to let her go. He would have to open his arms and he would have to watch her go, leaving him in the silence of a loneliness he no longer desired. She did not speak, she did not move, any mistake that could make her react from the position she was in would represent the abyss. Her delicate bare legs brushed against his and the warmth of her soft, rounded buttocks squeezed an area that was struggling to master the situation. Her full delicate face lay against his torso and he was able to feel the soft breath of her breath on the beauty of his skin and felt himself shudder as he felt the possessor of such a magnificent moment. If a year ago, someone had told him that you could enjoy so much something as insignificant as cradling the woman you love in your arms, he would have laughed in his face.

When had he first seen her? nine, ten? no, it was twelve, twelve months, three hundred and sixty-five days trying to restrain himself from looking at her, from needing to caress her, suffering from desiring her and begging not to love her. His rough hand trembled as he fearfully reached out to caress the silkiness of her hair. She was so soft, so delicate, and his broad, rough hand was so...so....

Akim tensed as he noticed that his heartbeat was getting slower and slower. At last he was resting. He sighed with a small groan and the man smiled at his luck, though this time he wasn't convinced whether bad or fucking good. His heart was beating out of control, in his arms lay the best and most unimaginable of his dreams.

"Sleep sweetheart. My Brin."

His wide, hard arms wrapped around her, preventing her from thinking logically. Reason screamed at her again and again that this was not right, that she should leave. When would a man like him ever have the opportunity to have someone like her on his body? And half-dressed! He smiled feebly so as not to wake her up. Today he would be canonized as a saint. He closed his eyes while he caressed her hair without restraint, she slept like a princess, a beautiful and exhausted princess.

-Sleep, my precious. Sleep, my Brin... Shall I tell you a secret? I like to call you that when you come into my room during my dreamy nights. It's something that exists only between you and me. Did you know that? No, of course I didn't...

Akim smiled imagining a thousand and one ways to have her under his body and smiled even more imagining the reaction of a woman as polite and correct as Brenda, letting him do everything he wanted to do to her if she were his. The man's mood improved instantly and it was mainly due to her, and that delicate touch on a torso hardened by too many hours of work. Dr. Klein had unique and magical powers, he thought amused. Quite a witch. His witch.

The young man breathed that sweet scent of woman and let himself be enveloped by the music of his heart that beat in rhythm with that of his muse, and dreamed, dreamed of a beautiful future of smiles and unique caresses in all its dawns.

-And you are? -. Akim cursed between his teeth when he woke up to a thick voice that rebuked him in a tone that was not at all friendly.

He opened his eyes a couple of times trying to clear his head, when at last he could appreciate the firm face of the one who was claiming his rights.

Wherever you are

They both looked at each other in a staring match and even though the guy hadn't introduced himself, Akim knew perfectly well who he was and why his gaze was silently screaming at him a, "Let's go outside."

The young man tried to get comfortable and stand up, but Brenda, who was still sound asleep on his chest, mumbled in her sleep in disgust that her soft mattress was moving. Akim hid his joy thinking about the patheticness of the situation. He could perfectly well say that this was not what it seemed, but he cared little for the man's forgiveness.

-I'm Akim, Akim Dudaev," he said as he moved to the side and Brenda leaned back on the couch totally oblivious to what was going on there. I work in the doctor's office and I stayed with her last night to take care of her.

The young worker got up completely and stood at the same level as the man who was listening to him without expressing any feelings. Was he so polite or was he an alien with an ice cap? he thought in annoyance.

He could yell at him, berate him, even hit him. Akim would have preferred that a thousand times to having to see him so perfect and correct controlling his every impulse. Damn him, he was angry, his gaze roared and his fists tensed at his sides, but he didn't say anything out of tune. He was stupidly perfect even in his reactions.

The architect was wearing impeccable light beige pants and a matching white polo shirt, embroidered with the horse brand, which he couldn't remember the name of because he never had enough money to buy one. Akim ran his fingers through his thick hair, trying to tame it from the morning's awakening, and spoke as calmly as he could.

-Inspector Gutierrez asked me not to keep her alone," she felt compelled to explain, though she hated to do so. She was afraid she might be attacked.

-Attack her? -Max, who only knew loose gibberish told by Rachel, put aside his wounded male pride to approach his wife. Rachel stood to the side in a silent attitude totally unusual for her.

He sat on the couch and stroked Brenda's hair trying to wake her up and Akim spoke quickly. He wanted to get out of there as soon as possible. It wasn't that she was afraid of that man, far from it, she knew perfectly well that he would fight a thousand wars if he could get her, but that was much more, she couldn't bear to see how his hands caressed her.

-She took some painkillers," he said hastily. She was very frightened, maybe I should let her sleep... -He commented annoyed when he saw how he caressed her with no qualms.

-What have you done to him? Gentuza, you're a riffraff!

The woman who had so far not spoken and whom Akim had simply ignored, cried out in annoyance.

-It wasn't me, se-ño-ra. He answered unwillingly and in his usual deep voice.

-Rachel, please... -The woman snorted, but obeyed Max's gentle, firm command.

The architect looked at him waiting for his account as he continued to stroke the hair of his still sleeping wife. Akim shifted nervously as he looked anywhere other than the man's hands on her delicate body.

-There is a patient who has certain problems and...

-I know that, but I don't understand why he was afraid? Last night he told me that he would order a couple of pizzas and then go to rest. I don't understand why he had to take painkillers.

Did he know that? had she called him? at what time? why had she done so?

Akim was disappointed. For a moment he thought she was with him as comfortable as he was with her. He hated to think that she had remembered him, let alone called him. Max rebuked him with a glare and answered unwillingly.

-That woman, or whoever she was, came into the house and left him a warning-Akim sighed bitterly. They killed her cat. They broke his neck.

-Pump... -Rachel covered her mouth and then crossed herself, and the architect closed his eyes pained by the information. He knew perfectly well what that kitten meant to her. They had no children and Brenda adored the pet like a baby.

The man ducked his head and murmured a few words in his wife's ear, waking her up. She opened her eyes drowsily and disoriented when she saw herself on the couch, but when she found Max in front of her, she hugged him desperately and started crying again.

-Max... Bonbon... Sweetie...

-I know, honey... I know...

The man was caressing his wife's back and Akim felt broken and completely helpless. He walked nervously to the window noticing for the first time that he was barefoot and wearing just jeans. He shook his head, that man was not from this planet. If another half naked man had the woman he loved in his arms, and on his couch, he would have beaten him out of his house. The perfect Max Brown, however, cared for her state of mind and caressed her tenderly. Damn... he thought, dragging his hand through his nervous hair. What am I saying! He loves her so much that he cares a lot more than breaking my face.

-You should get dressed, don't you think? Only Neanderthals go around other people's houses half naked.

Akim wanted to strangle the nasty woman who spoke behind his back, but he had to admit that barefoot, shirtless and wearing barely worn jeans was not a proper way to walk around the house.

-I was about to go to bed when I heard her scream and I didn't have time to put on my best clothes". She replied, leaving the snake unsettled, "I'd better go....

Max who listened attentively to her explanation was still speechless, and although his body seemed relaxed embracing his wife, his gaze was warning him very clearly to keep his distance.

Akim accepted his nonverbal threat without responding. That man stood up for his own and he couldn't blame him.

-Akim, wait a minute, we have to call the inspector. He'll want to see us. This can't go on like this.

Brenda spoke as she dried her eyes and pulled away from Max's arms. The young man stayed in place without moving. For some stupid reason he felt happy to see her let go of her husband to call him and say his name out loud. It was terribly stupid and he knew it, but he wanted to hold on to an illusion, no matter how idiotic it was.

-I can get dressed and take you. He replied enthusiastically.

Max, who kept his eyes on him, answered politely and firmly.

-Thank you for your help, I'll take it from here. What crew did you say you work for?

-Samuel's. He said, staring at the architect.

-Bricklayer?

-A little bit of everything," he replied uncomfortably.

-Well, I'll send word that you have the day off today. You can go home and rest. It is the least I can do for you after protecting "My Woman". He said highlighting the "M" of mine and woman.

-He owes me nothing.

Akim wanted to tell her to shove her gratitude where it would fit, that he was doing everything for her and only for her, but she bit her tongue until it bled.

-I insist.

-And I say no.

They both looked at each other defiantly when Rachel stepped in unbidden.

-Dear, you will have to listen to the architect, after all there is no proletariat bus service here. This is a top residential neighborhood. You will have to walk for a long time.

Both men continued to stare at each other without listening to any of Rachel's nonsense. Dr. Klein, who seemed somewhat recovered from her nerves, stood up with a firm posture and walked a few steps trying to mediate the tense situation.

-Akim, I totally understand that you don't want to miss your work day and attendance award, but if you would do me the favor of taking my car and dropping it off at the office, I would pick it up later. It would be a huge favor to me.

The young man who was about to protest was surprised by a silent plea in the form of chocolate eyes and accepted his defeat. She was winning him over with her every glance.

-It's fine, but if you need me to accompany you or if Inspector Gutierrez wants to see me or if....

Akim bit her tongue as she watched her perfect husband reach behind her small back to rest his hands on the woman's shoulders making it very clear who was to leave, and who was to stay.

-Don't worry, I'll call you. She replied gratefully.

He climbed the stairs with an enormous weight on his ankles. He didn't want to leave, he didn't want to leave her, what choice did he have? It was either that or kidnap her. "Maybe it's not such a bad idea," he thought smiling as he went into the room to get dressed and get out of there as soon as possible. The mere presence of the architect made him sick.

Back to

Brenda said goodbye to Akim with a heartfelt thank you and closed the door with grief still settling in her heart. She never thought the death of a pet would be so painful.

-Sweet, do you want me to make you something? some tea? Poor sweetie, he was so adorable, I can't imagine what he must have gone through. The doctor opened her eyes and Max intervened instantly.

-Rachel, I would appreciate it if you would leave us alone.

-Oh yes, yes, of course. I'm leaving in this moment. Talk to you later sweet -she said while she gave Brenda two kisses and said confidently -I'm leaving, but if you need me you know where I'm living.

-Thank you, Rachel.

Max waited for the woman to let go of his wife and walk out the door to ask.

-Do you have any clues as to who might have done it?

-I think so.

Her husband nodded as he hugged her shoulders.

-I'm sorry I wasn't here.

-You were working, don't worry," she replied, accepting the kiss on the forehead.

-I'll take a shower.

Max sat down on the bed to wait for her and head for the police station as soon as possible. He was a little nervous and that surprised him, because it was not at all usual for him, but neither was it usual for a madwoman to sneak into his house, kill his cat and threaten his wife. Brenda came out of the shower with her hair damp and wearing a perfect white lingerie set and he wanted to tell her she looked beautiful but he didn't, it wasn't the time.

-I heard Maria come in the house. Do you want me to order her a coffee or would you rather I buy you a latte macchiato and a dulce de leche cake? - Max asked, trying to get a smile out of her.

-You don't play fair," he said, smiling with hardly any desire.

Brenda was trying to recover, the image of Bombón with her eyes closed was still in her mind.

-It's my fault... If I hadn't taken Murray's case...

-Don't even think about it. That woman is crazy, period. They'll put her in jail and we'll go back to our lives. Max tried to hug her, but she let go too quickly.

-But it was Bombón... -she said with tears in her eyes.

-I know, honey, I know," Max hugged her and wiped away her tears.

She took a deep breath and headed for the closet.

The doctor's cell phone rang insistently and Max and Brenda looked at each other strangely. It was too early in the morning for such insistence.

-It's Connor," he said as he read the name on the screen.

-And who else... -Max said with a very bad look on his face.

-He must have heard about it and is worried.

-And how did you do that? Do you have cameras in the house? -he said with irony.

-Don't be like that. Maybe he got the information from the same source as you? What did he say to make you get a flight so soon? That they were killing me? -Brenda commented before answering her cell phone and calming her soul mate while Max wrung his fingers.

"Something like: you have to come home urgently, there's a caveman with Sweet and I'm scared for her." I had said to him in a loud shout.

Max shook his head. He shouldn't have listened to him and become so nervous. That young man was a poor boy. One of many in the work crew. Brenda hung up the phone and asked him curiously.

-Why are you smiling?

-Because of your friends, my dear. I still wonder what you have in common with them. Connor, Rachel, Johana...

-Max, please, I don't want to argue. Not today.

Brenda was a little tired of defending Connor and Rachel to her impeccable husband. They weren't as perfect, polite as Max, but she loved them and they loved her.

-And we're not going to do it. I was joking. Get dressed and let's go get that cake," he said as he gave her a little slap on the buttocks.

Brenda accepted the truce and finished dressing while he thought smiling.

"Only Rachel would see danger in a poor guy like that." He was used to dealing with bricklaying crews and Akim Dudaev was just another laborer. Tall and strong like everyone else. Short-brained and short-pocketed.

Looking for you without finding you

-No matter how hard you keep looking, he's not going to show up. Nikola grumbled in annoyance as he carried the full weight of the cement bags.

-I wasn't...

-Weren't you watching? Ha and Ha. He commented sarcastically as he threw the bags on the floor.

-Akim, that woman is not for you, she plays in another league, not to mention that she is a married woman and a few years older than you.

-I'm just curious," he lied cheekily. He hasn't been here for two days and they haven't picked up the car yet. Do you think he'll be all right?

The man began to make the mixture for the walls while he slyly looked towards the entrance of the closed office.

-I think you're dumb, that's what I think. If the woman were dead we wouldn't be fixing up her nice building or her practice would we?

-I'm not talking about anything so serious, but she still didn't fully recover, you should have seen her, so helpless....

-Yes, yes I know, and please don't tell me the dead kitten story again because I throw up. Now stop thinking about nonsense or we'll have to work on Saturday.

The man nodded and set off. The week had proved exhausting and he, like Nikola, had no desire to work on a Saturday. "I'll sleep in tomorrow." He sighed wearily.

The sound of footsteps from behind distracted him from his mix, but he didn't look up. His friend was right, they needed to finish the job so they could start their weekend off. They were at the end of the month, they would collect the paycheck and his son would get a new pair of sneakers.

-Akim, I need you to hand over the keys to Brenda's car. Connor commented authoritatively.

The bricklayer, who was squatting by the mixing bucket, raised his head to look at the artist who was watching him from above.

-No.

-How?

-I'm saying I can't give them to him. Dr. Klein told me she was coming for him and I can't give them to anyone else but her.

Nikola felt his jaw unhinge and Connor looked at him with wide eyes and then burst out laughing.

-You see, I happen to be Brenda's best friend, she and I are like brothers, so cut the crap and give me the keys to the convertible right now," he said, holding out his hand.

Akim got up from the ground and stretched his six-foot-plus frame to his full height to stand face to face. If he wanted a fight he would get one.

Nikola, who knew his friend very well and who were also like brothers, reacted instantly, trying to avoid the worst.

-The keys are on the desk in his office. He said loudly.

Connor stared at Akim for a long moment, but Akim was unfazed, in fact, he held his gaze without a moment's hesitation. The giant red-haired man shook his head and turned toward his friend's office, and Nikola wiped her forehead with a cloth.

-That was a close call, why are you trying to get us kicked out? -Nikola was hitting him over the head with a rag when Connor turned to speak to them again.

When Nikola saw him, he pretended to wipe his friend's shoulder and asked him in surprise.

-Did you forget something?

-The truth is yes. Tomorrow I need to take some works to a room where I'm exhibiting and the contractors have let me down, would you be interested in the job?

-No thanks, it's our day off." Akim replied in a deep voice and Nikola tried to soften the answer.

-We appreciate it, you see, this is an exhausting job, and tomorrow is Saturday....

The worker was about to continue when Connor cut him off with an offer that was impossible to refuse.

-I pay 80 pounds. Per hour.

Nikola felt his hands itching to catch those bills.

-The time? -he said enthusiastically.

-Yes. I need you to pick up some works from here, transport them carefully to the exhibition hall, and hang them in the gallery.

-We already told you that.... -Akim spoke confidently and Nikola interrupted him by raising her voice above his.

-We will be happy to help.

-Well, I'll leave the data with you before I leave.

The sculptor left for his friend's office and closed the door behind him.

-I thought we don't work on Saturdays? -. He said grumpily.

-For eighty pounds an hour? Brother, for that we'll even do it in our underwear.

Akim threw the rag he was previously hitting him with at his head and smiled cheekily. He had no desire to prove her right, and the truth was that the amount was well worth a little effort on Saturday.

-And don't be late with that painting. We have an appointment. Nikola spoke for sure.

-Have we? -He answered, raising one of his bushy, dark eyebrows.

-Yes, we have. And don't think about getting me bogged down. I'm on the verge of suicide, either I go out with a woman or I explode into a thousand pieces.

Nikola grinned with laughter and Akim followed suit. After all, he couldn't do without a date with a safe ending. He had been dreaming about the wrong woman for a long time. "And why not, I don't owe loyalty to anyone." He thought justifying himself.

-Where are we going? -Brenda asked her friend, who had put her in the car without informing her.

-It's a surprise. He answered for the umpteenth time.

-It's okay, it's okay...

Brenda's cell phone rang and she answered in earnest.

-Anne *Foster, how are you doing? I need you to calm down and talk to me without hiding anything.... No, I don't care how Reed is... I don't want to know how you feel about him.... Anne please, sit down and think for yourself, don't wait for me to tell you what is right or wrong... organize your mind and decide accordingly with your feelings... I know honey, nothing is easy, but you have lived long enough to know what you want out of life and what you don't....*

Connor continued driving without being able to take his attention away from his friend's chatter. Truly Brenda was a genius at recognizing conflict situations and channeling them with possible win-win solutions for those involved. Yes, Brenda was a complete genius for social psychology, even if she rarely used it to her own advantage. Connor shook his head in complete sulk. Just the thought of Max was driving him out of his mind. He would be her husband, but he didn't know her at all. Brenda wasn't the uptight socialite he was trying so hard to make her out to be. Her friend was pure sentiment and naturalness. She was solidarity and joy. Max had managed to bury under a layer of good manners and proper behavior a unique free spirit. He remembered her when they were still young students full of dreams and social demands. Brenda loved to participate in projects such as free assistance to battered women and was involved with every needy soul regardless of their social status. No, her spirit was not dead, merely lulled to sleep by a tyrannical wizard named Max, Max Brown. He may not have been evil at all and in his own way loved her. He disliked her friend's husband as much as he disliked a boil on his buttocks.

-What's on your mind? -Brenda said as she hung up on him.

-We are getting there.

The doctor looked around and instantly recognized the place.

-In the university district? You're not telling me that...

-Exactly that. We'll dine on two-pound tacos, drink soda in paper cups and get drunk on the cheapest tequila in the country.

Brenda smiled in amusement as Connor parked his wonderful convertible. As if abducted by other people's opinions, she pulled herself together and said in a serious voice.

-But we're not old enough, it's probably wrong for us. We don't fit in here anymore...

-We don't fit in where? Cari, you've had a shitty few days and crying for no consolation. Today's the day we're going to have a great time. We'll let loose and make fun of the world, are you in?

-I don't know," she said doubtfully. She got out of the car and clung tightly to Connor's arm.

-You leave it to me. Everything is under control." He commented with a loud laugh and guided her to the dining room. I want to see those eyes sparkle like they used to.

-What do you mean before?

Connor preferred not to answer and change the subject. That look of sorrow had been there long before Bombón's disappearance.

-I'm going to eat three double tacos full of hot sauce and I'm not going to treat you.

Brenda was no fool and understood perfectly well the sudden change of subject. She did nothing to continue the clarifications. Connor was right, it had been a horrible few days, Max was out again for that big project, and she dreaded going back to the practice. The Murray case turned out to be complex and dangerous and who knows what would happen down the road. The best thing would be to enjoy a good night and not think.

Do not say

Akim was enjoying his companion in the dark hallway of the local when someone in a very indelicate way bumped into them head on. With his eyes still closed in passion he cursed over his girl's lips to turn around as he was engulfed for the second time.

-Sorry, sorry.

The woman, with her hair a bit disheveled and in a complete state of inebriation, was trying to pass through the narrow corridor towards the bathrooms, but she was too affected to make it to the door.

Akim was about to respond to one of his usual tirades when he had to blink once, twice, three and even four times until he confirmed the identity of the beoda. The man cursed again and again as he cursed non-stop. This was not real. It couldn't be real. It couldn't be happening to me, he said almost sobbing. Brenda Klein walked totally confused towards the restroom of a sleazy joint while he, with his jeans zipped down, enjoyed the caresses of the always willing Lola.

-Shit, shit and a thousand shits together.

His manhood collapsed at the very moment he recognized Dr. Klein, who, somewhat dizzy, entered the restroom unaware of whom she had bumped into.

A part of him was relieved not to be recognized. He had no desire for her to see him in that state. He owed her nothing, she was engaged, but damn it, he hated to admit that he felt like a bit of a cad and quite a dick to see himself with his manhood in the hands of another. It was fucking stupid, nothing existed between them, she was married but he couldn't help but feel like a pig. He knew perfectly well who his heart belonged to and who he was using.

-What's up, baby?

Lola said in a honeyed voice trying to revive a part of her body that was collapsing without comfort.

-Stay here.

-You plan to leave me? -Like this?

The young woman pointed to her shirt fully open and the right side of her bra fully dropped leaving a rounded and very bulging breast free.

Akim ignored her captivating voice and headed for the women's restroom. Lola was urging him to go back, but he had only an image on his mind. She was there and in a very pitiful state.

"Fuck, what the fuck is wrong with your idiot husband! She shouldn't be walking alone in this joint. She's so sweet and different. Any asshole could take advantage." Akim was getting angrier by the second. If he were her partner he would always be by her side, he would never leave her, let alone abandon her in such a state, and in a place like that.

"You bastard." He thought as he remembered the perfect Max Brown.

He entered the women's restroom without caring if anyone was there or not. He looked for her with his eyes and found her refreshing her face with water. She wasn't wearing makeup and her hair fell messily over her shoulders, and Akim had to restrain himself from shouting out loud how beautiful she looked. Her little brown eyes glistened from the alcohol and her body was at its clumsiest with every movement, and that made her more earthy and adorable than ever.

She always walked so self-assured that to see her now so cheerful, so carefree, so imperfect, and so alone, he could not contain himself. Smiling he approached her and held her by the waist behind her back. She looked so dizzy that he was afraid she might slip and hit her forehead against the sink.

-Are you all right?

Brenda gasped as she felt strong fingers clinging to both sides of her waist and tried to turn away nervously but couldn't. The world was spinning too fast. The world was spinning too fast. At first she was afraid, though she felt relaxed in a moment. It was strange but she liked the feeling. She looked at the small, worn mirror with slanted eyes trying to put a face to those hands. Either the mirror was very bad or she wasn't in very good condition.

The doctor carefully straightened her back and gently turned around. When she saw him she smiled in such a way that Akim would have kissed her right there. She was drunk, yes, she may not even have been aware of the radiant smile she gave him when she saw him, or how her eyes sparkled when she recognized him, and the young man did not want to think and lose his few illusions. Those that dominated him every time he had her in front of him.

-Akim! It's been a long time!

The doctor threw herself into his arms and he held her even tighter so she wouldn't lose her balance.

"Why are you doing this to me?" He thought as he noticed the silky brown hair under her chin.

One, two, three, he had gotten to count to ten breaths before she released him.

-Brenda... -He spoke in a voice so hoarse that even he was frightened by his thick accent. What are you doing in this place? Are you alone? Is he with you? -She couldn't call him husband, husband, much less Max, in fact she couldn't call him anything at all. The woman continued to cling to his broad shoulders to keep from falling as she answered him in confusion.

-Yes, he is with me.

Akim instantly tensed. That was an answer he did not wish to hear.

-I'll take you to him. You're too dizzy to walk alone. I don't understand what that man is thinking to leave a woman like you alone in this dump. But what am I saying! I don't understand how he brought you here. This is no place for women like you.

Brenda walked him down the hallway while clinging to his arm. Why was Akim so angry?

-I'm fine... -He said with his tongue pierced.

-Not for the way she takes care of you. He grumbled in annoyance, not realizing that they were passing in front of Lola, who looked on without believing what she was seeing.

-Akim! What the fuck is this!

-Please speak up. I'm going to leave Dr. Klein at her desk. I'll be right back.

-If you think you can just leave me lying there like that, you're smart. You're a son of a bitch. The young woman fixed her black lycra miniskirt while chewing a piece of gum with her mouth open -. I'm not waiting for you, you son of a bitch... asshole... bastard.... You bastard!

Brenda's eyes widened like saucers at so many expletives and she wondered if she would be able to string so many expletives together so well and in such a short period of time. No, I'm sure she wouldn't.

-Lola... -The woman smiled as she saw him stop and thought that he would repent and return to her side.

-Yes, Akim? -. She replied sweetly hoping to see him turn around and return to her side as he let go of the stretched woman he was holding by the waist.

-Fuck you.

Akim continued walking toward the store without turning around while Lola continued her long and well-spun series of insults.

-I... -Brenda wanted to give her opinion. Dizziness prevented her from doing so.

The young man looked all over the tables for the presence of her husband, but there was no trace of the hated architect.

-Brenda, there is no one here.

-No, not for now... -he said and sat down, raising his hand to ask for another tequila.

The waiter nodded his head and left. The doctor, oblivious to Akim's doubts, began to hum the songs that those present began to sing in the space dedicated to the most pathetic of the Karaokes. The man sat down next to her and tried to speak to her slowly, thinking that this way he would receive a coherent answer.

-Has he gone and left you?

-Yes, but he'll be back. The poor thing has been so long without liking a man, that I couldn't refuse. But he will come back, he always does, he loves me very much and he will not abandon me....

Brenda shifted her body in the chair as she hummed loudly and received the two new tequilas.

Akim was totally baffled. It was clear that Brenda was drunk and quite a bit. Would they be such a liberal couple? Did her husband like men?

He scratched the back of his head in disorientation as a flash of clarity reached his brain.

-Did you come with Connor?

The doctor, who was dancing more and more in her seat, looked at him and nodded as she hummed. Akim smiled as he heard her tune her out of tune with such enthusiasm. She was alone, drunk, and with him. Fortune did exist. He sat happily beside her and was about to take a sip of his tequila when his jaw snapped back.

Brenda had stood up, and without warning, she zigzagged her way to the microphone. She burst into song with full energy and the worst of voices.

She moved a little dizzily, and it could be said that she wasn't dancing badly at all, if it weren't for the gash she was carrying and those little stumbles from the stage that almost scared him to death. Brenda was not at the height of her powers. The reality was that no one in the joint was. To be honest, neither would he be if it weren't for the fact that neither Lola nor he wanted foreplay.

-Brother, I'm going to accompany Sofia home.

Nikola, accompanied by a beautiful blonde who hugged him enthusiastically, approached his friend and spoke into his ear when he saw the woman climbing onto the wooden platform.

-Mother of God, it can't be true.

At that moment Dr. Klein raised her hand in the air and then directed it toward the table.

-And this one for the most handsome young man and best person in the room -Akim Dudaev!

Akim's eyes widened like saucers and he was petrified in his chair with a smile on his face. Never in a thousand years would he have imagined anything like this. Brenda Klein was calling him handsome and dedicating a song to him. Was he dreaming? His friend hit him over the head with a napkin and he knew he wasn't dreaming.

-Delete that idiot chuckle and tell me what the hell is going on.

-I swear I have no idea. He said as he watched her wave her arms around the crowd to encourage people to chorus her.

-He's like a drunk.

-He just doesn't know how to drink. Akim's eyes sparkled with amusement as he replied.

-What about your husband?

-He left her alone. Again.

The young man tensed at the response. She could have said she was alone, that she was waiting for Connor, but no, her anger was focused on him, always on him. She longed for what this man had and hated that he didn't value her.

Nikola watched him closely and didn't like it one bit. His friend was busted. That didn't mean anything good. Akim never showed interest in any woman and to tell the truth he didn't show interest in anyone. Only his father and his son were the center of his concerns, the rest of the world mattered little to him. Leaving his country, his future and taking care of an unwanted child had symbolized the beginning of the end in Akim's life.

-And Lola? -Nikola tried to distract him from the image of that woman who had him spellbound. For heaven's sake, you even smile at her! - she commented aloud. Akim didn't even hear him.

His aphonic siren sang to him and lured him into a world where no one existed but the two of them.

-Akim! -He raised his voice and turned around angrily.

-What fly has bitten you! Why are you shouting?

Nikola shook his head and asked again.

-What about Lola?

-That way... -He answered, lifting his shoulders.

-Brother, come with me, we'll look for her and the four of us will go to Sofia's house. She lives alone and we can have a great time. Get up and come with us.

Nikola wanted to lift him out of his seat. Akim smiled again at the woman who accepted the applause as if she were a true artist.

-I'm staying.

-Akim, this will not end well, come with me and end this stupidity while you still can..... - He said pitifully.

-What I start or not is my business. Now go away. Akim spelled each word with his deep and powerful accent, so powerful that Nikola accepted his defeat and left, but not before telling him loudly.

-I hope you know what you're doing.

Akim blinked with a bitter smile as he dragged his hand through his hair forcefully. No, he didn't know and he didn't want to know.

Brenda walked back to her chair and watched him with such joy and confidence that Akim felt himself melt. Damn his traitorous body but the blissful doctor gave him chills just by looking at him. She was dangerous, addictive and impossible to forget. He should run away from there, but his feet were anchored wherever she was.

-How did I do? Do you like music? I love it. I live singing. I don't do it much at home because Max doesn't like it. When I can, I sing. The woman took a sip of her tequila and continued speaking almost breathlessly. When I was in college, Connor and I signed up for a music course, even tried to play an instrument. We were so bad that after the first gig and a few tomatoes, we decided that drums and guitar weren't for us.

Akim's eyes widened in surprise, and the next moment he leaned back and burst into the deepest, loudest laugh he could ever remember. Brenda looked at him helplessly and laughed with him.

-I imagine what you're thinking, and I'm going to tell you that, believe it or not, my guitar and Connor's drums were a perfect match. Then I tried it with the ukulele, no way, it sounded terrible. I think they sold it to me as a failure, because after several months of rehearsing without a break, people insisted on tomatoes, they even added cabbages.

Akim broke down laughing and Brenda at first felt a little uncomfortable but then joined him in the merriment.

-You are unique.

-That's what Connor usually tells me, but...

-But? -he asked interested.

-Nothing. I think I'm going to go home, I'm so dizzy.

Akim stood up to help her up when Connor appeared through the door.

-Mother of mine, my dear, what a slice you have taken.

Brenda nodded without answering. She had gone from talking non-stop to not being able to talk at all. Connor looked at his six-foot-tall, muscle-bound companion apologetically because he had to leave, and Akim proposed without hesitation.

-You don't have to cancel your plans, I can take her home. Connor watched him closely trying to figure out where the catch was. I haven't been drinking if that's what you're worried about. He said trying to convince him.

-I don't know, I'm not sure.... -Although the company of his beloved fireman attracted him very much, his love for Brenda was much stronger than a good fuck. I'll take her home. Don't bother," he said unconvinced.

-It's no bother. Besides, I have no plans. I can leave it at home and take the car. Then tomorrow I could be very early for the transport of your paintings. If I wait for the bus I might not be on time...

Akim dropped the information hoping to convince him and hiding the detail on his motorcycle parked at the door. The powerful man of many muscles patted the artist's shoulder and Akim enjoyed his victory.

-All right, but please drive carefully. She is not used to drinking, do not leave her until you see that she is inside the house. If you see her getting dizzy or not feeling well call me urgently, I don't want her to feel sick and alone at home.

"Alone?" He thought in a millisecond.

-Don't worry, if I notice anything strange I'll call you.

"I wouldn't be caught dead letting anyone but me take care of her," he thought enthusiastically.

Brenda, who, totally dizzy and oblivious to the conversation, had leaned on Akim's shoulder, looking for some stability, nodded without understanding anything at all.

-Cari, Akim will take you home. If you feel sick or anything else you need, call me. It doesn't matter what time it is. She said as she handed the keys of her friend's convertible to the mason.

The doctor raised her rosy face from drinking and looked at her friend with complete tenderness.

-Yes, Dad," she said. She went over to throw herself into his arms and give him a big kiss on the cheek.

-I love you, baby.

-And I you.

The friends parted and the young escort felt the need to adjust her by the waist to bring her closer to his body. It was ridiculous, but for a moment he wished he was, if nothing else, her gay friend. Anything to get a kiss like that.

They walked to the door slowly when the screams of an uncontrolled Lola sounded behind them. Akim tried to ignore her. The woman ran and stepped in front to block the door to the premises.

-You're a pig, you thought you'd let me down?

-I have to go.

-With this one. He said contemptuously. But she's drunk and she's also a....

Akim didn't know what kind of insults Lola was going to hurl at Brenda. He raised his head and with all the hatred he was capable of sparking from his eyes, he shushed her.

-Don't say another word," he said with all the rage in his gut. Let me pass or I'll take you away myself.

The young woman let her pass, and Brenda, who could not coordinate much, spoke in half-words.

-That girl is furious. I'm going home, you go with her.

Dr. Klein released her grip and looked up, searching for a cab stand. She knew there was one nearby, but which way, right or left? Okay, let's try left, she answered herself amused. Akim grabbed her around the waist again and spoke to her tenderly and very, very emphatically.

-You're not going anywhere without me.

-But your girlfriend is angry.

-She is not my girlfriend. I don't have a girlfriend. He answered in such a bad mood that Brenda replied with pity.

-I'm sorry.

Akim, who at that moment spotted the car in the middle of the street, stopped to ask a curious question.

-Can you feel it?

-Yes, you are a very handsome and attentive man, you deserve to be in love.

Without explanation the woman reached up to give him a delicious, resounding kiss on the cheek leaving the poor man almost breathless.

-You are a sweetheart... -he said before collapsing again on her shoulder.

Akim noticed that her breath was barely coming into her lungs. He still felt the moisture of her sweet lips on his fledgling beard as he held her tightly so that she would not fall because it was obvious that she was about to lose consciousness.

As best he could, he guided her the remaining ten steps and put her in the car.

He walked around back to get into the driver's seat, but not before touching his face. He was about to open the door when he needed to rest both hands on the window trying to regain his senses and his breath. She had kissed him and his body still hadn't recovered from the impact. He got into the car and started thinking about how he would be able to take her home without committing anything crazy.

Dr. Klein's eyes were half open and the young man smiled to see her so relaxed.

-Brenda... Brin... wake up, we're home.

The young man stroked her mane trying to find her face when she lifted her sleepy little eyes and smiled at him with such affection that Akim felt the world would be so much better with a smile like that in the mornings.

-Thank you.

She tried to leave, became dizzy and Akim held her by the shoulders to keep her from moving.

-Wait, wait here.

The young worker ran to open the door for her, help her out of the vehicle, and get to the gate.

Brenda looked at the place with intrigue and Akim watched her quizzically.

-What's wrong?

-Are you sure this is it?

-Yes Brin, this is it. Let me get it.

-Brin? -No one calls me that.

-I do," he answered bluntly. Are you all right? Do you think you can?

"Say no... say no...". He thought nervously.

-I'm fine. Thank you.

Akim accepted her reply without taking his eyes off her. He couldn't. Every time he said goodbye to her he felt it was his last. Brenda was a dream he would never have, a whim he would never enjoy, and a sorrow that would never leave him.

-I owe you another one.

Brenda reached up to his face to give him a thank you kiss that happened to be too close to the corner of his lip. The young man didn't move, he enjoyed her perfume clinging to the soft skin as he closed his eyes drinking in every sensation. He didn't know if it had been one, two or twenty breaths, but what he was sure of was that they had been the best breaths of his entire life.

Brenda went inside and closed the gate and Akim needed to hold on to the steering wheel for a few minutes before starting.

-What is this? What's happening to me? God... Why are you doing this to me?

Preparations

-You haven't spoken to me all day. Will you go on like this for much longer?

-You don't need me. You're an idiot without help.

-You act like a jilted bride.

-And you as a complete brainless, what the fuck are you doing! Lola called Sofia and I had to take the rapapolvo and I say verbatim words of what she said: "Because of the son of a bitch pig who left me lying". Do you have anything to say?

Akim scratched the edge of his chin looking for an explanation that he didn't seem to have. Nikola, on the other hand, had a lot to say, so he continued to explain himself openly while resting the painting on the floor to make himself more comfortable.

-I didn't ask you for much, just to give me a hand to have a good time with a woman, but no! You couldn't do a favor to a friend and have a good time with Lola, who by the way has tits like a mechanic's workshop calendar.

-I wouldn't go that far," he replied, both angry and amused.

-Fuck you! Do you know where I slept last night?

-I sense from your nerves that not with Sofia. He replied calmly.

-And do you know why not? -. The friend denied as he placed a plinth on the wall. Because Lola showed up, sparking. Lola! The one you were supposed to entertain. Remember? But of course, you had to come to the rescue of a certain trouble-prone woman.

Akim climbed down the ladder and picked up the artwork from the floor to lift it up so he could hang it. He understood part of Nikola's anger, and so he knew he had nothing left to do but take the downpour.

-Do you know how long I've been cajoling Sofia?

Nikola sat on the floor as he looked at all the pictures hanging on the different walls of the room.

-Shall I buy you a few beers? -Akim sat down next to him, trying to get some redemption.

-Fuck you...

-But with beer or without beer?

They both looked at each other smiling and Akim knew he was forgiven. Nikola was all bark and no bite.

-Fuck, bro, at least I hope it was worth it for you because I'm about to explode.

Akim remembered the thank-you kiss and although it was not at all what Nikola might call "worth it," to him it had meant touching a star with his hand on a summer night.

The door to the room opened and a smiling Connor appeared admiring the walls.

-It's perfect. It's perfect. You guys are geniuses! - The artist said as they rose from the floor to accept the handshake.

-We are glad that we have placed them according to your taste.

-They are perfectly placed. I could say that they even have a certain coherence in the union of colors and motifs.

-The credit goes to Akim. He is an artist like you.

-Not at all.

-How?" Connor waited for an answer.

-In my country I studied fine arts for a few years and some music.

-And what happened?

-I had to abandon it.

-It can't be, really?

-Nikola spoke and Akim wanted to punch him in the mouth.

-So what happened? Why don't you do it?

-Why am I a refugee who took more than a year to be able to feed his child with his own labor?

Nikola saw the anger along with the sadness in his friend's eyes and regretted being so mouthy.

-When you leave your homeland because of political wars you have to leave everything behind, including diplomas. The government keeps the diplomas. Our studies are worthless without a certificate to prove it," Nikola said, trying to end the conversation.

Connor instantly understood the situation. Without the ability to prove his studies, no university or related job would accept him. They had no chance but to start over.

-Did you have a specialty?

-I liked restoration, but also creativity and design, I don't know, maybe I would have opted for one of those two branches.

Akim spoke up trying to leave the conversation once and for all and Connor took the hint so he reached out with two checks and a not inconsiderable amount.

-This is much more than I thought. Nikola spoke in confusion, but kept the paper in his pocket in case there were any signs of regret on the part of the artist. Akim looked at the figure and, like Nikola, was surprised, and instantly tried to return it.

-It is not what was agreed upon.

-But that's what they deserve. By the way, if you are interested in visiting the exhibition, the opening is at seven o'clock. There will be canapés, soft music and lots of art. I'd like to know what you think.

-You don't know me. The young man replied with some annoyance.

Connor was being charitable, and he didn't like that one bit. The rich were always happy to publicize their generous gifts to the poor who ducked their heads to accept them. No, he was not one of them. He was not rich, nor was he any wretch.

-But something tells me that your opinion will be most interesting and I would like to hear it.

-Thank you, I don't think we can. It's Saturday and we were supposed to...

-I will come. Said Akim cutting his friend off.

-We will come." Nikola answered very reluctantly.

-Great, I'll tell the organizer to add your names to the list of visitors.

Connor walked out the door and Nikola began to beat a rag on his friend's head.

-And now what have I done!

-Can you explain to me why the hell we're coming? You hate these kind of events of rich people showing off their finery and their fake knowledge of art. You always say they're idiots who don't understand a damn thing and now you go and accept. It's Saturday and we're supposed to get a couple of babes! What the hell were you thinking?

Nikola paused for a few moments as if illuminated by a divine lightning bolt, and instantly began to pummel him again with the rag. Akim held him somewhat confused and quite sore.

-What the hell is wrong with you?

-What's wrong with me? -Me! You bastard, you're doing it for her. You want to see her!

-I don't know what you're talking about.

-Don't play dumb, you know what I'm talking about. You want to see the doctor.

The young man began to put away his tools and Nikola attacked him again with the rag causing his friend's face to smile.

-You should give up this damned habit of hitting me with the first thing you find. Do you know that I'm six inches ahead of you and I know how to fight?

-Bullshit! I've been your friend since I was five years old. We got out of that shit together. We looked for a home until we landed here, I have the right to smash your face in for being such an asshole," he shouted loudly. And it's not ten but six centimeters. Six!

-Seven.

-What?

-Seven years.

-Fuck, Akim, this is not going to go well. That woman is no good for you. She's married, she has a home, you're making a mistake....

-There is no error because there is nothing. He commented furiously trying to deny what he hated to deny.

-But what the hell did you see in her? She's pretty, but she's not that pretty, and she's a few years older than you, because you must have noticed that she's older than you, right?

"I've noticed everything, her clear smile, her sincere gaze, her unmistakable scent, her spectacular intelligence, her sensual gait, her perfect curves, her elegant conversation..." He thought enthusiastically.

-You see ghosts where there are none," he lied shamelessly.

-So why don't you explain to me why you want to come tonight?

-Contacts.

-Contacts?

-I may meet some interesting people and get some kind of opportunity.

-Are you serious?

-No, but he could not admit the truth to his friend.

It was too humiliating to go to a place just to see her, he thought sadly. He should control himself, stay home and not meet her again, but he could not. Just imagining the opportunity to see her and not taking it hurt too much.

-If you promise me that's why I'll go with you, even if I'm bored out of my mind.

-Akim tapped his friend's shoulder as they walked towards the exit, each with their toolbox in hand.

-Are you sure you don't want me to come with you? Someone will have to help you escape when the doctor's husband shoots you twice in the balls.

Akim laughed in amusement. Nikola was not a friend, he was a real brother.

-No one is going to shoot anyone. I promise I won't do anything she doesn't want.

-Fuck, Akim!

-I'm kidding, I'm kidding," he said, raising his hands as he watched his friend remove the rag from the back pocket of his overalls. I promise, I promise.

"Nothing she doesn't want, now how she comes to want..."

The young man walked away with mischief in his eyes and pondering if at some point in the day he would stop thinking about her blissful smile and that soft wobble as she walked, or that sweet, thick gaze like the best of chocolates.

Brenda walked very carefully so as not to slip on the rounded cobblestones outside the front door of the magnificent early eighteenth century mansion. She was no longer dizzy as she had been first thing in the morning. At this moment her head was splitting in two. Her temples were throbbing like a thousand demons and the night light was penetrating her brain, taking away her will to live, but she couldn't complain, that's what it was like not even to remember the exact amount of tequila you had drunk the night before.

He thanked the hostess who was collecting his coat and entered the beautiful showroom thinking to get a refreshing orange juice and sit in a chair for the entire evening.

The exhibition

The colorful engravings at the entrance showed the wonderful paintings that visitors would encounter once they were inside. His work was based on a few portraits and different subjectivist scenarios, where the author demonstrated in his expressions, a reality completely different from the simple human vision. A complete exercise taken directly to the canvas in magnificent works where technique and feeling were hand in hand.

Brenda watched in delight for her friend as both the entrance hall and the main hall were packed with people. The exhibition was a complete success. Men in pristine suits and ladies in high heels were raptly analyzing each of her works. Brenda accepted a canapé and a glass of champagne as she stopped in front of her favorite canvas. That painting would never be sold, Connor loved to show it at all his exhibitions which, like some kind of fetish, he showed with the greatest of pride. In it, she and Connor were enjoying a quiet evening on the couch and television. The image had been captured by Johana's camera one college winter afternoon, and her friend had captured it in a painting where the winter browns stood out against the fire in the small fireplace crackling in front of the antique sofa. She rested on his shoulder while Connor, stroking her back, read a book in concentration.

Brenda smiled at the memory of that time. Her father was furious to learn that she would be studying psychology in London, so he did not hesitate to withdraw all financial support. Connor, for his part, had provoked the repulsion of his parents by making visible his, according to them, unhealthy sexual condition. Both, wounded and lonely, met on campus and brotherly love was born the very moment their stories crossed. They supported each other, never judged each other. The eternal source of a friendship that had many winters behind it was based on a love that overcame the problems of today, the here and the hereafter. In those days they worked as waiters, promoters and any other job that was offered to pay the bills, until, in the last year of their career, came the meager paid scholarships that were the first step to the level of magnificent young professionals. After that, it was all history.

Brenda wet her lips with just a few drops of champagne and thought somewhat annoyed if drinking that beverage was a wise thing to do after the previous night's gulp. It sure wasn't, she thought as she felt a small twinge in her head.

Were the little flashes I had from the night before true, or were they the fruit of an illusion drowned in alcohol?

"I sang on a stage and asked for applause from the audience? And what does Akim have to do with all this?"

-And here we have the new Beyoncé in pale! -Connor shouted at the top of his lungs as he squeezed her shoulders to kiss her effusively, making her head start to split again.

-Sh, don't shout..." He answered, narrowing his eyes.

-Come on audience! Those claps.

-Then it was true...

-Oh yes, honey, all of it, all of it," he commented with a broad smile, highlighting his strong Scottish features.

-What about Akim?

-The bricklayer? - He said with a smile on his face. Reality too. He took you home.

-I didn't dream it? -she commented worriedly.

-Do you dream about workers? You've never told me that before. With or without a shirt?

-Connor! Don't be silly. Did anyone I know see me?

-I couldn't confirm it, the place was packed to the rafters.

-God... -he muttered between his teeth.

-Cari, you were beautiful. Totally unbridled and free of prejudices.

-I'm not prejudiced, I just know how to keep my manners better than others. She replied ironically.

-You didn't keep them before.

-I matured.

-You got married.

-Connor... -he answered, stretching out the last "o".

-I didn't say anything. What do you think of my presentation?

-I love it. The way you have presented the pieces this year is magnificent, it's as if there is a coherence between colors, themes and feelings.

-Yes, it's perfect. It wasn't me," he said amused.

Her friend looked at him curiously and he replied enthusiastically.

-It was Akim. Turns out our bricklayer studied the arts in his country. Brenda shook her head in interest, and Connor continued to lower his voice as if in a little secret.

-I think that this dark and fierce character has to do with all that has been lost in the past.

-I can imagine. If you let me I could help you? -She said interested.

She could assist him out of that darkness, although I doubted he would accept anything from her, much less after seeing her always in circumstances unfit for a professional like her.

-I could do something for him too," her friend looked at him blankly. You know, one favor or another.... -She said, highlighting her beautiful smile.

-Don't be silly, besides, he's a lot younger than us.

-Honey, wrinkles don't matter much horizontally.

-Connor!

They were both laughing when her cell phone rang and she answered it.

-Michael, I can't right now. I'm at a friend's show..... His voice sounded so serious that Connor stood beside him, listening to the conversation. I'll make time for you in the office tomorrow.... I don't give a damn what... All right, all right, take it easy, I'll send you the address, do me a favor and take it easy...

When he hung up, his friend waited for her to tell him. Brenda drank from the glass still in her left hand and drained it in one gulp.

-Cari, what's wrong?

-That woman has threatened to kill Murray's wife.

-Shit... -He stammered angrily, "And what have you got to do with all this? The inspector said that the cat could have been just a coincidence.

"Or a compulsive obsession with me." He thought without saying it.

-I guess it's all nonsense," he lied. Now don't think about me. Attend to your guests.

A long-legged lady appeared with a folder in her hand and spoke softly into the ear of the artist who became instantly serious.

-Honey, I have to see some buyers. Wait for me here. If anything happens, call me.

-Relax, go get those rich guys and sell a lot.

Connor smiled and his wonderful green eyes smiled mischievously.

-Honey, you have to take care of yourself. Without you I don't know what I would do. Did I tell you that you are the only woman I love? -He said seriously.

-Are you sure you're gay? -he commented, trying to break the seriousness of the moment.

-One hundred percent," he replied amused. But I would make an exception for you.

-Go to your clients and show them what true art is. - Brenda's countenance changed as soon as her friend disappeared from sight.

Akim doubted that everything was in order, his face showed concern, again. As always, he watched her from a distance. He had seen her walk in cautiously and smiled as he imagined what a terrible hangover she would still have. She was amazing, so different from the night before, and so devilishly attractive. Brenda Klein was everything he wanted in a woman. Sweetness, maturity, and a spark of joy for life that only women like her had. Akim sipped from his glass as he choked back the laughter in his throat at the memory of her singing with such verve and dedicating the shrieks of her song to him. Normally these behaviors made him annoyed, he even found them distasteful, but in her it had been a simply adorable act. The young man sighed and took another sip trying to divert his increasingly sinful thoughts of Brenda Klein.

The doctor, oblivious to her observer, marched to one of the balconies of the mansion looking for some fresh air. Murray's call made her tremble with fear. The threats had not only been to Michael's wife.

Akim watched her walk and as if attracted by an invisible rope from which he was unable to let go, he followed her in the distance. He did not intend to greet her, he did not want to make her uncomfortable. He only wished to admire her from a distance. That was the only thing allowed to a man like him in a place like that.

Depressing thoughts began to overpower him again as he crossed the room and took a close look at the attire of the visitors. He was wearing his best pants and one of his best shirts, although none of his clothes could compare with the attire of these guests. She, his Brenda, wore a discreet and tight-fitting red dress, which surely cost the total of her monthly allowance. As for the other guests, it was better not to talk about them. Immaculate suits, outrageously priced shirts and jewelry worthy of being presented in another exhibition, hung from the most distinguished necks.

He wasn't an interested man, never had been. Dedicating himself to surviving turned out to be too hard a job to think about silly things like clothes or looks, but damn it, ever since he'd known her he'd never stopped lamenting to the mirror what he saw. A big, unruly-haired, deep-eyed big guy with tattooed shoulders. He thought angrily about his past. Surely the men there didn't have tattoos. I bet Max didn't either, he told himself hating himself even more for remembering the stuffy architect.

Dr. Klein took a deep breath in the coolness of the night, trying to relax. Just thinking about that woman made her tremble with fear. She had cruelly killed Bombón and who knows how many other things she would be capable of doing to achieve her end. An unsettling cold sensation ran down her back and she moved in confusion. She tried to turn around when she felt the presence of someone behind her. A hand grabbed her by the neck and pointed the sharp knife at her neck, which rested on the delicate skin of her neck.

-You fucking bitch! You're not going to take it away from me.

Brenda closed her eyes unable to speak, she knew that if she tried to call for help she wouldn't get through the first sentence before her neck was sliced like a steak.

Akim walked slowly. All his intentions of not greeting her collapsed the instant he discovered her alone on a terrace. The image of the two of them embracing and kissing under the discreet witness of the stars proved to be most tempting.

He was about to arrive when he cursed as he witnessed a second female figure on the terrace. Surely it would be a friend. He paused waiting for his chance when the woman's shouting threat made his blood run cold. He ran without caring who he ran over, his legs were clumsy trying to catch up with her.

"She didn't... she didn't..." He thought frightened.

The young man ran the last two meters, praying that his heart would not escape from his chest. Not without first saving her.

Brenda, who for a few moments had lost her senses, managed to regain her composure and, as if she were a patient, tried to speak in a calm voice while trying to face the door and ask for help, and she almost thought she had succeeded when they both met a pair of eyes as clear as the sky that flashed the hatred of the nine hells together, and that breathed as agitated as the fiercest of bulls.

-Let her go!

-Don't come closer or I'll kill her.

The woman, who seemed to be getting more and more mad, pressed the razor even harder and managed to make a small wound in the doctor's delicate skin, and Akim trembled just seeing her reddened skin damaged by the demonic woman. The young man possessed enough dexterity to take the woman down, but that damned knife was practically stuck in Brenda's neck, and the madwoman was too mad.

-What do you want? -he growled through his teeth as he watched Brenda's frightened gaze locked on his.

He wanted to scream his head off. He knew that any desperation on his part would end Brenda's life so he waited and prayed to discover a solution.

-She is not going to separate us!

-Let her go. You're crazy, you don't know what you're talking about.... -Akim's voice trembled with fear.

The unhinged woman moved her hand and Brenda swallowed hard as she felt the woman hold her from behind tightly and embed the sharp tip a little further into the base of her throat.

-No!" Akim cried out in agony at the sight of the thin trickle of blood.

-I'm fine, I'm fine.... -Brenda stammered, trembling. Roxane, that's your name, isn't it?

The doctor tried to calm her attacker. If she could distract her she might be able to separate herself from the knife long enough for Akim to pounce on her.

The woman did not answer. She squeezed the gun even tighter. Brenda raised her hand to tighten it on her attacker's wrist, stopping the pressure.

Akim, who thought he guessed her intentions, did not take his eyes off the women for a second. At the first opportunity he would take that bitch down and plunge the razor into her deranged heart himself.

-You have nothing to fear from me, I would never separate you from Michael. He said with total serenity and conviction that was beginning to take its toll on the woman's crazed nerves.

-You won't make it. She replied hesitantly.

-I'm just trying to help you.

-Bullshit, nobody loves me. No one has ever loved me...

Brenda took a breath and mastered her fears to speak as if the razor wasn't jabbing her neck and threatening to bleed her dry.

-I do care about you.

Akim tried to take advantage of the unhinged woman's distraction to step forward. The latter noticed and tightened her grip on the gun even more. Brenda looked at him trying to instill calm or Akim's nerves would end up killing her faster than they both wished.

-Tell him to stay away! -She ordered nervously, "Tell him to stay away or I'll slit your throat right here!

Brenda wouldn't know if it was the years of experience or the desire to survive, but she sensed that the young woman was as frightened as she was disoriented. A poor unbalanced woman who sought affection from someone she shouldn't have. Sexual ills camouflaged as lovesickness.

-Akim, please. Brenda pleaded, her throat almost dry. Leave us alone.

-No!

-My friend and I are going to talk and we'll be fine, won't we, Roxane? I can help you so you can see Michael. If we all relax we can help each other. You don't have to be afraid of me.

Dr. Klein fixed her pleading gaze on Akim hoping the man would understand her strategy, and apparently he did because Akim took a step backwards cursing over and over again at the top of his voice.

-That's it, my friend has kept his word, now it's your turn. Let me go and we can talk about whatever you want.

-I don't want you to take him away from me..... -She sobbed brokenly.

The young woman began to cry and Brenda grieved from a broken heart that was just begging for some attention. Roxane didn't want to kill her or anyone else, she was simply afraid. She was looking for love from a man who never valued her.

-I won't take him away from you, I promise. I can help you, and for that I need you to put the knife down and let's talk quietly.

-And why were you going to help me?

-I am a psychologist and my job is to help people like you. I help people who need me and I feel that you need me," the young woman sighed, still crying nervously and Brenda attacked with all her artillery of words. Michael has hurt you so much and I feel your pain, let me help you. You have so much love to give.

-He doesn't understand me... -she stammered sadly.

-But I do, I can show you the right way....

Roxane was beginning to loosen her grip and Brenda felt the trembling body pull away from her back. She was about to pull away when the thunderous burst of fireworks in the garden disoriented her. The young woman was frightened and Brenda, fearing for her life, grabbed the arm that held the weapon trying to free herself, but she did not succeed. The razor tore her a little more and she shrieked in pain. The frightened young woman seeing the blood running down her fingers pushed the doctor hard against Akim's body who lunged at her. Akim caught Brenda almost in mid-air and the attacker took the opportunity to flee through the back garden.

Akim clutched Brenda's body which collapsed on top of his. Both practically fell to the cold ground. Akim, in desperation, looked around crazily for help. Everyone was too focused on the fireworks to see them.

-Brin... Brin... -He whispered, choked with fear.

He turned his body and pulled his hair back to see his wound. His heart was pounding and fear coursed through his veins. The doctor looked into his eyes and smiled as she deepened his breathing. She tried to calm him down. He felt no pain, but his body was shaking, his heart was beating out of control and his head was spinning trying to fall into deep darkness. But there was no pain.

-This saving me is becoming a habit, isn't it?

Akim tried to smile, though he could not. He clutched her even tighter as if he could hold on to her forever.

-You saved yourself. Akim reached out his trembling fingers to bring them to the damaged neck and touch the wound. He could not see the depth. The blood had stopped and he knew that if it was serious she would have bled to death by now, but he still couldn't calm down.

-You scared me," he said, clutching her tightly in his embrace.

Brenda could not answer. She accepted the warmth of the embrace and tried to stop shaking. At that moment it seemed an impossible mission to achieve. Maybe because of fear or tension, but her world was spinning a mile a minute. The young man rested his mouth against the base of her head as he held her sitting on the floor. He couldn't let go, didn't want to let go. The dread of having lost her almost killed him.

They both remained like that for a couple of minutes when the thick voice made them look towards the entrance window to the terrace.

-What is supposed to...?

Connor spoke somewhat annoyed as he noticed the way Akim held his friend on the cold night ground. At first, seeing the rotundity of the young man's embrace of Brenda he came to think he was forcing her, but as he moved closer and saw her friend lift her head to look at him and see her bloody neck, he felt himself dying.

-What the fuck? I'm going to kill you!

Connor wanted to rip Brenda from Brenda's arms and beat her up, but Akim didn't move. He kept hugging her. Brenda raised her hand with difficulty to stop her friend's fury.

-That woman has been here. He said, his voice still trembling.

-Fuck, fuck, fuck... Honey, you're bleeding. I have to take you to a hospital.

Brenda separated from Akim and he carefully helped her up. Somewhat more recovered from the immense shock, she reached over, still trembling, and lovingly stroked Connor's face, which kept twitching nervously from side to side.

-Connor... Connor, please look at me.

The man made an effort as she locked her hands with his.

-I'm fine, it's just a scratch. Take care of your guests.

-Oh, my ass! I'm taking you to a hospital.

-No." She forced her throat dry. "You are going back to your event because you have been preparing everything for more than a year. I'll wait for you at my house because I don't want to be alone tonight and you'll come with me, is that okay?

-I can't leave you like this. I don't want you to be alone either. I'll move into your house. I'll say goodbye and we'll leave together. He said nervously.

-I will be with her.

Brenda looked at him gratefully. She was trembling, fear was in her body and her neck was burning. She couldn't be so selfish with Connor. He had fought for this opportunity and she couldn't let him throw it away because of her.

-See? Akim will be with me until you arrive. You don't have to worry. Please, Connor would never forgive me if you missed this opportunity because of me.

Connor scratched his head nervously. He didn't want to abandon her, but he also didn't want to make her feel guilty.

-A couple of hours. That's all," he said answering Akim. In a couple of hours I'll get free and leave this madness, I'll go to your house and stay with you.

Brenda nodded in agreement. Connor fixed his powerful green eyes on Akim to speak to him with menacing serenity.

-Do not separate from her. Don't leave her alone for a moment. She is a capricious woman who will try to get rid of you. If I find out that you have abandoned her, I swear that there will be no place in the world where you can hide.

Akim smiled at the threats that only those who truly love are capable of making.

-A 'please' would have sufficed," he replied amused, and Brenda wanted to die of embarrassment.

-Yes, well, that too. You'll have to take her to Stonebridge Medical Center. It's the closest one from here.

Akim nodded and, without asking, grabbed Brenda by the waist to guide her towards the exit. The doctor accepted his help gratefully because, although the wound was superficial, if she added fear and nerves, she was sure she would faint with the first step.

-We'll take the service stairs so you won't be seen. He whispered in her ear and Brenda nodded.

It was curious how in such a short time, so much had happened that Akim's presence at her side and his hands holding her around her waist, was not an unfamiliar sensation.

-Thank you... Again...

Akim did not answer, he looked at her with a tenderness so welcoming that his eyes became clearer than the most serene of springs. Both looked at each other for a few endless seconds and then left the place without a word.

Connor watched them walk away down the stairs and cursed over and over trying to calm himself. He took three breaths trying to regain control of his nerves before returning to the attendants. He adored Brenda, she was his mother, his friend, his sister, the woman he would never have. She loved him and accepted him. He never hesitated to accept her as she was and trembled at the thought of losing her. He walked determined to end it all as soon as possible and to be able to move to Brenda's house and kill that crazy woman with his own hands if he ever came near her again.

Mistakes that hurt

Akim helped her sit in the car and tried to take deep breaths to calm the nerves that were running out of control.

"You're going to kill me," he thought without a drop of joy as he recognized that since he had met this woman he had been living in a constant state of dissatisfaction. At times he felt at the top of the sky dreaming of the softness of her skin and the next moment he thought he would die of a heart attack.

The young man clenched his fists gripping the steering wheel trying to figure out what the hell had happened to him to make him feel like a drifting weather vane. Ever since he saw her for the first time something broke inside him, feelings were overflowing in his heart like uncontrolled waterfalls and he had no idea what he should do to get back to his old self.

He ducked his head and tried to start the car, but seeing her in that state was driving him to a madness unknown until today. The blood on her neck was drying. Her wound was a simple scratch, and she was safe and sound, so why the hell did he feel the need to press his fingers against that crazy woman's neck!

Akim kept seeing Roxane squeezing the throat of the woman he loved with that razor. He cursed loudly and hit the steering wheel because of the feelings of helplessness that kept overwhelming him. Helplessness for not having avoided those scratches on her neck, helplessness for wanting to hug her and not having the right to do so, helplessness for not being able to walk away forgetting her forever, helplessness for feeling stupidly in love. Brenda noticed his confusion, although she erred in her conclusions.

-I'm sorry. I keep getting you in trouble. She said apologetically.

-It wasn't you. You don't have to apologize. That crazy woman is the only one to blame," he replied, starting the car and without looking at her. I'll take you to a hospital to get checked out.

The man's muffled voice was so dry and deep that Dr. Klein felt sorry for him. Akim Dudaev was a good man and she could tell he had been afraid for her. She moved her hand closer to the arm that held the steering wheel and Akim blinked twice trying to hide the electric sensation he felt whenever she touched him.

-I don't want to go to a hospital.

-He answered seriously, "No way, don't even dream about it, you have to see a doctor.

-I'm not bleeding anymore and I'm in no condition to spend hours in an emergency room. Please Akim, take me home, I have bandages there, I don't need much more.

Akim looked away from the road to observe her and see that she was right. Her wound, very red and with dried blood, had only turned out to be a slight cut in the skin.

-Please Akim, I need to be at home.

The doctor looked at him with eyes so deep and sincere that Akim wanted to moan with pure desire.

-All right," he replied defeated, "we'll stop by a drugstore on duty and buy some bandages and something to heal your scratches.

Brenda was about to protest when Akim responded without giving her a chance to reply.

-Don't even think of telling me that it's not necessary because I swear you're going to make me angry and I assure you that you don't want to see me in that state.

Brenda began to smile quietly until she could stand it no longer and burst out laughing. The man looked at her wide-eyed and quizzical, but she guffawed even more.

-It seems you're getting to know that I'm a little stubborn.

-Poquitín? -Akim arched an eyebrow and continued driving without taking his eyes off the road.

Damn her, Dr. Klein was becoming more her Brin with each passing day. "With so many around the world and it had to be her?"

Connor was hysterical. She had to keep her cool as best she could in front of the guests, and although she brushed them off at lightning speed, she hadn't communicated with her friend for over three hours and needed to know she was okay.

On the way to Brenda's house he phoned Inspector Gutierrez who said he would come to the doctor's house as soon as possible. He also called the bland Max who promised to take the first plane and get there as soon as possible. He took a deep breath and entered the house using his copy of the keys. He was scared. He didn't know what state of nerves and hysteria his friend might be in, after all she had been attacked by a madwoman. He walked safely down the driveway when laughter from the living room stopped him in the doorway frame.

-But what...

She watched from the doorway as her friend with a small bandage on her neck and a cup of tea in her hand talked amused as Akim smiled enraptured with the story.

-Just as I say.

Akim laughed heartily and Connor took his first breath. He had been feeling so worried that seeing Brenda smile brought him back to life.

-A simple box of strawberries...

Connor smiled at the memory of the anecdote and continued the story as he walked over to sit next to Brenda and squeeze her in a long hug.

-It was not that simple, they had cost me a kidney, and I never thought the man was allergic....

Brenda laughed heartily and Akim felt a slight twinge of jealousy. He wished he could caress and kiss her as freely as the Scot did.

The three of them were laughing with their silly anecdotes when the doorbell rang insistently and Connor jumped out of his seat.

-It must be the inspector.

-Did you call him?

-Yes, and don't even think about talking back to me.

-At last you seem to know me too well.

She and Akim looked at each other and smiled as if they shared a secret and Connor walked towards the door arching an eyebrow trying to discover what those two were hiding. Gutierrez entered wearing his usual gray trench coat and closely followed by his loyal assistant Charly who was carrying an agenda, a pen and a tablet while adjusting his glasses so as not to lose them.

-Dr. Klein, are you all right?

-Yes.

-Have you seen your attacker? Can you confirm that she was the woman we are looking for?

The assistant took a seat and Dr. Klein tried to sort through her memories. She took a few seconds and was about to begin speaking when the sound of the doorbell distracted her.

-It must be Murray. Connor said with some guilt.

-Did you call him?

-Of course. He is responsible for all this mess.

Connor opened the door and Murray entered the room like an uncontrolled hurricane.

-How is she doing?

-Good night... -Connor mumbled. He didn't like that man very much.

-I am perfectly fine. Brenda replied with a rather tired voice.

-God... if something had happened to him...

The politician held his forehead with both hands and those present felt sorry for him. Gutiérrez resumed the interrogation.

-So you say you would be able to recognize her?

Brenda wanted to answer yes, but the truth was that she could not. Roxane had surprised her from behind and at no time had they been facing each other.

-I can. I would recognize her perfectly. Akim was now standing behind Brenda's couch like a faithful guardian.

-Is it this one?

The intern moved his finger quickly over the tablet and extended it to the man who nodded as soon as he saw the unhinged woman on the screen. The photo showed her face relaxed and less deranged, but she was still the same unbalanced woman she had always been.

-It's her. He affirmed emphatically.

Murray cursed loudly and the inspector celebrated the news. With confirmation of the woman's identity it would be easier to find her and charge her with a long list of crimes.

-Perfect, you'll help us catch her.

Brenda's eyes widened in horror at the idea.

-No. Not at all. Akim has already had too much trouble because of me. We'll solve it ourselves.

The young man reached out and gently held the doctor's shoulder as he answered the inspector without leaving any room for doubt.

-You can count on me.

-No! This is my problem. I can't allow you to get involved in this madness.

The woman moved her hand over his which was still resting on his shoulder and Akim smiled gawking.

The inspector was talking something to his assistant, ignoring what the doctor was saying, while Murray paced nervously around the room. Connor, standing directly in front of the pair, squinted quizzically at the image. Brenda sighed wearily, but accepted the hand on his shoulder without rejecting it. That wasn't something her friend did naturally, much less with a stranger. He used to hug her and overwhelm her with his kisses and although she often complained, he knew perfectly well that he was part of the select club of people to whom she allowed it. Brenda didn't accept just anyone into her world. Her relationship with her parents, or rather, the lack of a relationship with them, had led her to be a woman who was quite cautious with her affections.

Akim bent down to speak only into his ear and Connor straightened up even more as he watched them talk and smile as if they had known each other forever.

"This is not normal," he thought as he saw the gleam in the young man's eye.

The door opened and the artist was struck dumb. The third in discord was making an appearance in the house and Connor prayed that Max would be as blind as ever.

The husband entered and paused at the sight of his wife sitting on the couch with a narrow white bandage covering most of her throat. He rushed over and bent down to pull her into an embrace. Brenda noticed his concern and clung to him trying to soothe him in her arms as Akim closed his eyes and slowly lifted his hand from her shoulder to continue guarding her from a distance.

-I'm fine... It was nothing.

Max sighed in his arms as Connor kept watching Akim's movements closely. Akim moved towards the window with his back to the couple and Connor prayed that his sixth sense would fail him.

-So we all agree that we should bring that weasel out of hiding?

Everyone nodded to the detective, except Akim who remained with his back to the group looking out the window, the darkness of the night. The architect, who had picked himself up again from the floor, asked with some displeasure.

-What plan is that exactly?

Max stretched his tall, slender frame to stand in front of the inspector who was undaunted by the elegant gentleman.

-I take it that you are Mr. Brown.

-He guessed right. He replied roughly.

Max fixed his gaze on the inspector and Connor, although he didn't feel he was Max's friend, felt the need to explain the situation to him and calm him down. After all, the man would arrive home to find the party already set up and his wife as a piñata at a carnival.

-The inspector believes that the woman is dangerous and could harm Brenda. Connor replied with a serious look on his face.

-And why are you sitting on my couch and not going to stop her? -he grumbled grumpily.

-Mr. Brown, I understand your concern and believe me I share your wishes, but we have not been able to find her. This woman has disappeared from all the places she used to frequent, she doesn't use credit cards and she hasn't withdrawn money from any ATM. I suspect that someone may be covering for her....

Max dragged his hand through his hair and asked almost fearfully.

-And this plan, what exactly does it consist of?

-We will make noise. We will need to organize a big celebration and encourage her to participate.

-Next Saturday I'm hosting a cocktail party at my house," Murray commented. We'll do it there.

-We could bring agents in camouflage as guests, it could be.... -Charly commented, looking attentively at the inspector who listened to him in concentration.

-Russian! I'm going to need you.

-He is not Russian and his name is Akim. Brenda came to his defense, although to tell the truth she was barely able to speak.

The inspector smiled at the stupid defense and cleared his throat.

-Yeah well, I don't care where you're from, the important thing is that Murray will be busy and we can't arouse suspicion. I need you to shadow Dr. Klein.

Akim looked at the detective with a deadly coldness and although everyone could believe that he was offended by the confusion of his nationality, the truth was that he hated the rude way in which this jerk in a long trench coat spoke to Brenda. She did not deserve that patronizing tone, much less at home. If the situation were different, he would explain to that false Sherlock how he should treat a woman like her, but of course, for that there was already her perfect husband.

-No. He will stay at the construction site where he should be," Max's stern voice left too many reproaches in the open and Connor decided to intervene before the situation escalated.

-Akim was my guest. If it hadn't been for his intervention we would all be lamenting a major accident. He said in a deep voice.

Connor spoke emphatically. He needed Max to understand once and for all the danger his wife was in and the kind of support he should be giving her at times like this. Max heard his words, but did not interpret them in the same way.

Hearing him tell Connor that the bricklayer was a guest at the exhibition made him think that he would be the painter's latest conquest and that made him smile inside. From the first moment he met the young man he felt a small sort of threat inside him, which now turned out to be totally absurd. It turned out now that Akim was gay.

-Connor was surprised by Max's uncharacteristic change of mood. If anyone could be stubborn and even unpleasant in his fixed ideas, it was Max- but I'm going to that cocktail party too.

The inspector rose from the sofa and with complete parsimony spoke to the distinguished householder.

-I'm sorry, that's not possible.

-Then your plan isn't either," Max chuckled.

-Mr. Brown," the inspector shook out his trench coat as he put his old flip phone in his pocket, "let's get this straight, Dr. Klein saved your life today by a miracle and if we could name that miracle, I'd name it after the Russian," he said, smiling from side to side as he listened to the doctor's snort. Maybe next time we won't have the same luck and his wife will be wearing the best pine box in London instead of a bandage around her neck.

Max bit his teeth in anger, but didn't answer. He was a man of high enough status that no one would put him in his place, much less a three-bit detective. Brenda noticed his displeasure and decided to intervene.

-The detective is right. That woman has already been home and killed Bombón, we can't let her come near us again.

-Mr. Brown, if you are at her side permanently, the woman will not approach and we will lose the opportunity to capture her. I need you to believe that the doctor is alone.

-I still don't understand why I can't be by her side. I can watch her without going near her. Max spoke in defeat.

-Because Roxane thinks the doctor is my lover," Murray muttered.

Brenda, Max and everyone else's mouths dropped open. All except the inspector, who looked at his watch with impatience and some boredom.

-Is that why you are attacking me? -she said curiously.

-Yes.

-I don't understand." Brenda walked over to Murray who was ducking his head guiltily.

-Lorelaine has left. She has abandoned me. That's why I went to look for you at the exhibition, I needed to talk to someone. You are the only one who can understand me.

Brenda felt exhausted. Too much information to digest in one night.

-Please continue tomorrow..." He said feebly.

Murray accepted her affectionate look and decided to say goodbye. The detective and Charly followed him down the path to the exit, and Akim tried to slip away as everyone was saying goodbye, but Brenda managed to spot him and grabbed his arm before he stepped through the doorway. Akim cursed himself for feeling that kind of electric current, again.

-Thank you for everything.

-It's not necessary. She replied without looking at her when she noticed her husband's presence behind her.

-What's not needed? By God, you're always there when I need you most.

Max smiled and walked into the house, leaving the bricklayer to say goodbye to his wife. Maybe the young man was shy about saying goodbye to Connor in public and Brenda was a specialist in that kind of situation. Would anyone say so with those bullying looks of his?

-It's late, why don't you take my car?

Akim noted that they were alone and felt free to talk. When he was alone with his beloved doctor he felt like a different person, one less broken down by the misfortunes of society.

-I think I'd rather walk. I don't want you to get a scratch and report me," he said amused.

-You know I would never do anything like that," she smiled and Akim wanted to bite that precious dimple that was so tightly pressed to the corner of her right lip. All right, I'll accept that you won't take my car, only if tomorrow you agree to let me buy you breakfast at Starbucks.

Akim smiled so much that it was impossible for him to hide his silly, lovelorn grin. Could she still remember their unfortunate encounter?

-Won't that be a lot? I mean, it might save your life, but have you seen the prices of those cafés?

They both laughed out loud and Brenda, moved by a rare effect in her, moved closer and clung to the man's arm, who trembled at her touch.

-And if you're good," he muttered under his breath, "I'll buy you not only coffee but a slice of cake and juice.

-Juice too?

-Also...

-Then I'll have to behave myself....

Akim's voice was so hoarse that even he was frightened by the sound of it. He wished he could show her how good he could be to her.

Brenda loosened her grip and said to him with barely a voice.

-See you tomorrow... You fool...

Akim turned with a different light in his eyes as he replied in puzzlement.

-Dr. Klein, did you just call me a fool?

-Yes," she said amused, "Are you planning to do something?

-Nothing for now, snooty lady.

-Ah," Brenda squeezed her chest in irreparable offense, and Akim laughed with a laugh. Did you call me uptight? Stretched to me, Mr. curmudgeon?

-Sugar cube? But I'm a sugar cube, doctor, smug. He said as he walked away laughing like he hadn't done in a long time.

-See you tomorrow, kiddo!

-Don't provoke me, doctor, don't provoke me....

Akim's laughter was heard in the silence of the night and Brenda did not stop watching him until his image was lost in the darkness. She closed the door and tried to fit in what had just happened. She had deliberately provoked him. She was no inexperienced fool and had felt the tension and double meaning of Akim's words and although for a moment she was tempted to analyze them, she instantly decided to forget them. She was a woman quite a few years older than him, and married. "What nonsense," she thought downplaying the importance of the matter.

-Cari, is everything all right?

Connor approached her friend and hugged her tenderly.

-Of course. Are you leaving already?

-Yes, I'm exhausted. Besides, I don't want to face the beast," he said in her ear, making it clear that he was talking about Max.

-Don't be like that, he's just nervous.

-Something usual for him when things do not go according to his order and command.

-Connor!

-I didn't say anything, I'm leaving... I'm leaving...

He commented as he gave her a loud kiss on the cheeks and left, closing the door softly.

-You scared me.

Max hugged her back wrapping his hands around her belly and she closed her eyes sighing tiredly.

-It was just a scare. You should not have traveled with this urgency. The project needs you.

-Right now I just want to take care of you.

-I know how to do it myself.

-I know perfectly well, but knowing that that bricklayer was where I was supposed to be... I don't know, I don't like it. What would have happened if that Russian hadn't seen you on the terrace?

-His name is Akim... And he is not Russian...

Brenda tried to break free from his embrace. She didn't like the way Max talked about Akim at all. Was it so hard to call him by his name without any prefixes related to his nationality?

Max didn't answer, he simply took her by the hand and led her into the bedroom. He wanted to have her all to himself and show her how much he cared for her. He didn't want to waste his time arguing over someone who wasn't worth it. And Akim Dudaev, he wasn't worth it.

It's you

Akim cursed the bad luck in his life over and over again. "Can it be that you hate me so much! I'm no saint, but it's just that you never make it easy for me," he thought raising his eyes to the sky.

-Dad, are you okay?

-Yes.

-Shall we go to your work?

The little boy with wide cheeks and blue eyes even lighter than his own asked blankly, and Akim smiled with the same tenderness with which he was questioned. How could something so pure have been born out of one night's mistake?

-You'll come to my work, but first we'll have to find a friend.

-Do you have friends?

Akim smiled at the question. "Children and drunks always tell the truth," he thought amused.

-Very few, son, but that's information that's best kept between us, don't you think?

-Why? Grandpa says you have to get out more so I can have a mom.

-Grandpa talks too much. Now be quiet, we're almost there.

Akim entered the Starbucks holding the boy's chubby little hand tightly. He looked everywhere for Brenda, he had to apologize and stand her up but there was no other choice. Last night he was so excited about the invitation, he forgot the small detail that today his son would not have school due to a disinfection ordered by the ministry, or something like that. He found her sitting on a soft couch and wanted to groan at the sight of her. She was wearing jeans and a breathtaking white striped shirt. She had stepped out of the exquisite heels she usually wore and was wearing sneakers that made her much more desirable than when she was wearing her best suit. Brenda was typing quietly on her cell phone and Akim noticed that she had replaced the bandages with a pair of discreet band-aids. Her flowing hair shone like glints of sunshine on her delicate shoulders. Her features were not those of a Barby, but he never liked barbys.

-Is that her? -Lucien asked with a tug on his pants and his father came back to earth.

-Yes. Let's apologize.

At the very moment she saw them coming, Brenda gave them the best of her smiles.

-Hello, hello, but who do we have here?

The boy smiled so hard it looked like his teeth would pop out and his father was amused by his son's excessive expressiveness.

-Brenda, this is my son Lucien.

The doctor was disoriented for a second, but instantly bent down to give him two resounding kisses on the cheeks.

-Hi Lucien, you are very handsome.

-Thank you. She replied, blushing and thus highlighting even more her spring-like gaze.

-We came to apologize. I can't stay," he said ruefully. I forgot last night that Lucien was out of school and that he was coming with me to the play.

-I'm going to see how daddy is working. Grandpa found a job in the mornings, when he's done he'll come pick me up. He didn't have one before, but now he's a security guard at a shopping mall.

The boy talked endlessly and Akim wanted to bury himself right there. Was so much information necessary?

-So it seems to me that if Grandpa's got a job we should celebrate. How about a cup of chocolate and a slice of cheesecake?

-Is it possible to make dulce de leche? I've seen it on the bar. He commented a little embarrassed.

-Brenda smiled with amusement.

-No, we can't, we are leaving. Akim answered with a small mouth because he really didn't want to leave.

-Are you planning to stand me up and deny your son the cake I just promised him?

-I don't...

-Come on, don't be silly, he's a very rich boy and I need a coffee urgently.

-And here we go again with the bossy, starchy doctor. He replied smiling.

-Oh, I won't forgive you for that one.

Lucien looked at them in amusement as he noticed their smiles.

-Dad, then can I have cake?

-Yes, Dad, can we order? -she asked amused. I haven't had breakfast yet, and if I starve to death it will be your fault.

Akim felt he was losing the battle. He always did it with her in front of him.

-It looks like you're two against one," he said as he saw the little boy's beaming smile.

Brenda held the boy's hand between hers and looked at him with the same mischievous look of a little girl.

-We are. You sit down so they don't take our place while we go pick out some nice cakes.

Akim watched them walk hand in hand to the bar and thought about what she would be like as a mother. Surely great, he thought smiling as he went about the duty he had been given.

Akim accompanied Brenda to her office, repeating for the umpteenth time that there was no need to go to so much trouble, but Dr. Klein decided she didn't want to listen to him. She was delighted to be able to help them and Lucien's presence was a breath of fresh air after so many worries.

-I'll ask for the morning off," he said confidently.

-Not at all. Brenda squeezed the little boy's hand and went into her office with him. -If you do that, I'll miss the chance to meet such an interesting little man.

Lucien raised his little face, smiling and delighted with so many compliments. Brenda reached out her hand and couldn't resist to tuck one of those unruly blond locks that were shooting above his eye.

-I can ask for the morning.... -He said trying to be heard.

-If you do so, they will take away your attendance bonus.

Akim cursed to himself, he hadn't thought about it, it was true. Those bonuses, though they didn't mean much, were a not inconsiderable extra in a tight economy like his.

-It's okay, you can stay with him, my father will be here at lunchtime to take him home.

The man ducked his head with some annoyance. He hated having to talk about money with Brenda and accept that he needed her help so he wouldn't lose the damn extra pay he so desperately needed.

-I think it's perfect. We'll have a great time," he said, giving his undivided attention to the son and not the father. Lucien, do you like to paint?

-I love it," he replied euphorically, "and I like to sing, too. Dad says I'm very good at it.

-I sing pretty well too. Brenda answered confidently.

-Please don't lie to him. He's a child...-Akim answered amused and Brenda opened her eyes in horror.

-Doubts about how I sing?

-No. I confirm it. Akim's restrained laughter surprised her for the better. He was always serious and distant, but he seemed to be relaxing with her and she felt that she liked that feeling very much.

-Dad sings very well, he even plays the guitar," the boy bent his head with sorrow in his eyes, "he doesn't have a guitar anymore.

-We'll fix it as soon as we can," Akim replied earnestly, trying to cut the subject short. He did not want Brenda to discover another of his many sorrows. The woman understood the silence and wanted to break the ice with a touch of humor.

-Lucien, what do you say we tell your annoying father to let us have some fun and go to work?

Akim looked at her with fire in his eyes, ready to respond with full artillery.

-Heavy, Dr. Klein? If I'm heavy, what's left for someone like you?

-Wonderful, perfect, unsurpassed?

Akim smiled and prepared to leave, but not before answering.

-Authoritarian.

-Bitter.

-Stretch

-Niñato.

-Don't provoke me, doctor, don't provoke me....

Akim walked away enjoying the farewell they had just had.

On the way, smiling as he made his way to the bathrooms to change and put on his overalls, he met Nikola who kept staring at him as if he had grown horns.

-What the hell are you looking at?

-To you.

-And do you like it?

-I'm not sure... -his friend answered seriously.

-Stop this nonsense and tell me what the hell is wrong with you.

-That's what I say, what the hell is going on? Why are you smiling? You're not smiling.

Akim let out a laugh with a loud sound as he opened his shirt to take it off.

-You're an idiot.

-Maybe, but you don't answer me. Why are you smiling? And why are you looking so handsome?

-You're really going to start to worry me. Okay, if what you want to tell me is that you have fallen in love with me, I have to tell you that I love you, but only as friends. Akim smiled as he continued to change his clothes into his overalls, but Nikola didn't fall into his trap.

-You can say all the bullshit you want. You're different.

-Why am I laughing and not wearing a faded shirt?

-Exactly," he said as he too was getting ready to put on his work clothes. Well, not the shirt, but the smile? Now that's weird.

-Don't be silly and let's find the crew before they hand out the work and Samir leaves us with the worst of it.

Nikola hurried to zip up his overalls and run to his friend's side. If they were late for the activity distribution, they were sure to have to carry debris, and he didn't feel like it at all.

-By the way, I want you to know that Lola has forgiven you.

Akim paused to look at his friend in intrigue.

-You stood her up, remember?

-Ah, that.

-Yes, and she is willing to overlook it.

-Well, look how good it is.

Nikola shook his head and cursed with all the letters.

-With that help, I wouldn't sleep with her friend in a thousand years.... -Akim smiled and continued walking towards the work crew.

This morning the last person he wanted to think about was Lola. Her thoughts and dreams were sailing on other seas, one with eyes as warm and sweet as the purest of chocolates.

Wishes

-Why are you changing your clothes? I thought we were going to eat here.

Nikola picked up the sandwiches salivating as he imagined the delicious filling of tuna, pickles and a creamy homemade mayonnaise sauce.

-I have to pick up Lucien. He replied sparingly.

-Oh, I'm coming with you, I haven't seen my godson for days. Are you going to school?

-I had no class today.

Akim did not want to explain himself. He wanted to get rid of Nikola without any need for clarification. His friend was not making it easy for him.

-And where is he? I thought your father started work in the mornings.

-That's why I'm going to look for him. My father must be on his way to take him away.

Nikola walked beside him and Akim grumbled in annoyance. His friend would find out who Lucien was spending the morning with as soon as they turned down the hallway and....

-Fuck... Fuck... Fuck!

"You've seen it," he thought in annoyance.

-This is not right.

-Leave me alone. He answered, gritting his teeth hard.

-That's why the smile this morning. -Shit! Did you sleep with her? We're dead...

-Don't talk nonsense," she warned with apparent calmness, trying to shut him up. She only offered to look after him.

-You will crash...

-Fuck you!

Akim's father peeked around the construction site and smiled at them both, but they didn't respond so he chose not to ask.

-Well, where is my grandson?

A man with many gray hairs, with a very strong complexion asked in a friendly manner. Akim pointed to the office occupied by the doctor and her son, who were laughing in amusement and oblivious to the onlookers outside.

-They're having a good time. -Who is it? Lucien seems to like him.

-He is not the only one. Nikola replied in annoyance and left without saying goodbye to anyone.

-What's wrong with him?

-His usual nonsense.

-With Nikola, I'm sure it's just a flirtation. -His father smiled in amusement. He had known his son's friend since they were little. They grew up in the same neighborhood and their parents emigrated at the same time as they did. It was fortunate that after so much time and so many tragedies, life had not separated them.

-Let's go get that midget before he destroys what little is left of the building. Grandfather smiled at his son and walked toward the office.

Lucien and Brenda, oblivious to the looks that followed them from the door, were singing something that Akim could not define since the screams of both of them were too horrifying to understand anything.

-And now drum roll! -she said enthusiastically.

-Parra pam pan! -Lucien simulated the sound of a drum kit as he tapped some pens against some folders.

Brenda had her hair in a high ponytail and was smiling as she arranged some files in several piles.

-It's your turn. The boy nodded cheerfully and she accepted the challenge by slapping the reports with the palms of her hands.

Akim smiled, unable to look away from the picture. His son did not know his mother and no women entered his house. Lucien was growing up with only him and his grandfather, and Akim was saddened to note the little boy's joy at having the tenderness of a woman by his side.

-He seems nice. Grandfather commented with interest.

-It is. Akim answered without thinking.

-And he likes children.

-Yes.

-And she's pretty.

Akim felt a pang of jealousy when he heard that phrase from his father. Since his mother's death he didn't usually think about such things or at least not out loud.

-It's not for you. He replied annoyed with his father, believing him to be interested in her.

-I didn't mean it for...

The father tried to explain himself, but immediately realized that his son was least likely to listen to him.

-Hello Lucien. Said the grandfather stretching his arms out from the door when he noticed the boy's look at the door.

-Grandfather! -The little boy ran into his arms.

-Brenda, this is my father.

-Mr. Dudaev, a pleasure to meet you.

The doctor tried to fix her hair while Akim smiled at the sight of her, probably because of her singing session with drums included.

-My son and I thank you for the enormous favor you have done us.

-It was nothing. I had a great time. I needed some distraction.

The man accepted the kind answer and left, taking with him a little boy who promised to visit her again.

-Thank you again. I completely forgot I didn't have school today.

-Parents don't have to be perfect, don't worry. He replied, downplaying the importance of the matter.

-You don't have children.

-No." He said sadly.

-I'm sorry, I'm a busybody.

-No, it doesn't matter. I've got it figured out. An awkward silence settled between the two of them. I think I'm going to get something to eat before it's time for my next appointment. She tried to break the recent awkwardness between them.

-Eh, yeah, sure. -You're going out?

-No, I'll order a salad. Murray will be here soon and I don't want to be late.

The answer was not entirely to his liking. Deep down he had to admit that he had taken off his overalls in case the opportunity arose to have lunch together. An opportunity that, on the other hand, he was willing to find.

-I also have to get back soon and I have a sandwich, if you want some company?

Akim felt the heat rising in his body and scratched the back of his neck, trying to hide the nerves that were eating him up inside and out.

-I thank you, but I cannot. I have to prepare the consultation. Thank you very much for the invitation.

-Oh yeah, nothing's wrong. Akim stood petrified on the spot and Brenda watched him trying to figure out what was wrong.

He looked like he wanted to say something to her, though he didn't.

-Anyway, I'm going to order my salad and get to work. I'll see you around.

-Yes, see you. Akim managed to move without showing the helplessness he felt at leaving her.

In her mind's eye she had made the image of him and her having lunch and chatting animatedly, however, she was to return with the crew, as usual.

"What did you think, he's wasted too much time with your son to keep wasting it on you? Idiot." He sighed as he turned to leave.

-Oh, by the way," Akim stopped when he heard her raise her voice and turned around somewhat puzzled. Lucien said I sing very well.

Brenda's smile brought him back to life. A denial from that woman was death, a smile from her was the essence of eternal life.

-He is a very polite boy and does not like to hurt poor deluded girls.

The light in Akim's crystalline eyes sparkled with exaltation and Brenda, who had seen him leave in annoyance, loved to watch him regain his joviality with his joke.

-Did you just call her deluded? -He replied, exaggerating each word with melodrama.

-That's exactly what I said. He replied without a hint of embarrassment.

-You'll be a fool.

-Stretch.

-Niñato

-Don't provoke me doctor, don't provoke me.

They both laughed at a kind of farewell that was beginning to become commonplace between them. Akim walked away smiling and thinking about the way she called him a childish boy. If he only knew how many ways she wanted to show him what a brat he was. The young man went in search of his backpack and found a very serious Nikola. He wanted to pick up the sandwich and look as angry as his friend, but he didn't succeed. Happiness was pouring out of his pores.

-You're still smiling like a fool.

-And you're still behaving like someone else. What the hell is wrong with you?

Akim sat on one of the steps of the construction site next to Nikola as he unwrapped the sandwich.

-I'd better shut up.

The friend angrily bit into his lunch as he gazed into the distance and chewed each minute with more anger than the last.

-Well, it's about time, you don't stop talking nonsense. Akim replied an annoyed Akim.

Akim also bit angrily into his sandwich. His friend had managed to rub off his bad mood on him.

-Sandeces! -Sandeces? They'll be the ones you make.

-Weren't you going to keep quiet? -he commented ironically.

-Well, now I don't really want to shut up. What are you trying to do?

-I don't pretend anything. You're exaggerating. We met by chance," she lied, "and she offered to look after Lucien for a few hours. That's all there is to it. He said as he took another bite of his lunch.

-And I am a little sister of charity and I believe you," he replied angrily.

-What the hell is wrong with you! Why don't you leave me alone? In the end I'm going to think it's true that you're jealous," he spat angrily as he took a long sip of water.

-Don't be an asshole. Fuck Akim, you're in the moment to turn the corner and forget about all this. Don't get into something you can't control.

-You are exaggerating, between Brenda and me there is nothing....

-Brenda? Not Dr. Klein anymore?

Akim did not answer. The conversation was turning out to be most unpleasant and he had no interest in coming clean with his friend. He would rather lie a thousand times than accept that part of his reproaches had a fairly solid basis.

-Brother, stay out of this. You promised, remember? -Nikola commented anxiously.

-Yes. Akim mumbled as he drank more water.

-Fuck, you know that if it were possible I would be by your side, but I cannot. You're my friend, I love you, but I can't let you suffer for what you made me promise.

-I know, I know! -he grumbled as he angrily stood up and angrily threw the leftover sandwich into a bucket. He had no appetite anymore. His mood was the same as it had always been. Cold, angry and hopeless.

-I'm sorry, it's what you asked me to do," Nikola lamented in pain.

-You have nothing to worry about. Akim remembered that promise from years ago and had to accept his friend's words.

-I hope so...

Akim went to the toilets to put on his overalls and Nikola continued to chew less and less eagerly.

Another opportunity

Michael Murray struck twice before entering the practice.

Brenda observed his more than visible deterioration. Although she still looked as flawless as ever, the dark bags under her eyes showed her state of exhaustion and heaviness.

-Dr. Klein," she said just before leaning back on the delicate red leather couch.

-So now I am a doctor.

-You see. Changes are possible.

-I see. Do you want to tell me what happened or do you want me to ask?

-She has left.

Brenda knew because he himself had told her the night before. She needed to hear the politician explain himself without interruption. One of her main functions as a psychologist was to allow the patient to express his or her feelings out loud. Often that description had little to do with reality, but that was just the issue to manage. When feelings came to the surface. Fact and fiction had to be treated with the same level of importance.

-He says he can't stand it anymore," he commented bitterly. That damned woman has been harassing me relentlessly. He calls on the phone and hangs up when he hears my wife's voice.

Murray dragged his hand through his slicked back hair as he snorted in exhaustion.

-I swear I've tried everything. She's out of her mind. First Lorelaine and now...

-He blames me. He said calmly.

-Yes, she believes that my visits to your office are part of another type of therapy.

-What do you think?

The man leaned back on the couch and looked at her in confusion.

-There's nothing between you and me.... -he said scared, imagining that the doctor could be as crazy as the young model.

-I don't mean that. I'm simply asking what your opinion is about everything you are going through. Do you blame yourself?

-This mess has served as a lesson to me.

-What exactly do those words mean? -He said as he wrote in his notebook: Clear signs of regret. Treatment: Prolonged.

-I want my wife to come home and I will do everything I can to show her that I have changed.

-Have you done it? It's been a very short time since your last party, are you sure? -He said while performing a double underline on: Fact Check.

-Yes, yes, I understand that you don't believe me, this time it's different. I want to go back to my old life. I want these days to be erased from my memories and those of my wife. I want her to go back to the way she was before.

Brenda took notes and left long pauses between each of her comments.

-Michael, you say what you want from your wife, and you haven't said anything about what you expect from yourself.

-I've already said it, I want Lorelaine to come home and be the family we always were. Didn't you hear me? -he commented annoyed.

-All I hear are the words of a man demanding oblivion. I see no sincere repentance. I see," he said calmly, "a man who wishes he could take back what he had as if by magic, doesn't it seem the same to you? -Michael swallowed in annoyance, didn't answer, "You want to change your life? Would you give up the parties and your occasional conquests? Is that what you're looking for?

-You don't believe me...

-Michael, I do not believe or disbelieve, I simply ask you not to demand clarity that you are not able to offer. Before asking her to come back, think about whether you are willing to give what the relationship demands of you.

-I have nothing to think about! It's what I want. We had a home and I intend to get it back.

-When you were looking for other women, what exactly did they offer you?

Brenda adjusted her glasses on the bridge of her nose as she watched the politician's concentration as he leaned back and staring at the ceiling spoke calmly.

-Sex, passion, youthfulness, brazenness... plenitude.

-And when you crossed the threshold of your house, what did you feel?

-Security, friendship, comfort.

Silence fell between them. Brenda did not open her mouth. Michael threw his head back and replied in agony.

-I know what you are doing.

-And what do you think I do?

-Dividing my life into two pieces that don't fit together.

-I'm afraid I'm not the one who divided them. You say you want to change, in both answers you have offered positive references. You try to complete your life with bits and pieces you get from different places.

-And that means...

-That, if you want to get the pieces of different puzzles to fit together, you must choose a panel where you are allowed to assemble them or find a puzzle with all the figures you need. Do you follow me? -Michael thought in concentration.

-You mean that to get Lorelaine back I will have to return to my home and forget about any other kind of pleasures?

-Not exactly. What I am saying is that whether you go back to your world of conquests or back home, you don't have to give up the feelings that make you feel alive. If diversity is part of your fulfillment, but Lorelaine doesn't share it, then it's time for a panel change for your puzzle, now, if diversity is simply a desperate action in the search for passionate sensations, then your marriage may still have a chance.

-Sex, lust and marriage. Beautiful and absolutely unrealistic words.

-Maybe yes or no, that will depend on you.

-What if I don't want to or can't?

-Then go on with your life, but don't demand that Lorelaine accept it. Like you, she has the right to choose which panel to mount her puzzle on.

-And it may not be me...

-I haven't spoken to her and I can't know the answer, but what I do think I can answer, and without fear of being wrong, is that this Michael is not what she wants.

-Damn son of a bitch," he spat angrily. If it wasn't for her none of this would have happened.

Brenda shook her head as she wrote in her notebook: Third parties as responsible for our own mistakes. Therapy: Time.

-When you live in a castle of lies disguised as truths, the cards that hold it up sooner or later crumble no matter which way the wind blows.

Michael pondered his words and then asked bluntly.

-I'm not sure I can do that. You're asking for much more than an apology. You're asking me to change my whole life.

-I am saying that you cannot ask Lorelaine to quietly accept your demands. If you want to return you will have to accept a negotiation process where both of you will have to give in. If the losses outweigh the gains that is for you to evaluate.

-What if I agree to her terms and we go back? Who can assure me that it will work out between us? I know it sounds cliché, but Lorelaine hasn't always given me what I need.

Brenda imagined they were talking about sex and felt this was not the time to get too deep into the conflicts of marriage. First, Michael needed to recognize the pros and cons of a change in behavior. Later and being clear about their playing cards they could get right into their sexual behaviors.

-Michael, I want you to stop thinking about what you are asking Lorelaine to focus on what you are able to offer. You are used to asking and receiving and little to giving. I want you to do the opposite exercise. Don't ask for what you can't offer. Don't demand. Write down in a list what you are capable of giving to get what you are looking for. We will study it in the next consultation.

Michael accepted the homework and sat up on the couch to ask him expectantly.

-What if it turned out that I wanted to try it with her? Would you help us? Could I have a full and different life?

-If both of you are willing, of course I am.

-Lorelaine is not always an accessible person.... I can try, but I need a commitment from you. Not everything is my fault.

-I am in total agreement and excited to observe your findings. At last you begin to see the light and discover for yourself that this is not a task of just one.

Brenda was writing her conclusions when Michael stood up and slowly picked up his jacket hanging on the coat rack.

-Thank you Brenda, although I always leave here worse than I arrived," he said humorously.

-Well, I'm afraid I'm going to charge you despite your discomfort. The doctor smiled at her as she reached out to shake her hand in farewell.

-Women, they only give us trouble. He commented graciously before leaving.

Marriage had brought them to a state of habituation and acceptance in which both fulfilled their roles, even if neither was totally satisfied, she said to herself as she watched him leave. Brenda closed the door and unwillingly thought about her marriage and had to accept that many times she herself accepted what she would not like to accept and that many times she sacrificed what at one time seemed non-negotiable. She shook her head angrily at the comparisons. Her marriage was not the same as Murray's, Max was not Michael, and mostly she was not her own patient enough to be thinking such nonsense. She closed the folder and put it away in the filing cabinet trying to forget that last thought. It was late, she was tired and it was not the most opportune moment to psychoanalyze herself.

Akim worked throughout the day on the upper floors, avoiding Brenda's office. He knew perfectly well that if he did he would not resist approaching on some pretext. He held the wheelbarrow of debris tightly and made his way outside taking in the reality in Nikola's words. We are where we came from. No matter what you do to forget it, life always comes back to you on the closed path. The past may be past, but not at all trodden.

He promised himself not to follow in those footsteps, it seemed that his mother's sadness was struggling to be reflected in him. She had died with grief in her eyes, that which he himself was now unable to avoid.

Lost thoughts

-Max put some papers in his briefcase while he talked non-stop. I have to get everything on track, the flight is only in a couple of hours. I have asked Cintia to cancel the old reservations and change them to Saturday itself. I asked her to be especially careful about schedules. I hope she didn't get confused? - He commented as he reached for his cell phone on the bookshelf.

-I'm sure she's doing fine.... -Brenda thought of the poor secretary and took pity on her. Her husband could be insufferable when he was demanding.

-I don't want you to go anywhere and I want you to promise to take care of yourself. I don't want you to expose yourself. That woman is disturbed and can do anything, you must promise me you won't risk it.

-I'll be fine, now go.

Brenda offered him a tender kiss on the cheek as Max held her by the shoulders.

-I need you," he said as he hugged her tightly. You are everything. I can't lose you.

-Go or you will miss the plane. She said excitedly.

The woman accepted the hug, but did not express what she was really thinking. Are you my everything? The cab in the driveway honked its horn and Max sped off, leaving her alone with her thoughts and a cup of South African coffee in hand. Rachel walked in through the open garden gate and distracted her from her thoughts.

-Hello, hello... How is my super friend?

Brenda smiled and accepted the two kisses in the air her friend gave her as she approached.

-Perfectly, and you?

-Super, super happy. He replied, patting his hands together.

-I see, and may I know the reason for so much happiness?

Brenda approached the coffee pot as she raised it in an offer and accepted a yes from Rachel who kept talking.

-In three weeks it's my love's birthday," he took a sip from his steaming mug and raised his eyes to heaven. One day you're going to have to tell me how you make this drink so super.

Brenda sat on a stool next to her, shaking her head. They both bought the same brand, but Rachel always praised everything that came from her. She could seem cold and even empty, but Brenda knew very well the excellent woman who hid behind such a façade. Rachel was a former theater star and as such, she loved to be admired. Few knew her admirable background.

-Well, are you ready?

-Ready for what?

-Oh, no, sweet, don't tell me you've forgotten." Rachel clamped both hands over her mouth in tragedy and the doctor shivered at the thought of the storm that was coming her way.

-No, no, of course not." He lied shamelessly.

Rachel breathed in hyperventilating and Brenda desperately thought of something to make her remember. Anniversary, shopping, No! Birthday, it had to be something to do with organizing George's birthday. Yes! It was something to do with that.

-Do we have to be so careful with the details that I'm afraid I'm wrong? George deserves the best." He lied again, brazenly, hoping to get the cause right.

Rachel nodded in delight at her friend's words.

-It's the same for me. I am super, super stressed. I hope they prepare something according to the event or I swear I'll tear my eyelashes out. Brenda's eyes widened in horror and Rachel smiled in amusement. The false ones of course. I love my George, but not so much that I'm crippled.

-I doubt very much that not having eyelashes is considered a handicap. Brenda replied in a most unconcerned manner.

-Well, I should. Can you imagine how ugly it would look," he said, waving his hands in the air in denial. No, no, I'd better not even think about it. Let's try that cake and check that everything promised is real.

"Was it the cake? With everything that's happened I totally forgot about it."

-I pick up my bag and we leave.

They both left for a sweet morning hours session from which Brenda would not fare too well.

After a morning lost in cream and biscuits, the doctor entered the building caressing her aching belly. She stepped on some debris with little care and felt her heel break in half at that very moment.

-That's all I need. She grumbled angrily.

He walked with a more than obvious limp towards his office when Samir passed him with the sincerest of smiles.

-Dr. Klein, blessed are the eyes that see you, has something happened to you? - he commented as he saw her limping.

-Nothing serious - just a few manolos, she thought, sadly -. By the way, Samir, while I'm at it... -The man straightened up politely to attend to her as befitted a client of his kind, "I was wondering how long you have left to finish? It's been several weeks now and... -She was about to continue, but the foreman wouldn't let her.

-Two weeks, doctor.

-Yes, well, that's what he said a week ago and the other three weeks before that, although I don't understand much about construction," he commented, looking at the world war disaster panorama in front of him, "I'm not so bad at adding up and I don't think I can do the math....

-Don't worry, doctor. Your husband trusts me and I will not let him down," she replied with professional pride.

-No, I didn't mean... I mean, I didn't mean to offend you, it's just that all this is so much like....

-Don't worry, doctor," he said as he left the way he had come. Don't worry. Two weeks.

Brenda watched him leave without believing how he had dodged her without any remorse. The little man left behind a cloud of dust like a futuristic movie without looking back, leaving her just as he had found her. With nothing at all.

She entered the consulting room, leaned back on her couch and sighed in exhaustion. The day was just beginning and it was already proving to be too long. She took off her good shoe and threw it on the floor. She cursed aloud when she took off the second shoe and saw the heel was totally useless.

-Goodbye to my favorite manolos.... - She grumbled wistfully.

-What is a Manolo?

A deep voice increasingly familiar to her came from behind the desk.

Brenda smiled as she discovered Akim kneeling facing the wall with a screwdriver in his hand.

This time he wasn't wearing those hideous overalls and decided that simple jeans and a black t-shirt were one of his best looks. She had muscles, not exaggerated, wonderful height, some tattoos peeking out of her biceps, and a lovely suggestive look, of course all of those would be interesting qualities for a woman who was interested, not her, who was an engaged woman.

-A Manolo is a shoe.

-Do you give them names? -he said amused.

-No," he replied with a laugh. It's the mark.

-Ah, then it sounds like something extremely serious. He commented in amusement and continued with the wall socket without turning to look at it.

-Terrible and unsurpassable. She replied amused.

-They both laughed out loud and Brenda leaned back on the couch trying to relax.

Akim got up from the floor and turning around saw her in her fullness. She was lying shoeless on the wide red leather divan and a thousand ideas ran through his head, none of them expressible aloud. He had to make sincere efforts to focus his thoughts on something other than the usual. Her and her body, her and her smile, her and her intelligence, her and those full lips, her and her little chocolate eyes melted by passion, her and her moans of love, her without clothes and a life together....

-Difficult tomorrow? -She asked, unable to take her eyes off her dainty bare feet resting relaxedly on the divan. Her perfectly painted red nails matched perfectly with the furniture. He had his eyes closed and that allowed him to admire her with total indiscretion. She wore a black dress that fit delicately where it should and stood out elegantly where others would be coarse. Her breasts rose and fell after a tired sigh and he tried to imagine what it would feel like to caress them. They were neither too small nor too large, perfect for my hand, he thought somewhat agitated.

Brenda sat up to sit up and he moved quickly looking for something to do before he was caught snooping where he shouldn't be.

-Akim, you wouldn't happen to know where my teapot is?

The man who had his back to him and was nervously arranging the toolbox raised his men in a sign of total disregard.

-I'm sure Connor threw it away. He hated her. He said she was uglier than my grandmother, when I see him I'll kill him.

Akim was still on his back, concentrating on arranging his screwdrivers from largest to smallest and trying to calm his maddening heartbeat. She was so attractive lying on that couch that he could have stayed admiring her for hours. That and caressing every inch of her body until he felt her moan....

-Stop it... -he muttered between his teeth.

-You were saying?

-Nothing important.

She accepted his excuse and he repeated to himself for the umpteenth time how stupid he was.

-Well, you know what I tell you? I'll take a digestive or I'll die right here.

The young man turned suddenly in fear for her.

-Are you sick? Do you need anything? -His voice sounded so worried that Brenda almost ate him with kisses. The facade didn't match his essence at all. He was a badass on the outside, but undeniably tender on the inside.

-Let's say I was attacked by thousands of cakes and I can't recover.

-Cakes?

-You see, my friend Rachel took me to a pie tasting and I think I'm going to die of indigestion.

-Cake tasting? Does that exist?

-Oh yes, and I swear I'll never go to one again. My veins are clogged with sugar.

Akim looked at her with a smile on his lips. That smile that he had whenever he saw her and that he lost when she was not there. She might seem cold and arrogant in a first image, but nothing could be further from the truth, his Brin was not like that.

"My Brin? I'm delirious."

-I'd better go and let you recover.

Akim was about to leave when the doctor got up and intercepted him to stop him. He looked at her and stopped breathing. They were facing each other. Their eyes locked on each other. Her heels off, her little feet on tiptoe and two of her toes tapping against his chest. God, this was heaven. If he ducked his head he could possess her lips right there.

-You're coming with me," he commented with a mischievous smile.

-Where to? -He cleared his throat, trying not to think of the only thing.

-To have a cup of tea or something to help me.

-I can't... -. He said with a small mouth.

-I'll talk to Samir and you'll get your permission. I'm in a bad way and you can't leave me stranded.

Akim tried to think of the myriad reasons why he should reject her as he scratched the back of his neck.

-If you call Connor? -He stammered, instantly regretting offering her an alternative to him.

-He won't be here until tomorrow. It seems like a perfect match with the fireman.

"Fuck." Akim saw Brenda's winking eyes and cursed inwardly. What he was missing was sexual teasing with mischievousness. His crotch was beginning to harden as he imagined how well they could "fit in" too.

-Come on, you're not going to let me down when I'm so sick? -she said with her mouth half open like a little girl.

-Are you trying to manipulate me, doctor?

"Am I ever going to stop grinning at him like an idiot?"

-Absolutely.

They both laughed out loud and Brenda knew she had the battle won, but when she saw her shoes she thought better of the decision to go outside. The young man, who noticed her perturbation, picked up her still complete Manolo and asked her seriously.

-Can't they be fixed?

-No." She replied apologetically.

-So... -Akim ripped the heel off the heel of the healthy shoe and held it out to her as she stared in astonishment.

-Now you have a pair of Manolos without heels. Exclusive design," she said as she lifted her shoulders without giving it much importance.

-My Manolos... -She sighed as she put on both feet.

Although she now looked much shorter she had to admit that she could walk without looking like the hunchback of Notre Dame.

-Run! -Run! We have a free sofa over there.

Akim furrowed his brow as he shook his head. Why did people go to a coffee shop that charged four times as much as another and where they had to run to get a seat on one of the few couches?

-What do you want to drink? -. She asked enthusiastically.

-You're not bringing anything. I want you to sit on the much coveted couch and wait for me to pick you a drink that might suit you.

-Brenda remembered their first meeting at the Starbucks and felt guilty for making him spend money on her.

-Weren't you about to faint from discomfort? -. Akim arched one of his bushy eyebrows waiting for an answer.

Brenda bit her lip trying to think of an excuse that would make her look less taken advantage of.

-And if I said I was better, would you believe me?

She narrowed her chocolate eyes and Akim clenched his fists to keep from grabbing her shoulders and kissing her unconscious.

-I don't think so. Now doctor, are you going to be good, are you going to sit down and wait for me to bring you your drink or am I going to think that besides being uptight you are a phony?

Brenda opened her eyes trying to look offended but failed.

-I am not a phony.

Akim turned to the bar but not before answering.

-And stubborn.

-Niñato.

-Don't provoke me doctor, don't provoke me.

Akim left with the same smile she stayed on the couch with. That game was something she had only with him and she adored it.

Brenda knew she had been somewhat demanding in asking him to accompany her. She enjoyed his company more and more every day. With Akim, life was easy. The busy doctor gave way to the friend. The wife was becoming a woman and laughter was part of her daily life.

Smells of danger

-Green tea with a list of ingredients too long to remember.

Brenda thanked him as she picked up the lidded cup and gave him the best of her smiles.

Akim sat across from her thinking seriously about his current situation. No matter how many promises he could or could not make, what he felt for this woman was stronger than any past or any consequences. No matter how many times he denied it or cursed himself, she was a strange force that drew him into an abyss from which he could not pull away.

-You're going to tell me why you're smiling like that.

"Because you're killing me and I have no salvation." He thought in frustration.

-Are you psychoanalyzing me, doctor?

Brenda smiled and the man felt his bones melt into stardust. He was totally lost.

-Maybe a little bit.

He shook his head resigned to suffer her manipulations as he took a sip of his expensive coffee.

-I haven't seen you for days. He said regretfully as soon as the words left his lips.

-Commitments, nothing important. And you?

-The usual.

-Do you like what you do? I'm saying that because you told me you studied arts? -She drank, interested to know his answer.

Akim thought carefully about his answer.

-Now I'm also creative with cement in my hands. He smiled half-heartedly and hoped to end the subject.

-But if you had the opportunity to change, would you do it?

Akim looked at her with both curiosity and admiration. Did she pretend to be his savior? Did she think that by pulling a few strings he would become a happy and satisfied man? He shook his eyes, not knowing whether to be angry at her for being so nosy or to kiss her for being more tender than daisies.

-My only priority is to feed my family. He replied seriously.

Brenda knew that was an end point but she couldn't resist. Akim's presence aroused different feelings in her than she usually had with her patients. She wanted to help him. She wanted to fix his life and she felt she could do it. Their gazes met over the top of their respective fees and they both smiled like children caught stealing candy bars.

-You either ask questions or you bust, isn't that right?

-You know me.

-It seems so. He said amused.

-I'm sorry, I'm sorry, I don't want to seem like a busybody, your family is the one who should encourage you to find what you are looking for.

-And do you know what I'm looking for? -Akim's mischievous sideways smile diverted her from her plans for a moment.

Those eyes were as clear as the clearest of seas. Expressive and lustful like something I no longer remembered.

-How is Lucien. She changed the subject as she calmed a heat that rose in her body without understanding why.

-An unscrupulous rogue. He replied, accepting his detour in the conversation.

He knew his hints made her nervous. And seeing her blushing was too pretty a temptation to resist.

-Don't say that. He's a lovely boy. He told me that you are a perfect father, that you help him with his homework and that he can even sing.

-And now I must also add that he is a liar.

Brenda guffawed and acknowledged regretfully.

-He also said that I sing well.

-Liar and cheeky," he said earnestly.

They both laughed enjoying the moment. Brenda wanted to ask him a lot of questions, she wanted to know the little boy's story, she wanted to know what his history was, how long had he been in the country, did he have more family, did he have plans for the future, was he in love?

-And his mother abandoned him. He clarified, trying to discover something more than what he already knew.

Akim tensed and Brenda knew she had crossed the reasonable boundary between friendship principle and gossip, but the question just came out, it wasn't meant to be. She couldn't help biting her lip knowing she wanted the whole story. Knowing Akim's feelings, discovering his hidden side was turning from desire to undeniable need.

-Forgive me, I shouldn't have asked, I'm nobody and I understand that you don't want to answer.

The guilty voice roused him from his silence. He might not have liked to talk to anyone on the subject, let alone strangers. He was sure that with any other woman he would have given up on coffee. She was not just any woman. She was his doctor, his Brin. If there was anyone he wanted to share his secrets with, it would be her.

-She never wanted it. She tried to abort in very unorthodox ways. Lucien was stronger. When he was born she left him in my care.

-She just left him.... - He answered sadly.

-With two diapers and an old blanket.

-I imagine your pain...

Akim thought carefully before answering.

-I never felt anything special for her. You could say that Lucien was the fruit of a youthful mistake. At first I also refused the idea of being a father with a woman I slept with on weekends, then he won me over.

Akim's repentant voice ruffled every inch of her skin. Despite the harshness of his words she appreciated his utter sincerity.

-You wouldn't trade it for anything.

-I would kill to see him for sure. He taught me how to be a father. His love is so real and sincere that sometimes I think of it as a dream. His love is unique. No one has ever loved me like him. He commented sorrowfully.

-You are very young, you may not have fallen in love with the mother of your child, but you will feel something very intense when you meet that special woman.

-And what am I supposed to feel, doctor? -he asked, interested in the answer.

Brenda was surprised by the appellation. Akim wasn't kidding at this point. His deep gaze and that slight way of twisting his head showed her that he was looking for her most sincere professional opinion.

-You'll feel your heart beating so hard you can't control it. When you see her go you'll fall apart dreaming of seeing her again. Her smile will be your life and her tears your sincere sorrow. You will deny again and again her power over you. You will reveal yourself and you will want to scream with impotence, but nothing will help you anymore because the love for her will run through every drop of your blood.

Brenda sighed believing firmly in what she was saying and feeling a deep emptiness inside.

-Is that what you feel? -he asked in a hoarse voice.

-What? -. Akim woke her from her reverie. She did not answer, and he let her.

For a moment he thought a simple 'yes' would break his heart and shatter his illusions, but she didn't answer and his soul was reborn. She had not answered and he thanked God for the first time in years. He didn't want to dream of impossibilities, neither did he wish to stop living, and the question he had asked almost unconsciously, in a second became a gun to his temple that nearly killed him.

-We should go. Brenda picked up her bag, trying to run away from the cafeteria. She was supposed to be the professional of the mind, she was supposed to be the one to help him, yet for a moment, she felt exposed. She hurried to get up to leave as soon as possible. She had no desire to be therapist and patient at the same time. Her life was going too well to even consider it.

Akim accepted her flight forward, although she was unable to contain her thoughts. One moment she looked like an excited child, the next she was the perfect polite, serious, stiff woman after the consultation. What the hell had happened? Was it that her husband didn't love her as much as she loved him? Or was it that she didn't...?

"Akim stop!" he thought in a daze.

They crossed the street and entered the office doorway without saying a word to each other. Brenda seemed totally wrapped up in her thoughts and Akim wanted to shriek with pent-up rage. He would like to wake her up with hundreds of kisses and tell her he was there.

-See you. She said coldly as she entered his office. Akim stayed in place without moving. He couldn't say goodbye like that.

"What if she never wants to see me again? What if it was because of something I did?" The sorrow of feeling that she would never speak to him again pricked his heart too deep to bear.

-Brenda I... I was wondering if, I mean if we were left... I mean... that woman." He couldn't finish any of the so-called sentences he was thinking.

-How?

She turned around totally discomfited and Akim entered the office unable to remain indifferent for another minute.

-The crazy politician! We agreed that I'd go with you to the cocktail party," she said confidently, making it clear that she wouldn't get rid of him.

-Yes, of course. It will be on Saturday. Don't worry, I'll let you know when I have all the data.

The young man breathed a sigh of relief. This was not the last time he would see her. Oxygen entered his lungs again.

-Well, I'm off to work because we're not all snooty rich girls.

Akim jabbed her with sarcasm as he walked away trying to snap her out of her state of sadness and she accepted the joke as a sign of an increasingly common challenge between them.

-But I don't deny it, others claim to be good singers and who knows. He commented mischievously.

-Better than others for sure.

-Believed.

-Stretch.

-Niñato

-Don't provoke me doctor, don't provoke me....

Akim replied in a loud, clear voice as he walked down the hallway.

"What I would give for you to provoke me."

Countdown

Brenda was almost ready. In less than an hour she'd be at the blissful cocktail party at the Murrays' house. The doctor swallowed dryly as she finished combing her hair into a high ponytail. She looked at herself in the mirror and had to admit that the choice of the tight-fitting cream-colored dress was a wise one. It was to attract Roxane's attention and jealousy and she hoped she would succeed. This madness had to end once and for all and they all had to get back to their lives. She was tired of being constantly afraid and fearful for those she loved. Roxane had to begin treatment urgently or the consequences could be inevitable.

The morning had awakened with one of the worst spring storms in recent years and as the hours passed it had not improved one iota. Max was at the airport hoping for a miracle, she knew that was an impossibility. She would have to assume she was alone.

The doorbell rang and she took a deep breath to encourage herself before opening it. It was probably Connor. She opened the door with a beaming smile so her friend wouldn't sense her fears when the image she encountered struck her completely dumb.

Akim shook off the rainwater as he closed a huge umbrella. The man wore an elegant dark blue buttoned and perfectly tailored suit. The pristine white shirt stood out against a delicate blue and white striped tie that suited him to a tee. He looked up and focused his crystalline sky-blue eyes and smiled at her with enthusiasm.

-What a day. He said, wiping a few drops from his face.

He had to pinch his hand to come to his senses. His hair as black as night framed an angular, serious and seductively masculine face. He wore the same unkempt beard he wore almost every day, but today there was something different about him. That continuously disheveled hair, that eternally angry face, those shoulders in continuous tension, and the deep husky voice, were the same as always, yet he possessed something different. And no, it wasn't the suit or the shoes.

-The sky is falling. Brenda just looked at him. Are you all right?

-Hey, yes, perfectly.... -He said as he made room for her to enter.

-I know we agreed to meet at the Murrays' house, but the inspector told me the airports were closed and I thought you might be lonely and want to, well, anyway....

He scratched the back of his neck as he tried to get unstuck from his own jumble of words. "When I rehearsed it at home it seemed so much easier." He thought in disgust.

-I thank you." Brenda, recovered from the initial shock, began to reason and was able to speak out loud. The truth is that I'm a little scared. She acknowledged with sincerity.

-You have to promise me that you won't leave my side," he said, squeezing her strong hand on his shoulder. I don't give a damn what that damned inspector and his weasel have planned or said, you're not going anywhere without me. You can trust me, I'll never let anything happen to you, you know that don't you?

-Yes, I know." She didn't know why, but she did. You shouldn't be involved in this." She said with her shoulders slumped.

-But I do and I know you and I know you will try to do some of your own. You're a stubborn rebel who can't resist helping. Brenda's eyes widened in amazement and smiled. That woman is out of her mind, please promise me you will be obedient. My sanity depends on you.

The man clutched her shoulders with trembling hands and her eyes stung. She had begun to connect with this dark curmudgeon.

-I'll be good, I promise. Akim, I'm so sorry to get you into this mess.

-You didn't do anything. It's that crazy woman's fault," he said as he reached out to caress her delicate face with his hand.

They both looked at each other in silence for a few seconds until Brenda summoned some inexplicable strength to break the moment. She made an excuse and disappeared upstairs. She entered the room, closed her eyes and tried to calm her breathing.

What had just happened? Akim had caressed her face with tenderness, with pity even, but then why was her heart racing as if in some kind of hidden fear? He breathed once, twice, three, even four times until he managed to lower the state of excitement in which he found himself. Her face burned where he had caressed her, her heart was disoriented and her lungs exhaled with exaggeration.

"The nerves, the nerves.... I'm scared. That's it." She said shakily to herself.

Brenda took another four deep breaths and went downstairs, trying not to think about him and his racing heartbeat. Had she ever felt anything like this before? She tried to remember. No memory came to her mind.

Akim watched the storm behind the window and she was grateful that he was calm because it told her that his nervousness was unwarranted.

-I'm ready. He said with mock confidence.

-Perfect. You look perfect.

Brenda felt her heart start to gallop again, but she ignored it completely. Akim was gentle, as anyone else would be in such a situation, gentle and polite, that was all. Gentle and polite, that was all. He was much younger and with a future of possibilities, what could he see in her other than gratitude or admiration?

Convinced by her psychoanalytical reasoning, she accepted the man's arm to leave for one of her most difficult therapies. She had promised to collaborate in her arrest, she knew perfectly well that, if this woman finally appeared, she would do everything possible to help her. Roxane was one of the many women who were victims of a reverie that only existed in her mind. She believed in love and sought it in a night of passion with the wrong man. Yes, if he could, he would help her.

Akim, chivalrous, accepted her car key as he opened an umbrella to cover her. She looked like an angel. Her perfect curves covered by that delicate and fine dress represented the most subtle summer dream.

He knew his actions bordered on impertinence, at this point he cared little for them. Today would be the last day he would have her all to himself and he would make the most of it. The past and his sufferings could go down the drain for one night. Today he would launch all his artillery against his only target and may heaven have mercy on his lovesick heart because he needed to know what those lips tasted like and he was not willing to wait.

Look at me

The mansion shone brightly despite the heavy rain. The storm was raging relentlessly. The spotlights scattered all over the garden showed the might of the owners. The strains of the live orchestra could be heard from the sidewalk and Akim tried to loosen the knot of his tie so he could breathe. His legs went numb at the image of pomposity before him. He had never witnessed such an act.

With his calloused hand placed on the small of her delicate back, he was guiding a full-fledged woman to the reception desk and he felt exhilarated, and terribly nervous. He swallowed twice, thinking seriously about running away when Brenda gently pressed his arm as if sensing his dread and offering her full support. Would he ever look into those chocolate eyes without feeling himself falling into an abyss from which he didn't want to return? No, surely not.

-Nervous?

-Not if you don't walk away.

-I promise, now let's go inside and hope this night is over as soon as possible.

The bricklayer nodded and approached to go through the gate when a gray-haired, stiff man greeted them with a serious look on his face.

-Dr. Klein, sir, let me collect your coats.

-Thank you, Thomas.

Akim handed over his coat with great care as he even more delicately adjusted his suit, after all, the rental store owner had already stressed it to him, "if it suffers any damage we won't refund the deposit".

-Okay, here we go.

Brenda walked towards the main hall stunned by so much luxury and detail. It was clear that the politicians knew how to organize a good party. High society guests wore their best clothes while smiling properly. Ladies fresh from the hairdresser held in their hands an expensive crystal glass filled with the most exquisite champagne while they enjoyed chatting and drinking. The attendants smiled and ate the appetizing appetizers with delicacy, oblivious to the real reason why she was there. Roxane might appear soon and that made her shudder. She was no coward, but remembering that woman and her sharp blade on her neck made her rethink her solidarity. A soft touch on the small of her back brought a pleasant, soothing warmth. Akim gave her that shy, almost imperceptible smile he usually did and she was grateful for his understanding. The young man was becoming a pillar she could lean on and she liked that more than she would ever acknowledge to anyone. Many might consider Dr. Brenda Klein a feisty woman with character, style and confidence, only a few knew Brenda, the woman without the prefix of doctor in front of her. Akim seemed to see her as no one else could and she was interesting.

-That's our subject," he said in his deep, thick accent.

The orchestra, which was no longer playing jazz and was livening up the room with modern and very sweet musical notes, began to play. The women rested their arms on the shoulders of their companions while they guided them by clinging to their waists.

-I appreciate it, I don't think I can. I'm a little nervous. The doctor did not say that her nerves were not exactly coming from Roxane but from a hand on her back that made her feel an electric shiver.

Since she had seen him in his impeccable suit she had not been able to recover from her impression. Akim exuded an attractiveness that she had to resist with too much willpower.

-I'm sorry, I don't accept a refusal. That woman won't show up for a while and I don't see Murray anywhere. Either you dance with me or I'm the one who won't be able to handle the pressure. She knew she was taking advantage of it to make her feel guilty. At this point nothing mattered to him anymore.

Tonight was his and to hell with the cons of the whole world. Since he had seen her for the first time he had tried everything to forget her and he had not succeeded. The young man brought his hand to her delicate waist and guided her to the dance floor without waiting for an answer. Brenda gave in to his request in silence. Something inside her told her that it was wrong, that she should not accept it, a little voice in her ear wanted to warn her that she was about to make a profound mistake, but she did not listen.

Akim guided her to the center of the room and brought his hands to her waist to guide her. She lifted her hands to his shoulders and it was at that very moment that he felt that current of electricity run through him and mark him as a man of exclusive use. His own. He wanted to close his eyes and enjoy the sea of sensations from having her almost glued to his body. The urge to keep her forever in his memory was much stronger. Chocolate's gaze was fixed on his crystalline seas and he knew that his life would have a before and after tonight.

Brenda was the dream every man would have. Today he understood the Cinderella story perfectly because he felt like her. The clock would strike twelve and he would no longer be part of her world. Cement, dust and red numbers would fill her day to day life while she would fly into the arms of another prince, a more suitable one. Her fingers gripped his waist tightly wanting to freeze time. Anything to keep the clock from striking twelve.

Soft, slow music was enveloping the room as Akim discovered with some sadness the song they were playing. It was a Spanish lyric he knew perfectly well. His mother, an aid worker in Cuba for many years, had taught him the beauties of that beautiful language.

Without holding back he bent his head to be at the same level of his companion's delicate ear and whispered tenderly the only way he knew how to express himself. Music.

♪♫ You turn my world upside down

I walk the streets, I talk to myself all day long.

I am between a rock and a hard place

and I don't know what to do to be the owner of your life anymore.

I'd like to kiss you, but I dare not

Your love is forbidden...♭♩ ♭♩ ♭♩

He felt it tighten under his fingers. He did not let go. She would not understand a word. The warmth of his words would cross language boundaries.

Brenda heard the melodious voice singing sweetly in her ear, and she shuddered, although she was unable to recognize its meaning. At that moment she cursed herself for not having made an effort in her Spanish classes, she really wanted to know what Akim was whispering so tenderly and to decipher once and for all what exactly was being born between them. His melodious and harmonious voice was something exquisite. He wasn't able to recognize even one of the fragments, though he would swear that each stanza conveyed affection, warmth and a hint of, pain? He closed his eyes and enjoyed the moment. His conscience told him they should stop. He knew it didn't belong, so why did it feel so devilishly good?

"What is due is not always what is possible and what is wanted is not always what is convenient for us", he recalled his lessons to a patient and without looking for it he felt he was drinking his own medicine.

"Go away..." Pleaded his despairing heart. "Don't go on," his dazed brain vociferated. "Go away," her trembling body cried out to him. She would not listen to them. No matter how many falsehoods she wanted to disguise what she was feeling with, at last she felt herself vibrating and dreaming like a woman. In his arms she was not the strong, insurmountable Dr. Klein. With him she needed no disguises, no strength, no courage. With him she was only Brenda. A woman who wanted to receive without having the obligation to give....

Akim felt the touch of her skin on the tip of his nose and knew he would do it. He would kiss her there, in that little crease between her ear and neck. He would open his mouth and savor her like the most delicate delicacy. She had to know. He had to feel what her heart cried out when he was beside her. She may have had a life before him, but something was happening between them and Brenda would have to accept it. Because his heart may have been beating out of control at the sight of her, but there was something going on with her too. He had noticed it in the tension as he brushed against her or in the way she looked away when she discovered the hunger in his gaze. Yes, there was something between them and he would find out right now. She opened her mouth and let the warmth of his breath brush her skin at the base of her neck. He took a deep breath and felt her scent envelop him. He closed his eyes and was about to savor her when....

-Doctor.

Murray came between them breaking the weather and Akim wanted to break his neck.

-Brenda, I think it's time for us to play our part.

The politician reached out to take it from him and the young man had to use all his education to give it to him. He had had it. For a second he felt the taste of victory on his lips. "Damn Murray."

Brenda, still feeling dizzy from the sensations experienced with the song, and ignorant of the intentions of a stolen kiss, accepted his hand and prepared to leave, fearful of her feelings. Murray led her by the arm and the young man watched her walk away in utter disappointment. He prayed to heaven that she would turn and look at him. Just once, I'll settle for just once, he said looking to the ceiling for an answer from a god who didn't seem to hear him. She was leaving, breaking his illusions and his heart. Angrily he intercepted a glass of champagne and drank it in one gulp. He looked up sad, hurt and disappointed when she turned to focus her tender chocolate eyes on him.

-Yes, yes and a thousand times yes," I murmur happily.

Their gazes met and life began to course through his veins. It was only a few seconds, a short blink of an eye, just enough to focus their gaze on each other and Akim felt the sky open up. His heart began to beat again and a smile instantly settled on his face. Anger, disappointment and rage turned to devastating hope with just a small glance. She had turned, belatedly, but she had, and he felt exhilarated. It was maddening, his sanity or his happiness depended on just one look. That of her deep, radiant chocolate pearls.

She and Michael strutted around the room with rehearsed complicity. If Roxane was nearby she would have to make herself visible or jealousy would kill her. Murray explained to her that there were two plainclothes policemen at the door with the exact description of the woman. There was no way she would show up without being arrested. Brenda breathed a sigh of relief because, although she considered her a poor woman, she couldn't deny that she was quite afraid to meet her again. She approached whatever guest Michael insisted on introducing her to. She let Dr. Klein's figure take up positions and behaved as expected of her. She smiled at the impromptu banter and commented on important issues when asked, such as women in politics or private education and the underprivileged. She got into it with a backward politician about the traumatic situation of migrants and discussed human rights and even managed to forget about Roxane and her attacks. The only thing she could not forget was a sweet, deep voice singing in her ear. Had anyone ever sung to her alone? No, surely not. Max hated what he called cheesiness. Eventually he became convinced that, like flowers or chocolates, they were cold and unnecessary manifestations of love, today, after feeling a tingle go through his skin after a song in Spanish, he had serious doubts that he was right.

Pretending to be thirsty, he went off in search of a bar. He had to admit that it wasn't exactly a drink he was looking for. He wanted to casually look here and there trying to locate it, but nothing. He was nowhere to be found.

"Could he have gotten tired and left without me? Will he be getting used to the place? Alone or accompanied?"

Akim had been watching her behind a pillar for over an hour. Watching her in her environment was frustrating and devilishly sensual. She was talking, smiling, moving her hands and even snorting elegantly. From a distance he couldn't hear her, but from her movements he knew she was heatedly arguing about who knows what. He caught himself smiling and imagining those poor men trying to beat a big-headed girl like her. In this short time he had gotten to know her well enough to know that, behind her serious, correct and elegant facade, there was a strong, energetic woman with ideals and a heart so tender and feminine that even she didn't know herself. For heaven's sake! If that madwoman had been about to slit her throat and Brenda had only thought of helping her.

Akim enjoyed the moment. The first time he saw her he was attracted by her physique, today he had to accept that he was foolishly in love. Totally, madly and unconsciously in love. Murray turned away from her side for a moment and had to admit that he was jealous of this man. He was jealous of his partner, his friends, his joys, his sorrows and the life he was living without him. This was madness.

He always thought himself immune to feelings, or at least he thought them dead. Brenda had awakened something he didn't even know existed. She completed all his needs. Passion, desire and tenderness united in a single woman, the only one who by heart made him go crazy and who by right did not belong to him.

What woman would take a chance on a man who not only had a few years on her but was also poor as a rat? Well, he might not be a beggar, he thought in annoyance, but he knew perfectly well that his bank account next to Brenda's would run in shame without a backward glance.

He looked at his suit and was delighted with the effect it had on her, both his shirt, his shoes and even the knot of his tie, were still a mirage that would end the next morning when he returned them to "Sastrería Finos". Just like Cinderella, she thought with a wretched smile.

It had been five years since she had arrived in London with only a babe in arms and a tired father for company. In those years, the three of them had formed a quaint little family, with a more than decent roof over their heads and a plate of food never missing from their table, so why did he now feel more miserable than ever?

Akim scratched his neck trying to comprehend the blissful games of chance that life was playing, he didn't succeed. Of all the women he could have woken up to life with and it had to be her. He watched her from a distance behind a pillar. She didn't know he was around. He always was. Reason told her they would never be together but her heart always asked for a little more. Any time was a good time to sneak away and look for her. Like the sun that warms you just by feeling it, Brenda was his warmth, he didn't need to touch her to enjoy her sensations. He looked at her spellbound and smiled at the thought that a dress like hers should be forbidden. Who could remain indifferent to that image! And those heels? God! Pure essence of woman.

Akim leaned his back against the column and crossed his legs recreating himself with the print. The curves perfectly completed a dress with a long zipper in the back that he would gladly open with the same teeth. If she were his he would drag her to the darkest place in the house, drop the soft fabric to the floor and recreate himself with the precious image of her in lingerie on heels too erotic to be legal.

Brenda felt a strange coldness run down her back and, guided by a new intuition, she turned to meet Akim's gaze, who was watching her from a distance. She wanted to smile at him, to make a face of boredom for the company of the guests' plastas, any kind of joke remained choked in front of his blue and almost transparent gaze that devoured her with every blink of an eye. They both looked at each other and she couldn't translate any coded message. They were simply one on one end staring at the other. She couldn't tell if it was a few seconds or hours. It was the strangest sensation he had ever felt. Different, curious, exciting and new, very new.

A waitress handed her a message and Brenda thanked her for distracting her or she would continue to stand there watching without speaking. She read it and somewhat quizzically left for the upstairs rooms.

Where had she gone, why didn't she wait for him, and where the hell was Murray! Akim ran after her, but the hall was crowded and he couldn't catch up. When he reached the main hallway on the top floor he cursed loudly. All the doors were closed and there were too many of them. How many rooms do rich people have! he thought angrily.

I choose you

Brenda had to adjust her eyes to look for her. The room, dimly lit by the light from the street lamps streaming through the window, was not enough.

-Lorelaine? -He whispered, trying to figure out why the woman was hiding.

It was clear that the situation would not be to her greatest liking and she even understood the reason for not being present in the main room, but this way of summoning her to her room was intriguing and rather spooky. Brenda searched the vast room for some sign of life and relaxed when she caught a glimpse of the figure of a woman resting on a large single couch.

-There you are. I'm glad to see you, for a moment there I thought this whole thing had gotten the better of you. I hope that...

Dr. Klein's voice was lost in the dark silence when, as she walked closer, she could see to whom the female figure belonged. Her blood froze the instant she spotted it. The deathly cold jolted her to her core as she noticed a huge pool of blood on the floor. Brenda tried to run. She couldn't, her legs wouldn't move. Panic overcame her completely. Her brain was not reasoning. She was only able to see the huge puddle spilling under the feet of a woman maddened by madness.

Roxane pointed a gun at her while warning her not to scream or she would end up just like the corpse sprawled on the ground.

-What have you done? -I sobbed bitterly -How could you?

-She wanted to take him away from me. It was a hindrance between us.

The unhinged woman smiled with a lost look and Brenda, who until now had not been able to recognize the corpse because it was lying face down, knew instantly who she was talking about.

-Lorelaine...

-Yes. This bitch wanted to take him away from me.

-She was not your enemy. He said trying to get closer. Roxane pointed more vehemently at the center of his head.

-They were coming back! I saw them together!

Brenda ducked her head, trying to understand some of the madness. Michael had informed her the week before of his wife's abandonment of the home and his intention to get her back.

-I shouldn't have come. He said he wouldn't forgive him... -She screamed hysterically as she waved her gun uncontrollably through the air. I couldn't let him come back. She would entangle him again and he would be with her and not with me....

Roxane wore a black wig and a waitress uniform that she probably wore to throw off the guards at the gate. She paced back and forth, dyeing red wherever she stepped and Brenda could not hold back her tears. Fear, grief and deep pain tore at her insides. How could she not have foreseen this misfortune? She was a professional in human psychology, how could she not see the signs of an uncontrolled madwoman? Brenda thought she was dealing with a jealous and somewhat unhinged lover. This was much more. She had erred in her diagnosis and Lorelaine had paid the consequences.

-Roxane, I can help you...

-Are you going to call him? Are you going to explain that I love him?

The woman wandered between incoherence and despair. She was walking uncontrollably while she wheezed in agitation.

-First you must give me that weapon or someone else will get hurt.

-I didn't mean to... she was to blame.... -With every step she took and every trace of blood she smeared, Brenda held back her nausea. Pain, impotence and a terrible fear of ending up dead pushed her to try to take control of the situation.

-I know it perfectly well. You are a good woman. One who simply wants her man to love her. I'm sure you'll be able to explain and Michael will understand you, but you'll have to give me the gun," he stretched out his arm in a waiting gesture. Let me help you....

-Don't lie to me!

The scream that came from the last room froze Akim's heart and he ran like a demon-led soul. Without thinking whether it was right or not, he pushed the door with a blow that almost tore it off. When he saw them he felt like dying. Brenda held out her hand while the unhinged mistress looked at her with penetrating madness. A large pool of blood covered them both and the young man screamed uncontrollably as he threw himself on the woman who, being surprised in such a way, reacted in the only way she knew how. Desperate. Without moving from the spot and with an unhinged look, she aimed and fired.

-No!

Brenda ran towards Akim when she saw him fall backwards as a result of the power of the shot.

-What have you done!

Brenda cried as she tried to stop the gushing blood near the man's neck. She squeezed hard on something like a tablecloth she found nearby trying to stop the bleeding. Akim's gaze was vacant and somewhat lost. At no time did he stop focusing on her. He felt himself dying and she was the last vision he wanted to take with him. She would be with him until his last breath.

At that very moment a strong man entered in desperation along with the owner of the house who was following him closely. Michael seeing his wife on the floor approached her without caring about the consequences. The man bent down and began to scream between sobs and insults while rocking the now inert body of his wife.

-Darling... my love... I'm sorry... I'm sorry... -She said with her eyes covered with tears.

-Drop the gun! -One of the men shouted, but she did not obey.

Roxane's eyes focused on the image of her beloved crying for another woman. The one she hated. The girl felt her love break and her heart shatter. She heard each cry of Michael's like daggers stabbing into her soul. Hearing him demand her to come back, to not leave him, that he had been the biggest idiot was too much for her unhinged heart. He was suffering and it was for another. Not for her. It had never been her.

The pain of a heartbreak that she never wanted to accept possessed her and without thinking she took two steps backwards and approaching the huge window she leaned out to measure the distance to the ground. She was about to throw herself, or at least that seemed to be the idea that her deranged mind was suggesting, when she discovered that she could not even get his attention that way. Until the very day of his death Michael would ignore her. She tried to scream and say goodbye. He was on the floor holding a body that was no longer alive while Brenda, who claimed to be his friend, screamed for a doctor for a young man who was bleeding to death on the floor.

Everyone ignored her. Nobody loved her. They never saw in her more than a body to use...

The cold wind and rain coming in through the window wet her face as she closed her eyes, only to change her mind in a second. She aimed straight for Michael's head. She would die, but he would travel to hell with her. She pressed trembling fingers to the trigger as a thunderous sound filled the room. Brenda ducked her head as she held an unconscious Akim tightly to the floor, and that's when Michael Murray raised his head and saw her.

Roxane, for a thousandth of a second stood still in place watching the blood in her heart run like rivers of blood. Then she closed her eyes and slumped to the floor. From the doorway Inspector Gutierrez patted the back of young Charly who was planted just inside the doorjamb, gun smoking and pointing at the now inert body of the young model.

-Well done, boy. The young man nodded as Gutierrez watched the Russian being attended to, and a colleague tried to separate the politician from his wife's body.

Don't do what I do

-Isn't it too soon to run away? -Connor spoke in a tone that Brenda didn't like one bit. He seemed to be scolding her, and she was no child.

-Didn't you say I shouldn't have come? -she said, annoyed.

-And I keep thinking about it. It's barely been three days since the attack, but since you've come, I don't understand why you're in such a hurry.

-I'm going to the hospital.

-Again?

-Yes, and if you want to say something, you'd better be direct.

Connor was getting too pushy on the subject and Brenda began to get fed up with unsolicited advice.

-Cari, I don't want to seem heavy. I think you should stay.

-For not wanting to be one, you're being one, and very much so. You can stop this nonsense or you're going to make me very angry.

Brenda was talking as she reached for a huge bag that she hid behind the desk.

-What is that?

-Nothing that matters to you.

-Brenda, you have to stop! This is crazy...

-What's wrong with visiting a person who saved your life in the hospital!

-And that he's crazy about you!

-Don't talk nonsense. Akim is a charming young man and nothing more.

-Young and single!

Connor watched her for a couple of seconds and closed his eyes.

-You know it... -You don't answer me because you already know....

Brenda was not ready to recognize anything, much less when even she was not able to recognize her feelings. She knew that she

240

liked seeing him, that she enjoyed their conversations, but from there to feeling something more.... That represented an absurdity and she didn't understand why Connor was so worried. Anyone in their right mind could distinguish the profound differences that separated them.

-I remind you that I am a mature person and I know perfectly well the decisions I make," she replied annoyed. I don't need your advice. I am a woman fully aware of my actions," she said even angrier.

-You don't know what you're doing. You are making the worst mistake of all. He shouted, knowing he was the loser.

-I'm not doing anything wrong! You make a mountain out of a molehill.

Connor took a breath, trying to calm down. If it were someone else in front of him, his words and advice would probably be different, but it was Brenda, his Brenda. His friend and sister. She wasn't like him. She wouldn't jump from bed to bed forgetting in the morning what she had enjoyed at night. She would break more than a marriage, she would break Brenda herself.

-Cari," he said nervously, "that young man is a man and he wants you for more than just one night. I saw it in his eyes. You will play with fire...

-For heaven's sake, he's not a child and I'm not going to play anything. I'm just going to a damn hospital. He is a good, brave, risky and sincere man.

-You don't have to defend him to me. Brenda looked at him in surprise and Connor felt he had to ease the tension. - Honey, you know I support you in everything. I'm afraid you'll make a mistake.

The woman snorted in disgust and glared at him with a fire Connor was unfamiliar with that made him recoil.

-You've always hated Max. You've always said that his character made me feel self-conscious, that his character made me feel bad, and now you jump to his defense! Who understands you? If it were as you say, which it isn't," she roared, annoyed, "why are you so upset?

-I'm not defending Max! Or the firm on a stupid piece of paper. I'm defending you. He said annoyed with himself as he felt unable to talk sense into her.

Brenda leaned nervously on the desk trying to calm her vehemence. She shouldn't get that way with Connor. He was only looking out for what was best for her. She could tell him that Akim didn't care about her, that she was simply being grateful, but she couldn't. When she saw him bleeding out on the floor she felt faint and that fear didn't subside until many hours later when the doctors assured her of his stability. At first she thought her concern was a normal and even humane feeling, now she didn't know what to think. She wanted to go to the hospital, play cards as they had done the previous two afternoons. She would smile with her anecdotes and he would enjoy her busy-woman nonsense. Akim loved to listen to her and she would relax in his presence. Everything was easier with him. Ridicule or social conventions did not exist when they were together. In his company she felt free, unprejudiced....

-I'll be fine... You don't have to worry. We're friends, that's all." She said defeated.

-Since when did you become friends with a bricklayer? -he commented, trying to wake her up.

-And since when do you care about social classes! -she replied angrily.

-To me, never, in your world, they do matter.

Connor walked out the door. He no longer wished to argue. Brenda cursed angrily. A part of her was telling her that he was right. That she should listen to him. Something was growing between her and Akim and although she knew how to recognize it, she also knew she didn't have the strength to stop it.

"... I look for you in every corner waiting for something that never comes".

I need you, I want you back, but you don't listen to me. My heart screams at the top of my lungs and my eyes scream madly when you come near, but you don't listen to me.

I wait for you like a castaway for salvation. I express with gestures what my mouth is unable to recognize and I cry in silence when you leave me, but you do not listen to me.

I suffer for something I didn't seek. I curse over and over again the moment when my stupid heart decided that you were the sole owner of my desires. I despair at the thought of accepting that you are not mine and never will be. I lose myself in the darkness of an unrequited love, I throw myself into deep dark waters trying to conquer you, but you don't listen to me.

I wake up every day with the illusion that you do not exist and that my martyrdom is over like a bad dream of a small child, but my heart, bound and desperate, returns to look for you and find you.

No matter where, when or with whom you are, I look for you desperately because your perfume is my oxygen and your smile my breath to live, but you don't listen to me..."

Akim was writing in concentration when Nikola distracted him by entering the room. He was expecting someone else and his disappointment showed on his face.

-Have you started writing again? You haven't done it for years," he commented intrigued. How are you today?

-Well, I have been told that I will be discharged in a few days.

-That's cool! I'll throw a big party. Booze and good babes, all on me. You don't worry. He said as he sat down next to her on the bed.

Akim smiled half-heartedly. He didn't want any party, he was just waiting for her to walk through the door. He looked at the time and frowned. She said she'd be in around five. She hadn't arrived yet, had she regretted it?

Akim cursed himself for his doubts, he couldn't help them. The previous two evenings with Brenda by his side had turned out to be the best of bliss. Having her sitting next to him in the same bed was well worth a shot.

-Stop thinking about her.

-What are you talking about? -He answered distractedly.

-Whenever you talk or think about her, you always wear the same stupid smile. He confessed angrily.

-Don't start... -He chuckled as he heard the door to the room open.

-Is it possible?

A smiling Brenda entered with a large bag in her hand and Akim let out the best twinkle in his eye. He sat down trying to settle in and stretched the sheets with some nervousness. Ever since the day before she had left he had not stopped remembering her. He wanted to see her again. He needed to hold her close. He was unable to express in words what his heart felt when he saw her. His drafts were mere ink blots compared to the feelings that surged uncontrollably when he saw her. Nerves surfaced, his throat went dry and a strange current moved through his fingers.

Nikola made a sick dog face and left almost without greeting her. Barely a nod of his head before he slammed the door in the most obvious way.

-Angry? -he said, looking at the already closed door.

-I don't know and I don't care. What do you have there?

He commented pointing to the huge bag and Brenda smiled like an excited child.

-Not a good afternoon or what your day has been like.

Akim smiled mischievously and replied unabashedly.

-Good afternoon, Brenda, how was your day? You look beautiful. Now, what have you got in there? Is that for me?

She answered him with a huge smile and spread the bag on the bed. Akim sat up a little more and began to tear the wrapper. He was nervous. He couldn't remember when the last gift he had received had been. It was probably one from his mother. She had been dead too long to remember.

-I hope you like it... -he commented, biting his lip with obvious nervousness.

-It's... it's... -The man couldn't get over his astonishment. It's beautiful...

A beautiful Spanish guitar made of rosewood appeared underneath the bulky wrapping.

-But I...

The young man was unable to find the right words. In his country he had had one which of course was not half as pretty as this one. He had lost it in one of the many bombings.

-Do you like it? -she asked shyly.

-What if I like it? It's the most beautiful thing I've ever seen! I've never had anything like it... -He answered while caressing the soft wood and tuning the strings. But I don't understand. This is too much. I can't... How did you come up with this?

-Lucien... You see, it was given to me as a gift when I was in college. I never learned to play it. Well, not as well as I should. He answered gracefully.

Akim saw the light of amusement shining in her chocolate eyes and wanted to pounce and kiss her until there was no tomorrow, but he merely smiled at her with the same intensity with which his heart was beating.

-I guess you'll have to wait why... -I guess you'll have to wait why... Akim!

The man removed the bandage holding his bent elbow and freed his left arm to begin scratching at the ropes.

-You can't do that. If a doctor comes in, he will kill you. She said worriedly.

-Not to me, doctor, but to you who are the guilty one," she answered as she bent her head and extracted a beautiful melody from those tense strings.

-Would you blame me?

-Of course, stretched.

-Selfish child," she said with a giggle, and he joined her.

Akim continued to play as if the music was calling him. It had been so long since he had given free rein to his desires that he had almost forgotten to write his music. Supporting a son and a father was no easy task and did not leave much time for the arts.

Brenda sat on the bed pleased with herself. Seeing the man's joyful face was the best of payoffs. She watched him gaze raptly at the strings as he strummed them with enviable artistry. She admired him silently enjoying the moment and letting herself be carried away by the melody as he began to sing softly.

♪♫ I didn't want to love you and I couldn't help it

I thought I could defend myself, but you can't bind my heart.

I don't know my love what I'm doing looking for you....♫♮

He sang again in Spanish, as he had done at the party, and even though she didn't understand a word he was saying, the feeling he was conveying was so deep that her skin began to crawl. She didn't know a drop of Spanish and he seemed to love singing in that language. Brenda wanted to know what he was saying or why he was taking refuge behind Spanish to sing, but she kept quiet enjoying the beautiful melody. When he finished, she clapped her hands as his most fervent fan and Akim thanked her with a shy dip of his head.

-Why do you sing in Spanish?

"Because I can't tell you yet. Because I'm a coward."

-My mother was an aid worker in Cuba, you know about politics. She taught me. It's a language I instantly liked. She didn't lie at all.

-Were you very close to her?

-I'd rather change the subject. He commented, putting the guitar aside to rest it on the floor.

Brenda accepted his reply and began to tell him how the play was going and the hardships Samir was putting her through. She was joking freely and Akim was enjoying having her all to himself when the door opened wide with a smiling Nikola in the company of an explosive Lola.

"What is she wearing? Or, rather, what isn't she wearing?" thought Akim as he watched the young woman approach wearing something resembling a T-shirt cut just below her breasts and pants so tight that they looked more like stockings than jeans, but what really surprised him was a pair of heels with a hideous and terribly high platform. It was unnatural to be able to walk without hitting the ground. Yet, there was Lola, defying the laws of nature to spite him. No matter how many times he rejected her, she kept trying. She walked faster and jumped on the bed to embrace him, squeezing him against her breasts that cushioned the blow.

Brenda got up quickly so as not to be run over by the young woman, who didn't mind her presence in the least.

-Baby, you can't imagine how scared I was. He said loudly.

-I'm fine. He mumbled grumpily as Brenda stood watching them.

That girl hugged him like someone all too familiar and she was no inexperienced child to realize what those two had shared. A lump caught her throat and an incomprehensible ache settled in her chest. She shouldn't feel this way. She had a formed life, a complete home, and an incomparable professional accomplishment, and so why did she feel like crying?

In less than a minute she went from complete happiness to feeling like the ugliest, fattest, oldest woman on the face of the earth. She looked at the young woman with as much dissimulation as she could and discovered the impertinence of youth, one that she did not have. That girl would barely be in her twenties and that was a lot of years apart. Brenda felt that the weight of the years was like a great slab weighing heavily on her. She felt pain, shame and pity for herself. did she really think at any point that he might be interested in her? And what was she supposed to do if something like that was true? Would she leave a life, home and marriage to live a story destined to fail? No, she wouldn't. Many couples came to her office with similar doubts, and all the ones who took a chance on something crazy ended up going crazy. Without going any further, Michael Murray had lost his wife to a scorned lover. Lover? is that what I'm looking for? No! I'm not looking for anything, she thought, trying to fool herself.

Brenda reached for her purse to get out of there as soon as possible. She could no longer look at the image in front of her.

-I'd better leave you two alone. He said with extreme politeness.

-But you just got here. Akim spoke, pushing Lola's hands away from his body and trying to sit up in bed while protesting the pain of his shoulder wound.

-Honey, don't move. You're so strong, you look like a little baby. Lola spoke with amusement.

The luscious brunette leaned over him as a sign of helping him pick up the cushion, although in reality what she was doing was further embedding her breasts on his face.

"My life?" Akim was getting more and more annoyed. Brenda intended to leave, she looked uncomfortable, and if it hadn't been for the wound on her shoulder she would push Lola and throw her out the exit door.

Nikola, who was happy with the doctor's reaction, did not hide his smile. He was the one who put the icing on the cake, adding even more tension to the atmosphere.

-Dr. Klein, this is Lola, Akim's girlfriend, I guess you don't know each other.

The girl, delighted with her friend's description, jumped off the bed to sit up and kiss the woman twice, making her position clear, and Brenda accepted the strong embrace without saying a word.

Akim glared at his friend, but did not have the courage to deny his statement. He was too ashamed to cause any more scandal. Brenda was an educated, elegant woman and those two were behaving like two neighborhood boors.

-You don't know how grateful I am for your concern. We have been so afraid. Now that he's with me, I'm not going to let him do anything crazy again.

The young woman smiled determinedly making it clear who was the woman who was staying and who was the one who should go.

-I'm fine with that," she said as she tightened her grip on the handle of her purse. She never felt more humiliated than at that moment. She swallowed saliva and smiling with her best face of a polite, indifferent and cold woman, she spoke clearly.

-Now that you're in good hands, I'd better go," he said, patting his watch. It's late and I have a lot of work to do.

She was barely able to look him in the eye. She quickly made her way to the door when a thick, familiar voice stopped her just as she was about to jiggle the doorknob.

-Will you come tomorrow? -he asked pleadingly.

Brenda took a deep breath and installed the fakest of her fake smiles before turning to answer.

-I'm sorry, I have a very full schedule. It's a very complicated day, I'll see you some other time. Lola, nice to meet you, Nikola.... -she said, leaving as fast as her feet could carry her.

"We'll see each other..." Akim knew the meaning of that phrase very well. How many times had he been the one who had said them to get rid of the one he never wanted to see again?

The young man looked at Nikola's beaming smile and wanted to wipe it off. What the hell was wrong with him! He had never acted like this before with any other woman. She seemed to hate Brenda and what was worse, he was beginning to hate his best friend.

Day after day

Although the doctor suggested staying home for another week, he wasn't ready for a break. He needed to see her. He had not heard from her for almost three weeks and although many thought that distance meant oblivion, that was not what happened. Pain, rage, despair, addiction, those were feelings related to what he was going through. He sat on a visitor's bench located right in front of his office and waited. He looked for her as he had every day for the last few weeks, but she was not there. The office was locked up tight. Fury further dominated the man's sour temper. She should have arrived. She had to show up. He set aside an unwrapped sandwich and began to write. He was raging at the universe, his circumstances, and the mother who bore him. He hated his friend for taking Lola to the hospital, he hated that she told him she was his girlfriend, but mostly he hated her for being the root of all his woes.

"...don't go away, don't go away, not yet, not yet, not without first knowing my despair at not having you. Love, let me sing you the song my heart hums at the sight of you. Wait a moment, just a moment so I can tell you what I feel when I see your chocolate eyes caress my skin, let me explain how I melt when I see you.

No, please, I beg you, I implore you, do not leave me, not when I have not yet had the courage to tell you what you have done to my life. God! Forgive me, hate me, but don't leave me behind without first explaining to you how you have crossed my impassable boundaries. Your smile crossed any limit that my armor could sustain and your intelligence dazzled a blind virility that knew nothing else to do but surrender at the feet of your charms.

Honey look at me and find out how crazy I am for you. I don't feed, I don't sleep and I don't know how I still breathe. The days are endless weeks of a sun that no longer rises because you're not there. Come back, come back, ignore me if that's what you want, but don't take away my life that goes away the farther you go..."

Nikola approached without making any noise. Akim sensed his presence. He quickly closed his notebook, preventing him from reading anything. The only thing he was missing was more of that stupid advice that friends think they have the right to give, even if no one asks for it.

-I'm glad you're writing again....

Akim didn't answer, he simply reached out to tear the wrapper off his sandwich and start eating his lunch. At first he dismissed eating, now it turned out to be the perfect excuse to keep his mouth shut. He hadn't spoken to Nikola since the blissful afternoon when Nikola had decided to take Lola to the hospital and introduce her as none other than his girlfriend. Every time he remembered that moment and how Brenda ran away from him, he wanted to hang his friend with his own hands. They had known each other since they were little, they had lived through thousands of adventures and horrors together. They cried, laughed and became men together, but that didn't mean that Nikola could behave like a complete asshole by sticking his nose where no one had called him.

Akim bit into the tuna sandwich like a rabid dog ready to tear his prey apart. Three weeks had passed since the damned moment and the rage would not subside. Hatred was pouring out of his pores like an alien ready to strangle his loudmouth friend. She hated feeling this way but she couldn't help it. She was far away and someone had to pay.

Nikola sat next to him trying to calm some of his anger. He did not succeed. He knew Akim's dark character perfectly well and the rage that often managed to dominate him, but this was beyond any limit. He had never stopped talking to her for such a long time. Nikola tried to remember and the truth was that, despite his many blunders, his friend always forgave him. The young man snorted in annoyance and poked at his potato salad very reluctantly. That blissful woman was to blame for everything. She would end up pitting them against each other.

"What the hell has she seen him!" he thought irritably. She was pretty and by all accounts quite intelligent, but nothing comparable to Lola's luscious breasts.

Nikola chewed, shaking his head and not speaking. His friend was crazy. That doctor had driven him crazy. "Could that be it, could it be that being a psychologist she is able to dominate men's minds?" Nikola seriously thought about that possibility, though he dared not voice it aloud or Akim would skin him alive and without anesthesia.

-Are you going to talk to me at some point? - he asked between irritated and nervous.

Akim raised his head to look again at the empty office and went back to chewing another mouthful just as angrily as before.

-You can't take me away from you like this. We are brothers. He commented pityingly.

-We are not. He answered in a thick voice.

-That hurt.

-A brother does not stab.

-You were making a mistake, and you know it. That woman has disturbed your mind. For God's sake! That woman is...

-Don't even think about it. He warned between his teeth.

-Or what, Akim? Would you fight me for her? For a woman whose life is far away from yours and who is ca-sa-da.

-Go away," he muttered angrily.

-Brother, you're not like that. You've never fought for any woman, damn it! Why her? There are millions and very willing, why risk your head with such madness?

Akim did not answer, but not because he did not want to but because he could not. How to explain what has no explanation? Feelings don't, they just come when you least expect them and with whom you least want them. There they are, choking you inside like a long, thin needle that doesn't kill and hurts. Now I was able to understand what so many poets tried to capture in hundreds of sheets of paper moistened with their own tears.

The man dragged his hair back trying to regain the sanity he no longer possessed as a tremor of fear and hopelessness covered his heart.

-I can't... I can't... I can't... -He muttered exhausted and almost without thinking.

Nikola approached cautiously as he felt the warrior's armor begin to crack. His friend was a fighter of life and would come out of this with his help.

-What is it that you can't? What's going on brother? I can help you.

-No one can. He said with his body bent to the ground and holding both hands to the sides of his head.

-Trust me. We have come out of many together. Tell me what's going on?

-I'm in love. Totally, madly and madly in love," the young man continued with his head down, dominated by shame. I can't help it. I've tried everything to get her out of my mind. I can't. It's embedded here," he said, slapping his hand against his forehead, "If I don't see it I look for it, if it's not there I long for it, if it didn't exist my heart would invent it.

Nikola expected an explanation akin to a plot or a conspiracy, he would even have accepted witchcraft as a reasonable justification.

Any excuse would be more tolerable and less painful. What was he supposed to say to her? That was a relationship destined to fail. What would they be, lovers? Friends with bed rights? That at best. What made the man think that Dr. Klein would even deign to look at someone of lower social standing than the sewers of London itself?

She was nice and even seemed to care about them, but for heaven's sake! That woman would never have taken a cold shower or lit her meals with candles because her salary was not enough to pay the bills. They had lived through that and many other misfortunes. Days of searching for shelter, immigration paperwork and more paperwork, endless pleas and forms to get a dining scholarship for a motherless child. No, she would never live through half the injuries Akim had endured in his life. He was a young man but the experience of years is not always carried behind the wrinkles on his face.

Nikola took a deep breath and painfully said what he would not have wanted to say to a friend who is loved like a brother and who is fainting for his first love.

-You have to forget her. That road is not for you.

Akim looked up in pain. He was truly hurt. His friend never mentioned his humble origins and when he did it was always with joy and pride. Never as the closing of a door. Blue eyes as clear and transparent as springs filled with tears that he did not allow himself to release.

-And what is the path for someone like me?

-You know what I mean? -He replied, annoyed at having to show a reality that Akim also knew all too well.

-Say it. Don't be a coward," he roared angrily as he dragged his body on the bench to place his forehead almost next to his friend's. "Say it!

-It doesn't belong to our world, dammit! You know that. Even if he ever looked at you, you'd never get anything more than a roll in the hay. He'd sleep with you and abandon you like a stinking dog.

You think he'd leave one of the best architects in the country for a low-life bricklayer?

The young man stood up in a daze, not wanting to hear it. Truths are often too painful. He tried to walk away. Nikola continued to rage.

-Those kinds of women are not for us.

Akim lowered his shoulders in defeat. He turned his back on him because he didn't have the courage to look at him. Anger, pain, frustration, burned inside him.

Nikola also got up from the seat and continued talking from behind.

-I have no idea what hell you must be going through. You know me, I've never been in love for more than one night," he commented with little amusement in his voice, "it's best if you forget her. We can ask for a transfer. There may be another crew away from this building.

The young man in love felt the words like a bucket of cold water on a body feverish with love. To leave her just like that? Not to see her again? Not to say a last goodbye? Not to try? He considered himself an intelligent man, he may not have been able to finish school because of his circumstances, but he didn't feel like an idiot. He was hurting, in love and desperate. He could not consider himself defeated, not yet. He was an immigrant, a single parent, a breadwinner, with too much bitterness on his back. He was no coward. He may have been suicidal, but what man in love isn't?

He picked up his water bottle and the snack paper to throw it in the wastebasket when he heard his friend's annoyed voice.

-You're going to try." It wasn't a question.

-I'm sorry, she's the one I love.

-Fuck, then at least choose one with less com-pro-mi-sos! Find yourself a bland and boring doctor, but another one!

Akim smiled without amusement and with sadness in his eyes.

-She is the one I want.

Nikola cursed to the seven winds and loudly as Akim returned to work leaving him behind with his insults.

"Another bland and boring doctor?" He thought ruefully. "Not at all." Behind her polite and stuffy cloak, Brenda had proven herself to be many things, but by no means bland or boring. Funny, wry, intelligent, insightful and adorably attractive, those were indeed some of her qualities, boring? Not boring at all.

"Find me another one like her? Did she exist?" he thought as he walked. "Not for me anymore..."

You and I

He had been having a hard day. He tried to work hard trying to cheat a desperate heart. He had no luck. She was present in every second of his lost movements. He wanted to see her. It was not a request, it was a vital need. Twenty-three days without having her near, without being able to hear her voice was a hateful torture for a soul as much in love as his. He was about to leave when he wanted to check again her presence behind the glass. He was sure she would not be there. After all, he had been checking all day, every ten minutes to the minute. Brenda was not in his office and he had to leave. There was no point in staying there.

He looked up sadly thinking to say goodbye to a lonely office when he saw the shiny auburn hair moving behind a huge book she held interestedly in front of her face. Akim felt his breath catch the instant he saw her. Her little nose wrinkled trying to decipher who knows what was written there, and he wanted to reach out his hand to wipe away the small wrinkle on his forehead from his deep concentration.

A woman like any other, his friend had told him. If he only knew how wrong he was... She was like no other. A perfect combination of experience and beauty, that was Brenda Klein, capable of driving you crazy just by looking at her. Was she older than him? Yes, so what? Who measures the years more than one's own experiences, and he had more of those than anyone else. Married? Yes, so what? That only meant that someone else had come first, that didn't mark him as the loser.

He rapped his knuckles delicately on the glass and waited for her to illuminate his entrance with the preciousness of her gaze. By God, if he could only tell her how crazy she had him. He opened without waiting, he couldn't be another minute away from her company. The days without hearing from her turned out to be an eternity. He entered with desperation and a small touch of nervousness. Since Lola's cursed appearance at the hospital Brenda had not returned to the hospital nor had she taken any interest in his health. A small thorn of pain stuck in his chest. Instantly hope rose from the ashes like a phoenix ready to survive. What if Brenda's reaction had been based on jealousy? God, if only it were true....

How he would love to calm her doubts with hundreds of kisses. He would embrace her, tear off her clothes and make love to her until he convinced her that she was the only owner of his love. He would kiss her until her lips swelled and leave his teeth marks on every corner of her neck and then lick her until he reached the sensitivity of her breasts....

-You look great. She said somewhat confused as she watched him enter and close the door.

-Apparently...

Brenda watched him worriedly for any sign of serious injury. She had phoned every day to check on his condition and there was no mention of a relapse.

-Now it's better, but of course, since you didn't come back..." He commented without ceasing to stalk her with his eyes. He was looking for a reaction. He would cross the road, he would jump into the cliff, he would swim against the tides. Not letting her go, that was not a possibility. Not anymore. He found out when she interrupted his visits and the mornings became nothingness. Clock hands moving without destination. No, no matter whoever he might care for, he would fight for what did not belong to him and may God forgive him in the afterlife because in this one he would not apologize.

-I never imagined that your concern was limited to knowing whether he was dead or alive," he commented, feigning an anger he didn't really feel. Don't worry because I understand perfectly. A woman in your position is not in a position to waste her time on some insignificant bullet.

Brenda was starting to get annoyed with his statements. Akim was totally confused. She had indeed taken an interest in his injuries. She felt so stupid that she preferred to leave with her tail between her legs and her feminine pride in tatters.

-You were too busy to waste your time on a simple bricklayer..... -He continued to rack his brain.

Brenda watched him and felt herself dying. A part of her wanted to scream at him that it wasn't true, that she had remembered him from the first feeling of the morning to the last breath of the night. She tried to arrange the loose hair in her ponytail seeking serenity. If Akim wished to think the worst of her it might be for the best. It was already too painful to admit that a man much younger than you is taking away your sleep without any explanation.

-He commented, trying to provoke her to leave, and the young man cursed to himself. This was not the reaction he was looking for. He had to change his strategy and urgently.

-Have you heard from Murray? -She said as she diverted the conversation and leaned back on the patient's couch. The doctor shook her head unable to answer.

"What is he supposed to be doing?"

The young man groped the sides of the sofa with his palms verifying its excellent quality with a most mischievous smile in his eyes and she felt herself melt into the spot. His eyes were so crystal clear it was possible to swim in them. Her long body stretched into a relaxed position and she raised both arms above her head to cross them behind her neck leaving a wide view of her perfectly worked biceps.

"What's that?" he wondered as he saw the black color of a tattoo peeking out. She wanted to ask, tried to be interested. Every minute she spent by his side she wanted to get to know him a little more but again she didn't dare. They were nothing more than circumstantial friends. Time and differences would blow them apart like the wind to the leaves.

-Now I understand why people come to the psychiatrist. This couch is great for a little nap," he commented, smiling sideways and continuing to stalk her with his intense gaze, "or whatever comes up....

Brenda felt the heat rise up her back and wondered if this was something normal for women, after all she had never felt it before. Her hands were sweating, her heart was shaking rather than beating incoordinately, and words... words were hiding in the back of her throat, at least coherent ones. At least the coherent ones. What is he supposed to be doing? Am I interpreting correctly?

"No, it's not possible. It's just me being silly. He has a beautiful girlfriend, twenty thousand years younger. Brenda! You're silly. You look like a rookie." He thought conformist.

-Yes, and you are going to leave so that I can continue to take care of them. What's the matter, did Samir give you the day off today?

-No, but I can only do jobs without too much weight and I've done them all. He said cheerfully as he sat up on the couch to sit down.

-Well, I'm happy for you.

Brenda shifted, trying to find something to hold in her hands to conceal some activity before the young man's nervousness became apparent. His every movement was beginning to be exasperating to her feminine senses. What if the tension in his shoulders, what if his square jaw with a small dark beard a couple of days old, what if those sparkling eyes behind dense black lashes, what if those hands with long strong fingers clinging to the red leather of the couch.... God, if she wasn't so sure of reality she might come to think the man was performing the peacock strategy, yes, the one where he stretches out spreading his beautiful plumage to attract his female. Brenda shook her head and reached for some files trying to forget the stupidity of her thoughts.

-We had lunch together. It wasn't a question.

-I beg your pardon?

The man was already standing behind her so when she turned around they were face to face or rather face to chest because despite her heels he was still a few inches ahead of her.

She raised her head to look him in the eye and he ducked his head with the same intention. What neither took into account was the short distance. They were both a couple of lips away and although the right thing to do would have been to pull back, they did not. Their gazes clashed with deep messages. Neither was able to interpret them. The one was telling her how he felt, how he suffered for her while the other simply wondered why?

Akim was the first to speak up and separate himself by an inch.

-We'll eat together. You owe me. She said, her voice hoarse from the restrained caresses and the kisses not offered.

-I owe you? -Her sensual smile could not hide behind her usual mask.

-Yes," he replied angrily as he moved toward the door. For leaving me stranded.

Brenda felt angry at the situation. There they went again with their lack of sensitivity.

-Strengthen up with your girlfriend!

"What? What! God, what did I say..."

Akim smiled in delight and would have jumped with happiness were it not for the fact that she was at his back.

-At one o'clock. I'll pick you up, doctor.

He ordered without turning around and Brenda bit her lip, both angry at her clumsiness and surprised by his attitude.

Akim walked down the hallway with the most radiant of smiles as he closed his eyes when he met Nikola head on. "No, not again." He thought exhaustedly.

-I saw you," he said, pointing his head toward the office.

-Look how good it is. He answered trying to dodge him and continue on his way, but the latter stopped him.

-Are you going all out? -she asked as she held him by the shoulder to stop him.

The young man turned half sideways with a furious look on his face.

-Yes. Do you have an opinion? -he muttered through gritted teeth.

-I'm going to help you. Said a resigned Nikola.

Akim turned fully around to come face to face with his friend.

-You?

-Yes, we are friends," Nikola said firmly.

The young man froze for a moment with the news, but in a second he reacted by patting him on the back. Akim was his friend, his brother.

-But you know it won't be easy," Nikola said with a seriousness he never used to have.

-I know.

Nikola affirmed with an unconvinced nod of his head as they walked down the hall together.

-Thank you for understanding me.

-I don't understand you, I just support you.

Dreams

They were both walking through the park enjoying the beautiful spring day. She with shoes in hand enjoyed the warm sunshine while he walked up and down the stone curb that framed the immense lake. The flowers were happily displaying their beautiful palette of radiant colors while the pigeons were pecking at small seeds that had fallen from the leafy trees.

Akim watched her, recording every detail. Her loose hair snaked copper-reddish strands in the sun's glare. In her small hands she absentmindedly carried her shoes walking barefoot through the meadow like a child free from subjugation. She was radiant. She smiled without speaking, it was not necessary. Between them words were beginning to take a back seat. They spent the whole week together, when it wasn't for lunch they met for tea or dinner, the excuse didn't matter, they enjoyed each other's company. She talked about her family, her loneliness as an only child and her desire to help those in need with her therapies. He listened attentively, guarding every gesture on her face. He smiled at her shy forays into singing and died laughing at her exaggerated account of her failure in the performing arts.

Brenda sat in the meadow under the shade of a tree when he asked her intrigued.

-What lyrics did you sing? -he asked without answering.

-I should have known... -. She said regretting her confession.

-Come on, give me a name, I might know her.

-You're just saying that to make fun of me.

Akim sat down, sticking to her side and nudging her with his elbow.

-Come on...

-Ugh, okay, but keep in mind that she was a giggly young lady and...

264

-You were going for the vein-ripping love ones," he replied, laughing his head off.

-I'd better shut up.

-No way. Now more than ever. Either tell me the name or sing it.

-There were many...

-I want the most important one for you.

-I don't have any. Akim raised his eyebrow in disbelief, and she snorted wearily.

-All right... all right, but if you become deaf...

-I'll blame you. He said amused and she replied with a smile on her lips.

-I expected nothing less.

Brenda started to sing any song to trick him, but he knew instantly and asked for the real one.

Akim thought her notes could not have been more uncoordinated and her voice less melodious, although he had never witnessed such a delightful spectacle. His little chocolate eyes sparkled with excitement at the song as his hands moved, perfectly interpreting feelings that couldn't have been more accurate.

Akim lay back on the grass enjoying the most wonderful of landscapes. Her hair swayed casually in the breeze of the wind and there was no one else but her. At what point had it happened? When had she become the center of his illusions? How to be so in love with a woman you haven't even kissed? The young man wondered silently, recognizing that no answer mattered anymore. He had never tasted her lips and did not know her deepest secrets. He never heard the moan of her passions, nor knew the soft touch of her breasts between his rough hands, that didn't matter for his heart to beat desperately for her. He did not know her kisses, but he knew he would kill for them.

-What did you think?

-Fatal. He replied, stretching out on the grass and crossing his hands behind his head.

They both smiled and Brenda enjoyed the view. Feeling Akim so relaxed took her into a world she had never allowed herself to feel.

With Max everything was so different. At first he might have let himself go, but then work, routine and commitments made them walk a path of sanity and education where every move was the planned one. Dinner at eight, alarm clock at seven, out with friends on the first Saturday of the month, sex on Saturday night and fifteen minutes before bedtime. How long had it been since she had been with him the way she was with Akim?

-I'm losing you.

-I beg your pardon?

-You were far away. He answered hurt. She wanted to deny it. She couldn't.

-What's on your mind? -He asked, hoping it was something related only to him.

Brenda knew there was nothing wrong with it. Max was her husband and he knew she was married, but as if it were an unspoken contract, when they were together neither of them mentioned it.

-That tattoo," he said, pointing to his shoulder, trying to divert the conversation in other directions, "what does it mean?

Akim pulled up the short sleeve of his shirt to leave his shoulder fully exposed for her.

-It is a feather. It symbolizes the freedom I felt when I arrived here.

Brenda waited a few seconds before speaking to him.

-You and a small child in another country, with no resources, I imagine what you must have gone through.

Akim looked up and Brenda could see his gaze melt into the clear sky. His eyes as deep and clear as the sunrise itself were lost in the firmament as he began to speak unhindered.

-We had no future. Food was scarce. Adults crying over dead loves and children playing among soldiers disguised as friends. I didn't know what to do. One day I was preparing to study at the university and the next I became a single father trying to escape. I searched, asked and begged. There was no acceptance form for someone like me. When you are neither a politician, nor a singer, nor a writer, nor anything important, you become a simple refugee waiting for a permit that never comes. I followed the only way I knew how. We hid, ran and fled without caring where. I was ready to do anything to get freedom for Lucien.

-And for you.

-My life mattered little to me until...

-Until?

Akim was not about to reveal all his cards.

Although feeling her by his side had led him to talk more than he should and that had proved liberating he couldn't scare her away with his outbursts of sincerity.

-Are you trying to analyze me, doctor?

-It's not that.

Brenda reddened because the truth was that her curiosity was far from professional interest and Akim wanted to hug her, sorry to see the embarrassment on her face. If it were up to him, he would tell her his whole life story if it would keep her by his side.

-I promise to tell you everything you want to know, on one condition," he said gently as he stood up and helped her to her feet.

-Which one? -she said when she saw that he did not continue.

-May you never deny me.

-I would never do such a thing. I don't care about your origins, we're... friends. She answered doubtfully.

-Don't deny me, please. He stammered tenderly.

-I don't know what you're talking about? Deny yourself to whom?

-I don't know yet.

They both walked through the park on their way to the office. Brenda would pick up her bag and run off. What was a simple after lunch walk turned into a full afternoon. She wanted to regret it by thinking about what a married woman should or should not do, but she could not. The propriety that always accompanied her had left her and she felt delighted. She had enjoyed herself as never before. He opened his most painful memories to her and she cradled them like the most delicate of treasures. They both had a magical moment that, even if it would never be repeated again, she would nestle in his heart until the end of her days.

-Thank you. He said stopping in front of his office door.

Akim watched her curiously and she responded with the sweetest of smiles.

-For trusting me.

-I would trust you with my life if you wanted it. He said and left without waiting for an answer.

She may not have been a young girl and she had not been receiving the attentions of a man for some time, but Akim's signals were proving too clear to ignore. "What to do?"

The young man walked towards the exit when he discovered Nikola standing next to his motorcycle smiling wickedly at him.

-What happens now? -he asked amused as he put on his helmet.

His friend simply stretched out an invitation card and handed it to him.

-What is this?

-Samir handed it to me. It turns out that tonight is George Carrington's birthday party.

-I know. He replied annoyed. Brenda talks about it a lot. And he hated not being able to be by her side.

-Apparently it occurred to the lady that a representative of the crew might be present and Samir handed it to me.

-And you're giving it to me?

-I understand that a certain doctor will be attending all alone.

Akim opened his eyes expectantly when Nikola stated deadpan with laughter.

-What would become of you without me!

-I don't follow you," he replied nervously, waiting for clarification.

-You just tell me, do you want to be at that party alone with her? Yes or no?

-Fuck, yes.

-Then put the little card away and put on your best clothes.

-Nikola, are you sure? -Akim held the envelope with trembling hands.

-She'll be alone, leave it on my account.

Nikola slapped him on the back and Akim hugged him gratefully. The young man ran off after the bus that was just passing in front of him, but not before shouting at him.

-I fix everything!

Akim wanted to ask what the hell his friend was up to, but he couldn't, he was too happy with the news. A whole night to have her at his full disposal. That was too much to ask to spoil it with questions. He had to run before Sastrería Fino closed. That was if the owner would take care of him. After the disaster of the last suit, the old man said that not even the down payment would pay for the mess.

Akim hopped on the bike hopefully, the last thing he cared about was a cranky clotheshorse. Life was smiling at him and he didn't plan to waste it.

I will catch up with you

Akim entered the huge hall with a lump in his throat, and the tie was not the cause. The Carringtons could not have chosen a more dazzling and impressive site than this. Columns like giants held up walls decorated with the finest Italian stucco that could have been seen outside of Italy. Freshly polished mirrors reflected a tide of people that could not be real. Women in their best clothes strolled from one side to the other sparkling while they, impeccable and spotless, smiled politely at banal conversations.

The young man went in hard because, although nerves consumed him, it was not in his nature to let himself be cowed into cowardice. A few thousand more than his annual salary may have been wasted there, but he was no skittish boy. The noise of bombs and whole nights in the cold, and the heavy rain covered in worn, overcrowded green tents had taught him enough about the strength of courage.

He walked around looking for someone he did not see. A waitress with a wide smile and a more than professional interest offered him a drink and waited a few seconds looking for a proposition that did not come. Akim moved in disbelief and the woman did not cease her provocative glances. Could it be that she had recognized his humble origins despite his impeccable appearance? He stormed off with his defeatist thoughts leaving behind a waitress disgusted by the rebuff.

He walked and looked over the top of his glass as he took small sips of the soft drink trying to find the only sense of being there. And she didn't show up.

She leaned against the wall and looked at her reflection in one of the large mirrors regretting the expense of the rent. He had done everything for her and the woman was nowhere to be found. He had gone through everything, the two lounges, the main terrace and even found himself insulted by a lady as he peeked in the door of the ladies' room, but nothing. She was not present. He looked at the clock on his cell phone that was screaming at him that it was time to leave and stop waiting like a fool. He gulped down his third drink and was about to walk away when the sound of her laughter made him turn around like a shipwrecked sailor at the song of her siren.

Brenda was laughing with two other women and some men. She hadn't seen him but he had and she felt faint. Could such a woman exist? Her deep red dress could not be described. It was simply perfect. But it wasn't her fabrics, nor the perfect updo of her hair leaving a long, sinful neck in sight that attracted him like a bee to her flower, no, it wasn't her physique, she was so much more. There was something different about her doctor. She was authentic in her declarations and anger, she had no double standards like the others. He wanted to approach her, talk to her ear and confess to her what his heart no longer wanted to keep quiet. He wanted to explain to her that she was the dream of his long nights and the hope of his desolate mornings when other hands, not his own, rested possessively on his small back.

Akim watched as she turned sideways to listen and nodded her head to her companion and it took little for him to break the cup with the pressure of his hand. He knew jealousy was stupid and irrational, she belonged to another and he should accept it as part of a competition he brought upon himself, but he could not. His blood ran like burning lava through his veins. His heart gurgled with fury on all four sides.

Max wasn't supposed to be with her, tonight was supposed to be just for him. This would be a chance to walk a new path. He had so many things to tell her. He needed to awaken her most hidden feelings. She already doubted, he knew it, he had felt it in all those little moments he had managed to steal from her. It was time for the big step. He had to come clean and awaken her to a world of desires he knew she had forgotten. Brenda was sincere, transparent and passionate, he knew it and he wanted to be the one to awaken her to life again. He would make her vibrate with his caresses. They had looked at each other, sincere and flirted. This would be the night he would go further. His words would say much more than their looks. If she let him, they would do more than talk, he just needed that chance.

He thought himself fully prepared to fight her uptight husband, but he knew perfectly well that this was not the time. He was in no position to make her choose between the two, not yet. Annoyed, angry and choked, he tugged his tie tightly and tossed it into a nearby planter. He needed air. He couldn't breathe. The more he saw it near his love, the more he hated it.

He unbuttoned the first two buttons of his shirt and walked to the terrace desperate to light a cigarette. He had promised himself to quit. It was clear that this would not be that night. With his thumb and forefinger he held the fag, taking puff after puff as he let the smoke mask some of his discomfort. Her heart was breaking with his every caress on her slender back. She couldn't help but stare at them. He searched desperately for a sign that she didn't want him, that she wanted to be free of her husband. He did not find it. Brenda was talking to the group so animatedly that he wanted to walk up to her and snatch her right away. He wanted her for himself and no one else. He did not want to share her.

She continued to puff on the cigarette again and again and again when something caught her attention. Max, the husband, the architect, the perfect one, was concentrating on a phone conversation. For a few minutes he turned away from the group. When he cut off he took her by the elbow and pulled her aside to talk to her.

She gritted her teeth hating jealousy every time he brushed against her.

Brenda looked at him nodding, then Max left under the insistent observation of Akim who followed him with his eyes until he saw that he was leaving. He was leaving, at this hour, how and why? He was confused by the turn of events when one person came to his mind and he silently thanked. Nikola, I owe you big time.

Like Lazarus after the command of Jesus Christ, Akim felt revived from the dead. It was not that he was a believer, much less after the life he had lived, but if believing in God gave him opportunities like this, then welcome, because he needed them, and many of them. With recovered optimism, he waited for the right moment and it came when she walked away towards the canapés table. He walked slowly until he positioned himself behind her back like a wolf after its prey. He took a deep breath, intoxicating himself with the scent of jasmine, vanilla and her skin, when he spoke in a husky tone.

-Good night...

Wake up

The gravelly voice startled her so that as she turned she collided with a hard torso that held her by the shoulders to keep her from thrashing. Akim smiled brightly and she felt herself staggering again. He was managing to provoke in her an unbecoming instability in a lady. Never before had she felt so helpless, excited and disoriented in equal parts. They both looked at each other between nervous and excited about a night that had just begun.

Nothing could be better. Brenda was totally, absolutely and exclusively theirs. They smiled and gave each other hidden glances that only they were aware of. No one noticed their complicity. But there she was, like a sweet perfume enveloping them in the softest of her mists.

The night reflected on her face, she looked tired. A little more... a little more... he thought enthusiastically as he enjoyed watching her go out and admire the light of a radiant full moon in gardens he would never forget.

-It's beautiful... -She murmured in rapt attention as she looked up at the sky.

"You sure are," he thought as he watched her luscious shadow reflected in the green meadow.

Her tender figure rested on the stone railing with both hands admiring the horizon as if begging him to reach out to her. If only she knew that he would give her one by one each of those stars if she asked him to.

"If you knew that my world changed the day you looked at me for the first time. If you knew that my future stopped being a blank canvas from the moment your skin brushed my body. If you knew...

274

You would know, and may the sky be with me because today you will know".

The coolness of the night enveloped her. Brenda did not move. Her body glued to the railing asked her to extend those minutes forever. She had laughed, enjoyed and forgotten in equal parts. Forgotten who she was, what she expected and mainly what she owed.

Akim moved closer and could feel her warmth long before the strong chest brushed against his back. He closed his eyes taking a deep breath. He knew it would happen. He knew it the very moment he heard her deep, deep voice amidst the din. She asked her reason to subdue the treacherous one in her body. Her legs stopped in place and her smile gave him the most pleasant of welcomes, she was always like that and she would be a fool to deny it. She knew she had to leave, to get away from there, she had to run into the cold distance, she had to think about the mistakes and their consequences, she had to put an end to what had no beginning, but how to do it when a new and unknown energy runs through your veins screaming at you that you are alive, telling you that what you thought was lost, is there, with you, in your body, vibrating desperate to get out.

The man's strong hands gripped her waist and his moist lips burned her with their simple touch on a bare nape of her neck that stretched wanting to receive so much more.

She didn't move, she didn't open her eyes, perhaps thinking that by doing so she would be less guilty, who knows, maybe she simply wished to feel desired, at this point Akim cared little about the reasons. She was in his arms and his lips slowly and delicately traced each piece of her sweet neck. He held her life in his arms and did not intend to let go. Encouraged by her reaction, his hands moved to her belly enveloping her in a tight, possessive embrace while his mouth no longer disguised any of his kisses. His tongue savored every nook and cranny until it reached her ear and that delicate earring that barely hung down moved nervously with his kisses. He caressed, kissed and naughtily bit that delicate lobe, but it wasn't until continuing down her chin and hearing her moan as he brushed the corner of her lips that he could no longer bear it. His strong hands held her tightly and turned her to face them body against body, face against face.

When Brenda opened her eyes and Akim saw the sweet haze of passion envelop her then he knew he was lost. His moments of gentleness and waiting were over. He wanted her more than anything in the world and she wanted him. He saw it in her little chocolate eyes melting with desire, in her hands clinging to his shoulders, she needed him and he would give it to her. Passion, stars and life, he would lay it all at her feet. The whole world, with its pros and cons, he would give it all to her. His heart was pounding, his hands clutched tightly around her waist fearing to lose her, and his lips moistened eagerly at the delicious sweetness he would receive. He lowered his face and enraptured by the most tender lips he had ever felt, he sank into a mouth that received him expectantly.

Their lips caressed each other tenderly while their shy tongues were surprised to think they knew each other. Their bodies trembled wrapped around each other wishing that time would stop and the world would stop spinning.

Brenda could barely breathe. The kiss transported her to a world of fantasies that many spoke of and to which she no longer belonged. That world where the heart beat much stronger, the body loosened and the blood melted with its ardor wherever it went.

-Brin... look at me... Open those little eyes for me... Please do.

Brenda refused like a little girl and Akim wanted to kiss her. And he did.

His mouth possessed her firmly saying all that her words had not yet done. He heard her moan and sank even deeper into a sweet, wet mouth that made him tremble with passion. He stroked her chin with his finger as he kissed and nibbled her neck and the corner of her lips. God, that woman was pure feminine essence. She had him crazy with desire. She made him become the wildest of men, the one who wanted her all to himself and only to himself.

-You have to look at me," he said playfully as she closed her eyes tightly. Stretching her face back to give him better access to the smoothness of her skin, "You know you're going to have to look at me at some point.

-No. I can't... - He answered with embarrassment.

-Brin, this was going to happen. We couldn't go on like this. There's something between us, you know it.... -he said tenderly as with each word he continued his onslaught of kisses and caresses all over her face.

-I can't... no...

Brenda wanted to say many things. No single idea was transformed into a coherent sentence. Every brush of his lips distracted her and dragged her into that unknown and wonderful world.

-I can't... I mustn't... -he said over and over again.

Akim began to feel fear overpower him. She did not reject him, her delicate moans encouraged him to more, but her words drilled his courage. He could not lose her. This was his chance to show her that between them there was something that could be true and deep if she took the risk.

-Precious, look at me. I am here, you know who I am. I need you to recognize me... please look at me.

Akim stopped his kisses and waited anxiously. That look was everything. It would mean a sweet beginning or the worst of his defeats.

Brenda shivered just imagining it. If kissing him was terribly good she didn't want to think what it would be like to melt into that transparent sea gaze. The one that calmed down every time he looked at her. Yes, now she knew. Akim relaxed by her side and she smiled without prejudice next to him. She tremblingly caressed his wet lips swollen from kisses as Akim kissed the corner of her lips again pleading almost on the verge of desperation.

-Look at me, Brin, look at me and tell me what you see.

-I'm afraid." He murmured with his head down and accepting her delicate caresses on his face. This is not right. She said unconvinced.

Akim felt the ground crack under his feet. No! He would not accept defeat for the sake of duty. Not now. Not after feeling her body cling to his and tasting that honey mouth. Not now.

-What's wrong? That I'm getting crazier about you every day? -He said caressing her face, "Or that I can't stop kissing you?

Akim tormented her with small caresses of his lips running down her neck and face as confusion overwhelmed her.

"It's not right, it's not right," he thought as he prayed to heaven to know why his heart was beating wildly. She thought and thought and thought, she had no courage. He claimed to look at him, but she knew what would happen and refused to acknowledge what her body was screaming out loud.

-I can't...I can't...

Akim was going to continue his counterattack ready to achieve victory. She felt it in her body. She was melting in his arms. He just needed a little boost and he was ready to give it to her.

-He said no.

Brenda was ready to look at him when a thick, angry voice brought her back to reality the hard way. Connor.

Akim cursed at the interruption and although he didn't turn back, he didn't have to see it to know that the meddlesome Scotsman was in his life again. Always present where he was not invited.

-You should leave. He said annoyed and without releasing his strong grip on Brenda's waist.

-He said no." He repeated again, this time with more energy and more anger.

-I must go. The woman tried to break free, but her captor would not allow her to do so.

-Not yet, Brin," he said, his voice cracking. We need to talk.

Brenda raised her eyes to look at him as he had asked. She did not offer him what he sought. She spoke calmly and confidently.

-I can't." She put her small hands over his, who was still holding her waist, silently asking him to let go.

Akim acceded to her request as she muttered again this time more quietly before leaving.

-I can't...

Theft?

-Don't go near her again.

Connor was cursing and threatening him, but Akim wasn't listening. His sight was lost behind her. He had her. He had had her and like a spring through his fingers she had slipped away. He cursed over and over again his damn luck, life, and God who never listened to him.

He wanted to follow her, but his friend's cabinet stood in his way and although he thought he was capable of knocking it over he knew that such a fight would be sufficiently scandalous to attract the curious glances of more than one of the stuffy guests. No, he wouldn't do that. He wouldn't embarrass her. Brenda had seen in him the man he was not and wished he was for her.

-You are going to disappear from his life.

Akim looked up and Connor discovered the fury with the same color of sky.

-I won't.

-You will do it or I swear...

Connor approached menacingly. He did not touch him. Their faces looked millimeters away from each other like raging bulls ready to fight. Neither of them took a step. They both knew where they stood.

-Are you going to kill me? Then you'd better start soon because, even if you send me to hell, I'll be back again and again. And yes, I'll be back for her if that's what you're wondering.

-You asshole. roared the Scotsman between his teeth so as not to cause a scandal.

-You're not discovering anything new," he replied reluctantly.

Akim moved in punching shoulder to shoulder and trying to get the painter to let him out of there without a fight. Connor moved to the side allowing him to pass. At the last moment he grabbed him hard by the arm causing him to turn around in a rage.

-Let go of me. He barked between his teeth.

-If you think you have feelings for her, leave.

Akim jerked his arm from side to side to get loose, and looked at him with a mixture of fury and disappointment, that Connor felt sorry for him.

-Not that I believe it. I'm sorry.

-I won't take my eyes off her. Connor replied threateningly.

-Then you will see me soon.

Akim stormed off. Who was he to tell her what or with whom to feel! She had been in his arms, had moaned with his kisses and would have acknowledged his feelings if it hadn't been for his asshole friend.

He picked up his helmet and left. She was gone and that party no longer made sense to him. Excitedly he looked at her hand that hid a precious earring that he removed with his own lips. He accelerated his two wheels and sped off with a smile on his lips. He was close, very close.

Brenda showered and wrapped in the fluffy robe hoping the water and coffee would tell her it was all the fruit of a dream.

Max came in at that moment visibly tired and terribly angry.

-So nothing serious? - he asked, hiding his face behind his mug.

He had left due to a call from the police.

-Just a few broken windows. We had to verify the damage and file a report. He commented as he took off his shirt and threw it on the bed. They were probably vandals, I don't understand why they broke the windows and didn't take anything. They did it just to annoy me and make me lose the night at the police station. He said taking off his shoes.

Brenda nodded at his side. Who would break the windows in an office like Max's just like that?

-I'm dead," he said, hugging her around the waist. I'm taking a shower and I'm going to sleep for a while. Don't you mind?

-It's still too early. It's still too early.

Max noted that it was barely dawn and nodded with a yawn.

-How was the party? -He asked before turning on the faucet and stepping inside.

-Nothing special. He replied, closing his eyes and trying to forget what he could not.

Brenda paced up and down the room looking for an explanation to a situation that was upsetting her more and more. How could she be so oblivious? Had she learned nothing in her practice? Didn't she know that crazy things only led to more crazy things? Was she so stupid as not to discern between reality and stupidity?

She was furious with herself. What woman in her right mind would do such a thing? She remembered the warmth of his lips and shook her head in denial over and over again. It wasn't possible. Akim and she lived in different worlds. Their universes were opposites. Nothing united them. Everything was differences: their youth, their social environment, their jobs.... So why did her heart beat wildly when she remembered him? And why did she keep reminiscing about him over and over again? His memory assaulted her over and over again without giving her a break. His face was reflected in the coffee, on the computer keyboard, on the pages of a book. Always there, stalking her with his hard gaze. She was distracted by the landscape of the garden in the huge kitchen window, but Akim resurfaced again, this time in the blue of the lavender.

"He always is." She thought perturbed and with the tear about to fall rolling down her cheek. She had to stop this madness, how?

She was an intelligent woman, she considered herself a professional psychologist, she knew the human mind better than anyone else, so why didn't she feel able to heal herself.

Max appeared with the smile of the rested and guilt instantly overcame her. Any woman would kill for a man like that and she kept thinking of a crazy thing that would make her do crazy things. This wasn't right, she wasn't right.

-So it's okay with you?

-I think so... -. She answered doubtfully.

-I think? -he said intrigued.

-Well yes, why not?

-Great. After all you've been through you need it and I'll be glad to.

Brenda smiled, feigning an eagerness she didn't feel.

-Then I'll tell Cintia to book you for Monday itself. Will that give you time to get organized?

-Yes. He answered without further explanation.

Max looked at his watch in disgust. I have to pack my suitcase. I leave at eight o'clock. I'll have dinner on the plane.

-You're leaving on a Sunday? You've only been home for a couple of hours?

-I have a meeting first thing Monday morning, then I'll get organized. I promise," she kissed him on the forehead, "Will you take me to the airport? That way we'll have some extra time for you to tell me all the party gossip.

Brenda took a deep breath, hiding a guilt that even in the worst of her nightmares she never thought she would feel.

I cannot

She checked her small suitcase, both nervous and excited. In a few hours she would be in Paris with Max. They would spend the whole week together. She would rest from a year full of endless therapies and hopefully forget the one she couldn't, she told herself annoyed as she folded the blue wool sweater, as blue as her eyes...

Brenda shook her head as she zipped up. She had to accept her mistakes, that didn't mean she couldn't get back on the lost path. A kiss, it was just a stupid kiss, she said over and over out loud to herself as the doorbell rang loudly and in a moment her mind snapped back to the present and she smiled in amusement.

-Since when do you use the door? -He thought as he remembered that Rachel always slipped through the garden door into the kitchen.

She opened smiling when she knew that her good intentions to forget had vanished. There he was. Wearing a simple black T-shirt, worn jeans, and disheveled hair because of a recently abandoned helmet.

-We need to talk. He said, feigning a calmness he didn't feel.

Akim waited for her all day. He looked again and again at the office waiting for her to appear. She did not come. He rehearsed thousands of speeches and used hundreds of words, but they all stuck when he saw her face to face. If he found her attractive before, now she was radiant. Those jeans, those three open shirt buttons, and that silky hair lying on her delicate shoulders. That was too much.

He spent the whole of Sunday reminiscing about the softness of her skin and caressing an earring that still held her perfume. He imagined she was by his side and thought he was going crazy knowing it wasn't his bed he was sharing. He needed to wake her up. She had feelings for him and he was ready to prove them to her.

-You didn't go to the office today, and I... We need to talk. He said firmly.

They both looked into each other's eyes and Brenda felt herself trembling from head to toe. Akim was eating her with his eyes and knew perfectly well that her body was responding to him.

-Pasa.

The woman closed the door and leaned against the wood before turning and facing her own decisions. Taking courage she turned to face the truth when in a single movement Akim imprisoned her in his arms and kissed her with an ardor and desperation he had not shown the night before.

She tensed up trying to refuse. She had to run away.

-No... please... -He begged as best he could.

Akim was ready for anything. She might not be alone at home, he didn't care about that anymore. It might even be what he wanted.

He deepened the kiss even more energetically. He wanted to show her how much he had missed her, how empty he felt without her and how his body trembled at her touch. Their tongues fought with passion and a lot of anger. Rage of feelings that shouldn't exist. Their teeth clashed and Akim smiled triumphantly as he noticed her desperation matched his own. Brenda needed him the same way he needed her. He held her by the waist and carried by some sort of higher power lifted her up and leaned her against the door leaving their heads at the same height. He wanted to eat her, taste her, feel her and arouse her.

His mouth ran passionately over her from lip to neck as his strong arms lifted her off the ground as if on a cloud inhabited only by the two of them.

-When I didn't see you in your office.... -I felt like I was dying....

-Akim... I...

-If you're going to lie, don't speak," he commented gently, "You want me as much as I want you, and I'm not willing to accept any lies.

Their mouths collided again and Akim's ever-tightening grip lifted her off the ground as if her body was flying next to his. to lie? Yes, that was her first intention upon seeing him. To deny everything she could deny, now, here in his arms, lies had too short a run.

Did I want to? Of course I did, but should I?

-Please...please...please." He begged for some sympathy.

-No, don't think, just feel," he said, dragging her to a sofa and letting his body fall on hers. Feel what you do to me when you are close, feel how you tremble in my arms.

Akim spoke and a cloud of unconsciousness enveloped her, taking her to that world she thought lost or non-existent. There everything was sensations. There a deep and suggestive voice promised to awaken her to an unknown universe that she desperately desired. She closed her eyes ready to fly wherever he wanted and accepted his body to dominate her for the first time in her life. Enveloped in a sea of sensations, she listened to a man talk to her and tell her so many marvels that she felt the most beautiful of women. No one had ever, ever, whispered so much affection and sweetness to her with simple words.

-You drive me crazy. You are beautiful. The softest skin. The sweetest mouth.

Akim spoke without being able to silence what his heart was screaming unrestrainedly. He had been loving her in the solitude of his room for so long that having her here, under his body, and with his shirt half open was driving him crazy.

His body tensed screaming desperate to possess her. He slipped his hand down her cleavage, afraid of damaging her smooth skin with the roughness of his hands. This was heaven. His chest hardened interested in her caresses and he was on the verge of fainting with pleasure. He looked up wanting to remember every detail of his passion when he saw her and felt himself dying of bliss. Her eyes were open and she was looking at him just as he had asked her to the night before. There were no eyes more delicious than those. Chocolate melted by a passion that clouded his reason. A passion that he was capable of awakening and that almost made him howl with happiness. Maddened by her response, he threw himself desperately on her body to nibble at her wherever he passed when a shrill voice from the kitchen woke him from his most lustful sleep.

Brenda tensed instantly and Akim knew his moment was over. He lifted her as if she weighed nothing and laid her on the floor trying to calm uncontrolled breathing while Brenda stroked her hair nervously.

-And they don't go and tell me only twenty kilos? What do they want me to do, walk naked through Paris?

Connor and Rachel were walking through the kitchen door into the living room smiling when the smile was wiped from the Scotsman's lips to give way to a scowl of displeasure.

He and Brenda were standing in front of the couch without looking at each other. Rachel kept moaning without being aware of anything, but Connor had noticed it in her nervous hands and in their misaligned hair. The situation was going from bad to worse.

Connor greeted her friend ignoring the guest and Rachel, who would not shut up, kissed her enthusiastically.

-Sweet, won't you have room for one of my little things? -Rachel asked with a laugh.

Brenda shook her head almost without answering. She was still in shock and her heartbeat was impossible to slow down.

-It would be just a couple of dresses, for the night. You know how Paris is. Demand the best and we'll be the best of the best.

Akim who so far looked like a painted figure, walked two steps to ask him in a direct way without caring about the presence of the others.

-Are you traveling?

Rachel, who had not even noticed the young man's presence, replied haughtily.

-What are you doing here? -she asked curiously. She instantly seemed to find the answer herself. Max sent you? I get it, you're carrying our bags. I think that's great because I hate tugging on those things.

-Rachel, Akim is not here for that," Brenda replied with barely a voice.

-Oh no? Well, I don't care and I don't give a damn. I'll go up to your room and you can keep this little present. After all, we are on our honeymoon and we can't be shy. She said pointing with her eyes to the black satin nightgown she was holding in her hands while she headed for the stairs.

-Honeymoon? - he asked almost out of breath.

-Yes worker, we are going to Paris to enjoy our darlings. He said happily as he went up the stairs.

-Are you leaving?

Akim felt his heart shattering into hundreds of unrecoverable pieces. Only a few minutes ago she was moaning in his arms and he imagined something awakening between them, when the truth was that he had planned a direct escape with the one he hated more and more.

Connor was about to answer when Brenda stopped him with her hand on his chest.

-Please leave us alone.

-Not a chance. -Why is he here? Brenda, this isn't like you. You must be...

He was about to continue his speech when his friend stopped him in an authoritative voice.

-I know perfectly well what I should or should not do. I have known my duties of conduct since I was a child, and it will not be you who comes to give me moral advice.

Connor shut up instantly. It had been many years since he had seen this Brenda. The one who raised her voice without caring who heard her. The one who wouldn't take advice from anyone she shouldn't and who wouldn't let herself be manipulated. I was totally amazed.

-I'll be close by. He said more in support than as a threat, and she understood him as such.

Akim, who kept looking into her eyes, wanted an explanation, he was looking for something that would give him hope. Her gaze did not bode well or at least not for him.

Brenda approached knowing that her words would dictate sentence and she was not convinced if she was really acting justly, that no longer mattered. Akim deserved freedom and she represented a prison that would end up destroying him.

-Don't say it," he anticipated as he walked nervously. You're going to regret it. Don't say it.

Tears tried to well up in her eyes. He would not allow it. He had to feel the robustness of her decision. It didn't matter what she did or didn't begin to feel. Whatever it was that was started, it had to stop. This was a path that would lead them both to destruction and although she wasn't sure how she would save herself, right now her only concern was him. She raised her head with that assurance of women who knew their duty and with the greatest pain in her soul spoke to him with all the coldness and haughtiness she was able to bear.

-I am sorry for having confused you and I understand that you do not understand me, I am obliged to make it clear to you that between us....

-Don't do it... -He roared in pain.

Akim stopped her as with two strides he reached over to grab her by the shoulders.

-Don't do it. You promised. Don't deny me.

Brenda remembered the one she had made weeks ago and now took on the worst meaning.

-You say what you should, not what you feel. Give me a chance. Give us a chance. Our destinies are in your hands.

-I can't.

Akim approached her trying to kiss her, she turned her head away refusing his caresses. She knew perfectly well the power that his kisses had over her body and she could not allow it. The man tried a second and a third time but this time she not only refused with her face but said what he didn't want to hear.

-Nothing exists or will exist between us. We are from different worlds. Did you think I would give up everything for you? -Her heart was torn for being so stupidly harsh, but it was the only way she could think of to set it free.

Akim felt a dagger thrust straight into his heart to break him from the inside. His hands fell defeated to the sides of his body and the hopes of a life with her died at that very moment. She would never gamble on a man like him. There was the blissful reality.

-You're not like that. You're not... -. He said madly looking for an explanation.

Brenda felt tears starting to well up in her eyes so she opened the door silently asking him to leave. It was either that or throw herself into his arms apologizing on her knees.

Akim accepted the invitation to leave the house. She made her position clear. She may have liked his caresses, but not enough to choose him over society, its rules and comfort.

-You know, I was willing to do anything for you.... -. He said before leaving without looking at her.

-I can't... I can't... -. He answered with barely a voice.

She closed the door and her legs gave out. She almost fell if it weren't for Connor's arms holding her tightly. Rachel entered the room and screamed in fright. Connor calmed her instantly.

-It's just a drop in blood pressure. Why don't you go home and bring me the blood pressure monitor?

Rachel bolted to carry out the orders without question and Brenda wept uncontentedly as her friend held her tightly in her arms.

Akim drank two, three, four, and it wasn't until he reached the sixth glass that he discovered he couldn't forget it or get drunk. He was a fool even for that. Rage roared desperately through his veins. She was not what he thought, he was. The most imbecile of imbeciles. Did he really think he could play and win? What could someone like him offer a woman like her? Hadn't he seen enough pain in his mother not to make the same mistakes?

He slammed the wooden table of the bar as he left the money and left, furious with his stupidity. With her, and with the damned life that was once again beating him mercilessly. He sped off on his bike at full speed, not caring if he crashed into a car or a lamppost, maybe this would end his suffering. For a change, life didn't help him here either. He arrived at his destination safe and sound. His body ached, his heart was broken and his eyes burned from so many tears. He approached the doorway and leaned his head against the frame and rang the doorbell.

Lola received him smiling and he felt like the dirtiest and most disgusting being on the face of the earth, but he desperately needed her.

-Make me forget her.

Don't miss Book II Dr. Klein Series . Wild.

... Akim walked naked to the restroom feeling the cold under his feet. His insides churned inside him, he felt dirty and disgusted. He felt dirty and disgusted. How many times had he called her name? How many times had he pronounced her name, ramming hard into the one who had no claim on him? He could no longer remember....

He leaned against the sink and ducked his head so as not to see himself in front of the mirror. He was disgusted. Lola didn't deserve treatment like that.

"Damn it! Even I don't deserve it."

-Come to bed. A honeyed voice whispered with his lips pressed against her back.

The young beauty hugged him around the waist trying to pull her man back to where she wanted him.

-Lola... -She murmured trying to apologize. Trying to say with a word what her soul could not.

-I don't care. He replied without regret.

Akim closed his eyes, knowing that he should not accept it. A good man would understand that this was wrong and that he should leave. Lola wanted him and he had already taken too much advantage of her.

-Lola..." He whispered again asking for some understanding and a hint of forgiveness.

-You can call me whatever you want, I don't care, don't go away. He said, gluing their naked bodies together. You need me...

God, he hated to admit it, but yes, he needed her. Lola was offering him what another was denying him and he...he was not a good man.

With strength and broken by the pain he drowned his sorrows in a hard and unromantic kiss. He needed to unload and she was his escape valve.

-I'm sorry..." he said, hoarse with desire and holding her too tightly in his arms, showing that it was not love he was looking for.

Lola smiled, accepting the challenge. Whatever she was looking for, Akim would always find it in her.

...Brenda watched through the airplane window as time passed. Senseless memories were relived over and over again. The blue of the sky, ungrateful in its sincerity, described to her a deep look that she had to forget. His exhausted head rested on the rigid frame. How could it have happened? He asked himself again and again trying to explain what reason did not know.

-Thank you... -He murmured almost feebly.

-We are friends. Rachel commented.

-But I...

-You don't have to talk," she said sympathetically, "it's not necessary.

-I would like to... now I can't." He commented, justifying his silence.

-I will always be here. He said showing his unconditional friendship.

Brenda looked at her with such deep sadness that Rachel stroked her hand resting on the armrest trying to comfort her.

-Whatever it is. It will work out.

-Are you sure? -Brenda shook her head, "I shouldn't have dragged you into my problems.

-Nonsense. You didn't drag me anywhere. In fact, it was my idea, wasn't it? -he said, smiling.

-Yes, and you're crazy. He commented, trying to smile and not succeeding.

-You leave it to me.

-Max and George... -she murmured regretfully.

-It's all arranged. You take it easy. She said as she remembered her lies behind the phone.

Rachel had lied and lied a lot, but this was not the time for sad regrets. Brenda's recovery was her only priority.

The doctor went back to looking out the window at the houses that were beginning to revolt below the plane when a friendly voice spoke into the microphone.

"Gentlemen passengers, we are about to land at the International Airport on the island of Ibiza. Please fasten your seat belts, straighten your tables and put the backs of your chairs in an upright position. Please remain seated until the announcements have been turned off. Cabin crew..."

Rachel adjusted her backrest with real concern. Brenda was not well and she hoped she could help her.

The annual convention of the Amazons in Ibiza had been the first idea that had occurred to him to run away. Desperate situations, change of destination, she thought with a smile.

If Brenda needed a friend, there were hundreds more than willing to help.

"Yes, between all of us we will help her, but from what?". She asked herself with real concern.

Milton Keynes UK
Ingram Content Group UK Ltd.
UKHW041950291124
451915UK00001B/81